les. How closer to and, and ....ze move from her cheek to her ....s another man on earth whose appearance could have her so unsettled.

His bronzed hand moved to her arm and she was sure he could see her heart's erratic pounding. His long tapered fingers forced her to lean into him as he raised himself off of the pillows.

His warm lips covered her own and she felt like she would explode by the awareness of his body touching hers. Her mind raced with the knowledge that he was actually kissing her! She pulled back for the smallest instant and looked at him—sure he had made some sort of mistake.

He broke away with a sigh and whispered into her ear, "Miss Kittridge, I must apologize. Do forgive me."

In her flustered state, Charlotte could not think of a single thing to say. To occupy her shaking hands, she began unwrapping the bandage that was to go on his lordship's leg.

"Perhaps it would be better for your father to wrap my leg, Miss Kittridge. I daresay, not even a saint could be trusted in this condition. I am sorry."

She flew from the room, leaving behind the stiffened bandages, her pride, and the scene of her first kiss in all of her spinsterish seven-and-twenty years of existence.

A
Passionate Endeavor

Sophia Nash

A SIGNET BOOK

SIGNET
Published by New American Library, a division of
Penguin Group (USA) Inc., 375 Hudson Street,
New York, New York 10014, U.S.A.
Penguin Books Ltd, 80 Strand,
London WC2R 0RL, England
Penguin Books Australia Ltd, 250 Camberwell Road,
Camberwell, Victoria 3124, Australia
Penguin Books Canada Ltd, 10 Alcorn Avenue,
Toronto, Ontario, Canada M4V 3B2
Penguin Books (NZ), cnr Airborne and Rosedale Roads,
Albany, Auckland 1310, New Zealand

Penguin Books Ltd, Registered Offices:
80 Strand, London WC2R 0RL, England

First published by Signet, an imprint of New American Library,
a division of Penguin Group (USA) Inc.

First Printing, August 2004
10 9 8 7 6 5 4 3 2 1

PUBLISHER'S NOTE
This is a work of fiction. Names, characters, places, and incidents either are the
product of the author's imagination or are used fictiously, and any resemblance to
actual persons, living or dead, business establishments, events, or locales is entirely
coincidental.

To Ralph

Acknowledgments

I would like to thank the following people for countless hours of support and encouragement: fellow authors Kathryn Caskie and Diane Perkins Gaston for their insightful comments on the first draft; my agent, Jenny Bent, at Trident Media for guiding me through the publishing process; Signet/NAL Senior Editor, Laura Cifelli, whose superior editing skills enhanced the manuscript; Bill Haggart and other experts on the Beau Monde/Regency loops who so generously shared their knowledge of the regency period; Ingrid Lindquist, my top-notch riding teacher of long ago who provided firsthand information on the foaling process; Dr. Jere Daum for making available a text on the history of medicine; and Mary Noble Ours, an outstanding photographer who captures everyone at their very best. Finally, I would like to express my appreciation to my family who makes it all worthwhile.

Chapter One

*"Nobody who has not been in the interior of a
family can say what the difficulties of any
individual of that family may be."*

—*Emma*

Wiltshire, England—April 1814

Sir, wake up!" The young boy shook the broad shoulders
of the gaunt man beside him on the landau's perch. The
vehicle swayed as the gentleman regained his faculties.

"Blast it all, I am awake—now, at least." Rain sluiced
down the back of Lord Huntington's hat between his greatcoat and neck cloth, drenching the last bit of dryness on his
person. "We'll be at Wyndhurst before dawn, barring any
further disaster," he said, trying to calm the boy by making
light of the matter.

"Yes, sir. Shall I keep readin' the signposts to you, then?"

"That's the most important part of your job, Charley. And
poke this infernal leg of mine from time to time. That'll
keep my wits about me." He wondered if his mind was
going off-kilter as the droplets falling on his face seemed to
sizzle and turn to steam amid the blanket of darkness. A
fresh wave of pain seized his leg and he shivered uncontrol-
lably.

"Perhaps you will let me take the ribbons, sir," said the
boy.

Nicholas looked down at the all too serious eyes of
Charley Picket, whose innocence was lost too early. "Nay,
son. These post horses have mouths of lead. It's just a few
more miles . . ." A rush of wind sent a heavy downpour from

the leaves of the branches arching overhead as a nocturnal creature scurried across the road. One horse whinnied its displeasure at the mysteries of the night.

If not for himself, he must try to focus on the road for his small companion. Time seemed suspended as the horses splashed mud in every direction. Finally, the almost forgotten form of the stone gatekeeper's house loomed ahead. Dim candlelight flickered in a distant window—the only sign of welcome he would encounter.

The darkness started to close in on his mind once more as the unbearable cold turned hotter than Hades. A throbbing seared his leg and hip as the sweet calm of unconsciousness flooded his being. He tried to hold onto the young voice calling to him, but he could not. The warm world of darkness was too inviting.

A feminine voice was like a pinprick of light in the dark abyss. Nicholas shivered as he grasped the slippery world of the conscious, floating above what looked like the acrid smoke of the battlefield. He slipped away from the haunting halls of his mind and focused on the calming voice amid the babble of hushed murmurs.

"Lord Huntington? Sir, you must awake," the voice insisted. Coolness bathed his face. He opened his eyes and encountered two blurry, small faces staring at him.

"Lord Nick, I'm 'ere. Don't you worry, sir." Charley brushed past hands trying to move him away. "There be not a sawbones in sight 'ere. Won't leave your side, like promised."

A man with a nightcap askew moved into sight. "My lord, the doctor has been sent for, despite this pip's impudence. But Miss Kittridge is the good doctor's daughter. Perhaps she can ease some of your suffering until her father arrives," said a man whose bearing suggested a butler's command of the household.

"Stevens, is that you, man?" Nicholas peered around his bedchamber of old.

"Yes, my lord." The elderly retainer responded with a slight smile.

"It is good to see you," Nicholas said, trying to keep the wobbling in his voice at bay. "No need for the doctor. Charley Picket will provide all the doctoring I need," he said, nodding toward his young charge.

Charley puffed out his chest with pride. "I tolds you. They daren't listen, sir." The thin boy reached for Nicholas's hand. "I won't leave, sir, without a fight."

Nicholas coughed, his throat parched. Immediately, a cool hand slipped under his neck and raised his head to meet a glass of water. As he gulped the liquid, he looked at the huge gray eyes in a diminutive girl's face, the visage of the person who supported him. Her mouth was very odd-shaped; small, full-lipped, but with a slightly puffier top lip. Almost a doll's mouth. She looked away when he continued to stare at her. They were employing very young maids at the abbey.

"My lord, Charley is your stalwart champion, I know. However, you are very ill," she paused. "Might I, at the very least, unwrap your leg to see if we can lessen your pain?"

He tried to fathom why a young maid would ask such a thing.

She became defensive. "I am my father's assistant."

"And who might your father be?"

Stevens interrupted before the girl could speak. "This is the Miss Kittridge I spoke of. She is a nurse and the daughter of His Grace's doctor, recently arrived from London. She was watching over your father tonight when you arrived."

"Well, you may return to your post, Miss Kittridge," Nicholas said, as the pounding in his head returned with a vengeance. "And tell your father I have no need of his tinctures and leeches. Charley will do just fine."

A cool, damp cloth replaced the hot one on his forehead. The gray eyes met his again. He was sure she would insist. Doctors and others of learned professions never failed to press ministrations on their victims.

She said not a word. Gentle concern etched the corners of her eyes. Eyes, like Charley's, that had seen too much of the world at too young an age. She turned to glance toward his lower legs encased in muddy boots. Her gaze then moved to Charley, who instantly sprang toward the end of the bed.

"I's going to leave off your boots, sir." Charley grasped the tight top of the boot and heel then pulled.

Excruciating threads of light flooded Nicholas's brain, and he tried to cling to reality.

"Sorry, Lord Nick."

"It's all right, Charley," he bit out as he closed his eyes against the pain.

Gentle touches relieved the pressure on his injury. He opened his eyes to find Charley and the girl removing the long, blood-encrusted pieces of cloth from his thigh. Blood had turned parts of his dark-green 95th Rifleman's uniform a muddy brown.

"I told you to leave me be," he said.

The two young people continued to unwind the cloth. Miss Kittridge refused to meet his gaze. "Yes, my lord."

"I am not in the habit of being disobeyed."

"I am sorry to displease."

"Beggin' your pardon, Lord Nick, Mr. Stevens said we could 'ave new bandages if that's to your way of thinkin'," said Charley.

Nicholas kept his eyes trained on the small, untrustworthy frame of Miss Kittridge, but aimed his question to the lad. "Is it bleeding?"

Charley peered at the thigh wound then wrinkled his upturned nose. "Nay. But it don't look so good, sir."

"Leave it be, then. We'll bind it later," he said, reaching for the water glass again.

Miss Kittridge handed it to him. "Is a ball lodged in it, my lord?"

"No." He was sure her girlish curiosity would force another query.

Her damnably calm dark eyes peered at him. She was not

a pretty girl. Her homespun brown wool gown was the same dull color as her hair pulled back into a severe knot. Not a childish curl in sight. He was annoyed with himself for not being able to find pity or at least kindness in his heart for this young creature forced into night duty.

"Then my father still lives, I take it?" he asked. "I feared I would not make it in time."

Stevens stepped forward. "You arrived much earlier than expected. His Grace has taken a turn for the better since Dr. Kittridge's ministrations this past fortnight, my lord."

"I see you have been taken in by the good doctor's luck, Stevens." He glanced at Miss Kittridge, sure that the jab would let loose a torrent of familial defense.

But Miss Kittridge merely glanced toward the pile of dirty bandages. A slight flush appeared on her cheeks as she began gathering the cloth.

"You are to be commended on your fortitude and patient character, Miss Kittridge." Stevens gave Nicholas a dark look—a look not seen since his prank-filled youth. "The master here knows not of your father's excellent work."

"You needn't show concern, Mr. Stevens. From what I have heard of the butchers on the battlefields, I am quite sure I would have formed an ill opinion of surgeons, as well, had I been wounded."

And now he had nothing to feel but heartily ashamed of his antagonism toward this kind yet plain young nurse.

"However, Lord Huntington, most learned gentlemen know there are exceptions to every rule," she said.

"Perhaps I am not a 'learned gentleman.'"

"As you are in great pain, I shall not argue the point. I would, however, ask your forbearance and courage in a short meeting with my father. Surely a man of your great heroism could endure that much?" she asked, finally displaying some emotion, which allowed Nicholas to lessen his guilt.

"I shan't allow you to bully me, Miss Kittridge."

Nicholas noticed Charley tugging on Miss Kittridge's

gown. She turned her ear to his dirty, cupped hand. A smile creased the corners of her mouth before she hid it with her hand.

"And what, may I ask, is being said? Certainly nothing kind. Whispers never portend comfort."

"I mayn't tell," she responded.

Charley's red face loomed large. "I told 'er you weren't usually so pigheaded. I think you should give 'er a chance. I mean, Lord Nick, it's not like she's carryin' a saw on 'er."

"I'm surrounded by a turncoat, a believer, and a perceived performer of miracles. How can I refuse?" he asked, dryly. "I must insist, however, that you do not apply any potion, or leech, or knife to my person." He hated to appear the coward.

"Agreed." She moved forward to examine the wound. "May I ask how you sustained this injury?"

"I was thrown from my horse during battle and fell on an exposed rock, breaking my leg."

"And a surgeon on the field set it?"

"No," he said, as a fresh wave of pain radiated from the flesh wound. He looked toward Charley and blinked rapidly to regain control.

"You depended on Charley to set it?" she asked with a horror-struck expression on her face.

"It was that or the surgeon's method. And as my batman had been killed in the same skirmish, I chose Charley. He is an admirable fife player." He turned to see Charley grinning. "And he agreed to accompany me home as a batman-in-training."

"And proud I am of it, too," said the impish boy.

Nicholas was annoyed he had submitted to the will of the nocturnal group, but had little time for thought as Miss Kittridge pushed him back and tucked under the ripped edges of his breeches. He closed his eyes to prepare for the pain. She was so gentle. And her hands were so little. Nicholas concentrated on . . . on anything except what she was doing.

"How long ago did this happen?"

"About a month ago. It was magnificent timing." He paused to concentrate on his words instead of the pain. "A day after the battle, a letter from my sister found me, informing me of the advanced ill health of my father. I secured leave—easily enough with this injury—and set off with Charley's help. It was only a matter of traversing parts of France on a poor version of a wagon, and swimming the channel, don't you know," he said with a wry smile.

Charley giggled.

The girl was immune to his attempts at humor, unfortunately. She pressed her thumbs into the upper muscle of his leg. Lost in a morass of pain, he tensed involuntarily.

"Try to relax, if you can. If you can't, it's all right," she said.

She ran her hands along the length of his thigh, feeling first the top and underside. She changed positions and moved her hands upward and around to encircle his thigh. He felt an uncomfortable tightening and groaned.

"I'm sorry," she said.

Nicholas opened his eyes and watched her slim hands move perilously close to, well, blast, to his unmentionable parts. If not for the unbearable pain and chills, he was sure he would have embarrassed himself if this lasted much longer. He had abstained from women of the willing persuasion for many months.

Miss Kittridge was so close that he could smell the clean, feminine essence of her. He felt paralyzed by the entire scene before him. He was in a truly laughable situation— with pleasure and pain vying for control. Her hands stopped, and she glanced at him. He could feel her breath on his face. He pushed her away.

"Enough with the examination, *Doctor*."

She avoided his gaze, and moved to the end of the bed. Without a word, she picked up his foot and ran a finger up the sole. His toes curled. She rolled his foot, then ran her hands up past his calf to his knee, feeling the top knobby part and the sensitive underside. He squirmed.

"Ticklish are you?"

"No. That is undignified."

She leaned back. "Well, you've certainly sustained a considerable injury to the femur, or rather the thighbone."

"A magnificent display of medical deduction, miss," he said. He moved her hand from his knee as he sat up. "Well, what is your diagnosis?"

"You will, of course, have to allow my father to perform a full evaluation. But, I believe your little fife player performed a commendable job. There seems to be a small splinter of bone that might not have adhered itself to the main formation. I daresay that only time will tell if it will heal properly."

"And what is the alternative? There is always an alternative, is there not?"

"The alternative, which my father might recommend, would be to reset the bone. That would entail breaking the bone again."

"An unappealing choice. But would it promise to relieve the pain?"

"Possibly," she said. "But, you must allow my father to give you his opinion. You know, he really is the most talented physician in all of Europe."

"Ah, the recommendation I expected many minutes ago," he said with a small smile. "What a proud, good daughter you are. But I thought physicians never touched a surgeon's job."

"My father has progressive ideas. He believes a gentleman entering the medical profession must become an expert in both areas."

"Most progressive. He must not have been popular in the Royal College of Physicians."

"Yes, you are correct. But the College of Surgeons respected him greatly."

Nicholas shivered as he struggled to sit up. All the former waves of heat left his body.

Miss Kittridge grasped his wrist at the pulse point. "My

lord, would you allow me to prepare for you a pot of chamomile tea? It is most calmative and has antispasmodic properties. I daren't press upon you an infusion of wormwood for your putrid wound, for fear of distressing you," she said with an innocent expression on her face. He was sure she was mocking him.

He hated feeling so weak and faint. It was with considerable effort that he had managed to converse. He forced himself to continue, for fear of losing his grasp on consciousness.

"What is your age, Miss Kittridge?" he asked, turning the subject. She was so little. Really, like a mere flighty bird.

She met his gaze and appeared flustered. "I beg your pardon. I am advanced enough in years to prepare tea."

"You cannot be more than fifteen."

"I shall tell you, if you agree to the tea *and the infusion*."

He laughed before a series of coughs constricted his throat. "All right, *Dr. Kittridge*. What have I to lose? You are not hiding any barber's knives in those pockets of yours, are you?"

Charley grinned. "No, sir, I checked 'em when she was lookin' at yer leg."

Miss Kittridge's eyes widened and she felt for her pockets.

"We have provoked Miss Kittridge long enough, Charley. How about if you go with Stevens to the kitchens to fetch a pot of boiling water for the good nurse?" he said to the boy. With a shake of the head and a murmur of agreement, the two figures, one portly and old, the other small and young, disappeared, shutting the door to keep out the growing crowd of curious servants.

"And now, you must fulfill your end of our bargain," he said, looking up at her.

She looked back at him sheepishly. "I had hoped you had forgotten," she said, while picking an invisible piece of lint from her sleeve.

"I never forget."

"It's quite rude to ask a lady her age."

"But I am confused. Your stature and physiognomy suggest a woman not past her girlhood. But your eyes speak differently."

"I am past my prime, if you must know. Soon to be past seven and twenty to be exact."

He was shocked. And now embarrassment flooded him for having forced a spinster to reveal her age. No gentleman beyond leading strings would have dared to stretch the barriers of society's unwritten rules of behavior toward the gentler sex.

She was looking at him. "I'm sorry to have embarrassed you."

He forced himself to form some words. Any words. "No, no, it is I who must apologize. I should never have presumed to ask."

"It's all right. Now you do not have to worry about shocking me. I am quite the old maid."

"Certainly not—"

She interrupted. "No, you misunderstand. I am not asking for you to refute the fact—just explaining that I have no maidenly airs to worry about. My work with my father has taken away any silly sensibilities I might have had in my youth."

There was a tap on the door. "Enter," Nicholas called out.

Chapter Two

*"A woman of seven and twenty . . can never hope
to inspire affection again."*

—Sense and Sensibility

*C*harlotte Kittridge knew she was just as firmly on the shelf as the book she tugged in vain. She was the fool who had overstuffed these inadequate shelves in the small front parlor just two weeks ago. Charlotte looked down lovingly at the tonsured crown of her father and the full head of black hair of her only brother as they sat before a roaring fire meant to displace the early morning darkness. She smiled with good humor.

She realized with a small shrug that she also had only herself to blame for her ill-natured thoughts about her station in life. Charlotte had read a novel, for the first time, during the trip from London to Wiltshire, much to her father's horror and her brother's laughter. It was all about Elinor and Marianne Dashwood, and it had filled her mind with heretofore unknown thoughts. Given that Charlotte felt Elinor so akin to herself, she wondered whether that practical lady or the author herself, a mysterious "Lady," would have approved of Lord Huntington, he of the wild hair, arresting green eyes, and impossibly broad shoulders. Surely not. There was not a trace of the subtle gallantries of Edward Ferrars in the novel *Sense and Sensibility*. Lord Huntington had a compelling presence that made her feel unaccountably awkward when he spoke to her. A feeling that happened but rarely in her small, familial world.

Charlotte would have liked to be surrounded by lots of

sisters and a mother of the Dashwood ilk, but fate had chosen a different course for her.

Her father, seated in the worn leather chair near the hearth, turned and peered at her over his spectacles. "So, my dear, did Lord Huntington survive despite the dreaded chamomile tea and infusion?"

Charlotte gave one last yank and finally dislodged the massive volume. "Yes, Father, when I left him two hours ago, he was sleeping. His Grace was also resting comfortably," she said. "But, the son is very weak and the fever continues. I thought a restorative draught might help. I've searched through the English texts, and am now into your books from Paris. What do you think?"

"Methinks it is a good idea. Let us try the one I have been administering to His Grace." He lowered his book and got up to help her down the last rung of the small stepladder. He kissed the top of her head before looking at the volumes at eye level. "It helped lower the father's morning fevers, although the duke's condition is much more grave than I expected when first we arrived. As soon as we prepare them, we should return to the abbey. I fear we will be ensconced in that cold, barren fortress for the duration of the illness."

"How much longer before the consumption overcomes his defenses?"

"I cannot tell yet if he will rally. The severe fever and chills complicate a recovery. If I cannot cure the evening fever within the next few days, the duke will depart this mortal coil, and we will have a critical, new younger employer."

Her brother looked up from his book. "Especially if you continue to force your perceived poisonous ministrations on his lordship, Charlotte."

She was used to her family's plain speaking. "Father, you know we could return to London on the next mail coach if need be. Why, we even had a handful of letters yesterday from several patients begging your return."

"Yes, I'm for all that if the old man does kick off," her brother said.

"James, a little respect, thank you," Dr. Kittridge snapped. "Nevertheless, a calming stay in the country is what we all need. A country practice is all I've ever really wanted. After France—" Charlotte's father stopped speaking and looked down at his book.

"It's all right, Papa," she said as she walked toward him. "*Elle me manque aussi.*" *I miss her too.*

"I've asked you not to speak that . . . that language, Charlotte."

"I'm sorry, but when I think of Maman, I think in her language." Charlotte gazed at her father's faded blue eyes.

"It is dangerous to forget. To forget is to court folly. It is one of the very reasons I wanted to leave London. The English are foolish to think they are immune from the power of an angry lower class. If they would but open their eyes and see the dissatisfaction of the masses, they would fear rebellion, fear revolution."

"Yes, yes, I know, Papa." His favored topic had long ago lost its fervor for her. She and James exchanged knowing glances. Her brother rolled his eyes.

"Charlotte and James, you must listen to me. Do not ever discuss your heritage with anyone here. There is no benefit to anybody knowing. Only detriments."

"Father, we've discussed this ad nauseum. Your fears are unwarranted. There are so many displaced people in England. And what do you expect to happen here in this small corner of England? You could not have found a more remote place—unless we had flown to Yorkshire," said James.

The father paled. "Your nonchalance surprises me, given the past."

"Father, I've begged you and begged you to let me make reparations."

"Ah, James, you know not of what you speak. I'll not let the only son of mine think he can avenge his family by shedding more blood. I'll hear no more from you on this subject."

"But Father . . ."

"NO, I say. I forbid it."

Charlotte gave a cautioning glance to her brother as she moved to touch her father's shoulder. "Father, do not exert yourself. We are all in perfect agreement," she said again, as she gave her brother a nod toward the door.

James snapped his unread book shut and stalked toward the exit.

Upon James's departure, their father pulled Charlotte into his lap. "Charlotte, I am grateful to the Good Lord for giving me you. At least one of my children is levelheaded, with enough intelligence for ten siblings."

"But no beauty."

"Fishing are you? That is unlike my Charlotte. Beauty does not save lives, nor take care of the less fortunate. It is what is inside your mind that matters, not a good complexion and sparkling wit."

Charlotte's soul constricted. Fishing had never been good in these waters. And for good reason. She knew the answer by looking in the tiny cracked looking glass in her small chamber above stairs. Her father had just confirmed, as he always did, the truth. She was as plain and bookish as ever. She was too small, her eyes were a nondescript gray and too far apart. At least her freckles had faded, except the one under her eye. Her only points of pride were her long neck, delicate ears, and tiny ankles—areas others never noticed or cared a wit about.

It was only that she had not minded being plain so much before, really. Well, maybe not too much—except when Mr. Cox had stopped calling, and perhaps worse yet, when Alexandre had not responded to the letters. But Elinor Dashwood had taught her all about patience and its reward.

Lord Huntington had instigated something altogether different. Something that was sure to lead to dashed hopes yet again.

*   *   *

It was his favorite time of day, the hour before dawn. As a child he would slip into his oldest clothes, sneak through the kitchens for yesterday's baked remnants, and head into the fields or streams, fishing tackle in hand. More often than not, he would end up side by side with the laborers to make hay, harvest the grains, or oversee the livestock. It was the one time he had been happy here. He looked down at his useless leg. At least he was feeling better—maybe still feverish and tired, but not exhausted to the bone nor plagued by hallucinations. Yes, it would be a few days before he could contemplate a predawn jaunt. But, perhaps a trip to the window?

A knock sounded at his door, and before he could respond, his sister flew into the room.

"Oh, you *are* home!" Rosamunde said, running toward the bed. "Stevens had me woken early with the news." She hugged him, and his throat tightened as he grasped her thin back through her nightdress.

She pulled back. "You are a scoundrel for not sending word. I would have waited up for you," she said, as her wide green eyes, so much like his own, filled with tears. "Oh, I am so glad you are here. I have missed you so."

"And, I you."

"Still the barefaced charming liar, I see," she said, laughing until she looked at his bandaged leg on top of the down coverlet before Nicholas could cover it with a sheet. "But what is this? Are you wounded?" Her face paled.

"I'm afraid I made the mistake of cracking it," he said as he reached for her long brown braid, which snaked over her shoulder. "At least that is the opinion of our new resident doctor and his nurse, although I must say I came to the same conclusion within moments of having my horse shot out from under me."

"Oh, Nicholas, not Nimrod!"

"You show much compassion for my horse, I see," he

said, forcing a lopsided attempt at a grin. "And little for my poor leg."

"You are as wretched as ever. Don't try to pretend you didn't love that horse. Father gave him to you." Rosamunde snatched her braid from his hand when he tried to tickle her nose with the end of it.

"Yes. I thought I would never 'earn' him."

"It was the first time he went against the wishes of Her Grace. You have to give him that," she said.

"Yes. And you paid dearly for that too, as I recall." He grasped her hands, forcing her to lie next to him on the bed, his shoulder offered as a hollow for her head. Stroking her small head brought a remembered feeling of love.

"Let us not dwell on the past," she said, snuggling against him. "I have good news. Did Stevens tell you that Father seems to be recovering a bit? When I wrote to you, I was sure the letter would find you too late. I am so glad you are come. Will you stay?"

"At least until this blasted leg has healed," he said. "I am going to miss all the wild celebrations in London when old Boney is routed, as he is sure to be shortly. I will miss all the cakes and champagne after eating all that mud for so many months."

"Well, I have at least one good thing you can look forward to, as well as one more bad thing."

He stopped stroking her hair. "Yes? The bad news first, if you please."

"*Mother* has invited a Lady Susan and her grandmother for a visit. She is quite . . . unusual, and of course a heiress. Perfect for Edwin, according to Her Grace," she said. "At least you will have me and my dear friend Louisa to buffer the attentions that might turn toward you, if my guess is correct. The actual heir will prove more attractive to that lady than the spare."

"Her Grace will be doubly delighted then to learn of my arrival," he said, one brow arched. "I shall have to try not to become an impediment to Edwin's future good fortune," he continued. "And the good?"

"My favorite mare, Phoenix, is in foal—due in a month's time. She is a dream to ride, and I have decided that her first progeny will be my homecoming gift to you."

Before he could reply, a knock sounded. "Enter," he called out, as Rosamunde scurried to her feet, and smoothed her gown.

The diminutive Dr. Kittridge entered, along with his daughter. Before she looked away from him, Nicholas noticed dark circles cupping her large gray eyes. At least now he could focus on her face. Last night seemed to have happened in a sort of delirious daze. He could not remember much. Except he did recall that her delicate hands, clasped before her now, had touched most of the bare skin of the lower half of his body—and she had smelled like the fields of lavender he had seen in France.

"I am sorry to have disturbed you, my lord, Lady Rosamunde," said the doctor, bowing.

"No need to be sorry."

"Are you feeling better, my lord?" asked Dr. Kittridge.

"Much. In fact, I must go to my father now that I have rested. It is why I am here, after all."

"His Grace would not want you to be moved in your condition, just yet. Your leg needs to be in a raised position and immobile for many weeks."

"Sir, I was the unwilling recipient of your daughter's cunning maneuvers last night to keep me confined, but not so this morning, when I have sufficiently recovered my senses," Nicholas said, fashioning an easy smile.

"But, my lord—" Miss Kittridge began.

"Please offer me a dressing gown and slippers, Miss Kittridge, not arguments," Nicholas interrupted. "It is fruitless, you know. I will not be put off." Instantly, he regretted his words. He didn't want to offend her. After all, she had been quite gentle and kind to him last night. And whether it was her care or luck, he did feel better for the first time in longer than a month. He opened his mouth to apologize, but she had disappeared from sight.

She returned with the requested garments. He could barely fit into his old blue brocade dressing gown. It had grown hopelessly tight about the shoulders since the last time he had worn it more than a dozen years ago.

Stevens was called, and between the doctor and the butler, Nicholas was helped to his sire's chambers. The first dizzying wave of pain made him question the sense of his plan. Soon enough he was settled on a lounging chair next to his father, his leg extended.

He grasped the elder's wrinkled old hand. A large signet ring swam on a finger of his cold, clawlike hand. His watery green eyes opened halfway.

"Ah, it is you, my son. I did not think to see you again in this lifetime," he said hoarsely.

Panic gripped Nicholas's stomach. His father had withered. The sparse hair covering his skull had gone white, and his once robust frame was frail.

His father's gaze moved to focus on the doctor. "But we have Dr. Kittridge here to thank for keeping me alive. Percival Smythe, that damned apothecary, almost poisoned me."

"Actually, I think it is your tenacity, Your Grace." Dr. Kittridge moved forward. "I've brought a draught for you this morning, and one for Lord Huntington as well."

Miss Kittridge appeared at the other side of the bed and moved the Duke of Cavendish into a sitting position, rearranging the bedcovers all in one smooth movement. She brought to the elder's willing lips a steaming brew. At the same moment, the doctor handed Nicholas a cup. It tasted of anise, honey, and almonds—very strange, but not unpleasant.

"I take it from the looks of your leg that the Frogs did not let you go unscathed?" the duke asked a minute later.

Nicholas's explanation glossed over the harsh details.

"But I must know more. Dr. Kittridge, what is my son's prognosis?"

"I examined him late last night, after some . . . discussion. It is an ugly break with a red swelling in the open area. But your son is an otherwise strong and healthy gentleman. It should heal in the next two months with elevation, proper rest, and a slow rehabilitation."

Ha! Nicholas was at least glad the doctor did not worry his father with the second part of the diagnosis and the mention of his fever, a fever he could feel already returning with a heated vengeance. Dr. Kittridge had concurred with his daughter on the possibility of rebreaking the leg should it not heal properly. But Nicholas would be damned if he was going to stay in the sick room for the prescribed eight-week period—although, he wouldn't have minded lying down for a few minutes right then.

"Will he—" began the duke, before becoming overwhelmed with a coughing spasm. Miss Kittridge hastened to his side with a handkerchief.

After a full half-minute, Miss Kittridge removed the fine linen covering his father's mouth and offered the liquid again—but not quickly enough for the flecks of blood to escape Nicholas's notice. He breathed in sharply. If his father's physical appearance had suggested the end was near, the blood confirmed it.

As he looked into his father's sad eyes, he prepared himself to carry out the duke's wishes uttered so long ago. He was not sure he should have come back. . . . But then again, what did he have to lose? Except a father. A dear, dear, father.

The shadows were beginning to creep toward the center of his vision again. Blast. He was not going to be able to hide it. The heat turned to an icy flash. His head swam, and the last thing he saw was Miss Kittridge rushing to his side and lowering his head to his knees.

*   *   *

As Charlotte walked up the last small rise before Wynd-hurst Abbey came into view, she sighed and was grateful that within the beautiful limestone walls, the last patients of her wretched day awaited her. She was weary from attending to the various aches and pains of the laborers, tenant farmers, and villagers. They only ever had an apothecary in the past—an ancient man named Smythe, who resented the newcomers with their newfangled notions. His ghastly ideas for curing the duke had included pills made of cobwebs and snail water!

Being a stranger and a female, Charlotte still had a long road to travel in gaining trust in the countryside. Mrs. Pierce had voiced doubts concerning the hot camphor compresses prescribed for inflamed breasts due to new motherhood. Then there had been the penniless widow from the village with a boil that had needed to be lanced. She had become indignant when Charlotte suggested she could pay her fee by spending one day the next week helping the overwhelmed Mrs. Pierce.

She had yet to have a man agree to discuss any ailment with her. Mr. Gordon had refused even to tell her what his complaint concerned.

"Only a gen'lman doctor will do for the loikes o' me," he had said with a big grin as he chucked her cheek.

All this she must endure along with the recalcitrant new patient, Lord Huntington, who refused to trust her and took delight in goading her. It was a disheartening business.

She promised herself an hour working with her clay sculptures or bird-watching when she was through with this afternoon's shift with the duke or his heir. At least Lord Huntington's fever had broken, and the infection was clearing and less inflamed after a week. But in some ways it was easier to care for a delirious patient than a stubborn man who was weak and too determined to deviate from the lengthy path to recovery.

Charlotte greeted the busy servants and young Charley as she made her way to Lord Huntington's chambers.

"He is asleep, Miss Kittridge. He must be making up for all the tossin' and turnin' he done last week," said the ever-faithful youth, who sat slumped in a chair outside the chamber's door. He was always within earshot of his master.

"Charley, you are a most loyal batman. But everyone must take a lie down from time to time. I promise to care for your master. But you must be at your best when he needs you. Please go and rest."

It was the first time he had agreed to her suggestion. Either he was exhausted or he trusted her, at last. One battle won, on to the next.

She entered the room and stood over the form of Lord Huntington. The small pile of books on history, farming, and law stood untouched. She had brought them to him two days ago, when the fever had broken. He allowed her to read to him and discuss the worldly topics for many hours each day, but refused to read alone in his solitary hours.

His breath came evenly in slumber, and his forehead looked dry. She gently felt his pulse and resisted the urge to touch his face to check for any remnants of a fever. He needed sleep more than anything now.

Lord, he was so very handsome. The classic lines of his face reminded her of the engravings in her book on the sculpture of Michelangelo. Even in sleep, he looked like a mythological warrior in stone—although somewhat more gaunt in the cheeks, if she was truthful. His jaw was square and strong, with just a hint of a cleft in the chin, his lips full. With a sigh, she realized he was like a Greek god no less, perfection—the antithesis of her childish female form. It was a thoroughly depressing thought.

Charlotte jumped back in surprise when his lips opened and his breath quickened before he groaned. His shoulders twitched, and she could see he was dreaming.

"No, no, NO—please don't . . . don't take her—" he whispered.

Charlotte woke him immediately. He sat up and grasped her arms in a painful grip, gasping for great lungfuls of air.

"Oh, dear God . . ." he said in a rough voice.

She put her arms around his shoulders awkwardly when he did not release her. Lord Huntington rested the side of his head against her breast while he regained his senses and regulated his breathing. "Thank you for waking me."

"I am glad I could be of service." His head on her breast made her insides feel strange and wobbly. "I have known the fear of many a bad dream or three."

He released her, and she was sorry to lose the contact of his warm arms.

"Have you been plagued, thusly? What could possibly invade the sweet dreams of a sage innocent such as yourself?" He was still groggy and struggled to reposition his pillows to allow himself to sit up.

In a trice she arranged them to his liking, and looked down at him. "Mostly the revolution, my lord," she hesitated. "Sometimes, my mother, the crowds—" she stopped, unwilling to say more, and wondered why she had dared to reveal even that much.

"I am sorry. Your family was in France during the revolution? Were you exposed to any of the . . . ugliness?" he asked, but then put up his hand. "No, I can see by the look on your face that you would rather not speak of it. Just as I choose not to dwell on scenes from the battlefield." He smiled. "We are two veterans, I see."

"You are right." She was grateful he had not asked more. "War leaves such deep scars on the mind. I've seen it on the countless numbers of men my father treated in London after they returned."

"Ah, it is strange, but I rarely dream of the war. It is more often about here—the abbey."

Charlotte possessed a keen sense of when a patient wanted to talk and when they did not. She looked at him and said nothing, willing him to continue. He looked past her shoulder toward the window.

"It is a cold, awful, damp place, Wyndhurst," he said, passing his hand over his forehead. "And many a night my sister and I were convinced it was haunted by the long-dead religious, who, we guessed, frowned upon our escapades."

He looked at her with a slight smile and continued, "I would hear my sister's little bare feet padding down the hall at a dead run a full half-minute before she would fling open the door and jump into my bed," he said, laughing. "She hated to be separated from Edwin and me at night—left all alone in the dark in a room down the hall and one floor above. Our nurse, who was quite hard of hearing, slept in a small chamber off the room Edwin and I shared."

He paused, and a shadow crossed his features. His eyes became unfocused.

"And then the day arrived when we were caught. Her Grace arrived much later than usual one evening to say her goodnights. She was very fond of . . . of children. Well, of her son at least, and she made a habit of coming in every night to coddle and kiss him goodnight, then sing a lullaby to him."

Charlotte was confused but remained silent. She watched him swallow before continuing.

"And of course, she noticed the large shape in my bed, as Rosamunde had hidden, pressed against me, when Her Grace had entered. There was quite the fracas. Rosamunde was banished from being near me—a harsh punishment we managed to circumvent often, but equally often received hefty punishments for. My stepmother said it was—unnatural—our attachment." He almost stopped altogether, then added, "Perhaps she was correct."

Many moments passed before Charlotte knew he was finished. "Her Grace is not your mother?"

"Yes, well, she tries to insist that we call her that, but no, she is not."

"When did you lose your mother?"

"When I was six, and Rosamunde, three."

He had been almost the same age she had been when her mother died in France. "I am sorry."

"So am I, Miss Kittridge, so am I," he said, looking down

at her hand that had grasped his during the awful story. He covered her fingers with his other powerful hand and squeezed.

"And your stepmother did not feel compelled to show you and your sister the same affection she gave her son each night?" Charlotte's composure shriveled with anger.

"No. But I could hardly expect it. I was not her flesh and blood."

"You consider it normal to kiss and cuddle one child while leaving the other half-orphaned child in a darkened corner of a room with nary a word of affection?" Now fury was upon her. "Your stepmother was wrong, you know. There is nothing unnatural about two motherless children seeking comfort from each other—especially in the pitch darkness of night, when fears run amok in a child's mind." Charlotte stopped for a moment to collect herself. "I'm sorry for my outburst."

"I am honored to have a defender." He appeared pleased by her spirited words. "I would have liked to have you in my darkened corner, I think," he said, his eyes crinkling in the corners.

She could not stop. "I myself spent many a night in my father or brother's arms when night fears took hold. I was more fortunate than you. They never turned me away. Many would say I was spoilt beyond redemption."

"I would not say you were poorly reared by any means, my dear Miss Kittridge. Except when you are intent on disobeying my every command," he said, smiling.

She opened her mouth to disagree.

"Now you are not going to play the contrarian, are you?" he interrupted. "I thought we made strong headway today, against our poor start. Don't you agree?"

"Well . . . yes. In fact, since I am agreeing with you in this case, I will be much obliged if you allow me to encase your leg in this linen, stiffened with egg whites. I could not obtain plaster of Paris, which is a new technique being used in some parts of Europe now, so this will have to do." She knew she was rambling. She did it in an effort to avoid his certain censure. "It will help keep the limb immobile and hasten recovery."

"I am well aware of the necessary annoyance of immobility, Miss Kittridge, as I have had you to remind me of this every day during the last eight days. All right, I shall acquiesce, but only because, well . . . well, because you are right!" He laughed.

His humor was contagious. Charlotte smiled.

"Why, Miss Kittridge, I didn't know you had dimples. How charming," he said, grasping her arm and pulling her close.

He touched her cheek with his other hand, and she held her breath. She watched his intense green gaze move from her cheek to her mouth and wondered if there was another man on earth whose appearance could leave her so unsettled.

She was sure he could see her heart's erratic pounding. He dropped his hand from her face and lightly pulled her to meet him as he raised himself off the pillows.

Please, oh, please God, let this happen.

His warm lips covered her own, and she felt like she would explode by the awareness of his body touching hers. Her mind raced with the knowledge that he was actually kissing her! She pulled back for the smallest instant and looked at him, sure he had made some sort of mistake. Something in his hungered expression reassured her, and she quickly lowered her lips to his again, mimicking his gentle exploration.

His lips parted and the intoxicating heat of his breath flowed onto her cheek. His tongue traced the edges of her lips and she shivered. Was there a more divine feeling?

His hand stroked down her arm and back up her waist, coming to rest against her breast. The pressure was wicked and heavenly all at the same time.

He broke away with a sigh and whispered into her ear, "Miss Kittridge, I must apologize. But dimples drive me to unconscionable actions. Do forgive me. Best keep them hidden from now on, or you shall be in danger again."

In her flustered state, Charlotte could not think of a single thing to say. To occupy her shaking hands, she began unwrapping the bandage that was to go on his lordship's leg.

"Perhaps it would be better for your father to wrap my leg, Miss Kittridge."

Her eyes flew to his thigh, still covered by the linen sheets, and the shape above it. Her embarrassment increased tenfold.

"I daresay not even a saint could be trusted in this condition. I am sorry, Miss Kittridge."

She flew from the room, leaving behind the stiffened bandages, her pride, and the scene of her first kiss.

Oh, it had been heady. Quite, quite divine. Why hadn't that novel mentioned anything about kisses?

Chapter Three

"Even the smooth surface of family union seems worth preserving, though there may be nothing durable beneath."

—Persuasion

*O*h, no, my dear brother, I must relinquish the head of the table in deference to you, now that you are on the mend," said Lord Edwin, drawing out the aforementioned seat and motioning Nicholas to it. "This is your first appearance, after all, after three weeks."

Nicholas glanced at his father's wife out of the corner of his eye. Her Grace paled, her lips thinning in suppressed anger.

"I prefer to leave it vacant in deference to Father," he replied.

"Always the proper one," Edwin replied. "Always thinking of others. How I admire you and wish to be more like you," he continued with an easy smile.

Not wanting his brother to feel uncomfortable, Nicholas offered another solution as he turned to one of their dinner guests, the elderly parish vicar. "His Grace would be most comfortable knowing a man of your high morals was warming his seat, Mr. Llewellyn."

The duchess appeared infuriated by his decision.

The tall, white-haired gentleman bowed. "I would be most delighted to accede to your wishes, Lord Huntington."

Nicholas hobbled on his new crutch to a seat offered by the butler.

"I am most pleased you were able to join us for dinner, Dr. Kittridge," said the Duchess of Cavendish as she took her seat along with the other ladies. She nodded to the doctor's two offspring, "and of course your family as well," she added with stiff, condescending hauteur. A smile skirted her tight lips as she surveyed with distaste the unbalanced group of seven ladies and five gentlemen at table.

"It is an honor, Your Grace," replied Dr. Kittridge.

"We are indebted to your tireless care," added Edwin, as he served himself a sizable portion of the boiled loin of veal and braised asparagus.

Nicholas glanced at Miss Kittridge, who had been placed opposite him. She looked up to meet his gaze, then returned her attention to the plate in front of her with haste. What was she thinking? He had not seen her in the last fortnight, although his faithful batman had told him Miss Kittridge often watched over him while he slept. Charley and Rosamunde had been his only source of companionship since that morning. Had his boldness shocked her so much that she dared not converse with him again lest he ravage her?

For the hundredth time, Nicholas wondered what had possessed him that morning. Since when had he started pouring his heart out about his past and taking to flustering innocents with unabashed lust? But she had tasted so sweet, and he had been unable to deny himself, even though he had no right to indulge.

He must return to the battlefield, a place where it was easy to forget all about the pleasures of the flesh amidst the horrors of war. She was everything he was not, and he had made a promise he would not break—no matter how tempting. The fever was, without doubt, to blame for his momentary lapse.

The ancient formality of this massive stone dining chamber, whose coldness matched the mood of so many of those who inhabited it, brought him back to the scene within it.

"Perhaps I could sit with Papa this evening to give a rest to Miss Kittridge," said his sister, Rosamunde.

"Whatever for? Miss Kittridge does not mind her duties. And you are needed to entertain the other ladies. Louisa and

Lady Susan would be inconsolable without your company," Her Grace said. "And now that your brother is well enough to join our evening circle, we will have quite the gathering of young people," she concluded without looking at him.

Seated next to him, Louisa Nichols, Rosamunde's dearest friend from Miss Polinaught's School for Young Ladies, looked ready to add to the meager conversation, but then lost her nerve as she toyed with the spitchcocked eel and roasted pigeon in front of her. She appeared much the same as when he had accompanied the girls cub hunting, fifteen years ago. Except Louisa's freckles had disappeared and her carrot-colored hair had mellowed.

The petite lady sitting on the other side of him giggled, displaying very small teeth evenly spaced. Her curled blond hair formed a picturesque halo around her dainty visage. "Your lordship is very quiet tonight," she said. "I am honored you chose me to lead you in to dinner, and happy to find you are much improved in health."

Rosamunde's assessment of Edwin's rich prospect had proved correct in every way. The vixen had been unrelenting in her new pursuit during every visit. And he had felt very much like prey, unable to move away from the miserable, calculating girl.

"Yes, it seems several weeks under the care of the Kittridges does indeed produce miracles." He turned and winked at Miss Kittridge.

"Miracles, my lord? I think not," said Miss Kittridge. "We leave to God alone those tasks. However, my family and I are much relieved to see you so quickly on the mend. You are not the sort who enjoys the idleness of the sickbed."

"I am sorry I was such a trial on your patience, Miss Kittridge."

"My dear, you were always a trial on the patience," inserted the duchess as she cut into the veal with vigor.

A thick silence intruded. Nicholas resisted the urge to fill it by turning the subject. It was a tried-and-true method he had used doggedly throughout childhood. But, he would not revert to his former ways.

Suddenly, he felt a slight tap on the tip of his boot. He looked up to encounter Miss Kittridge's clear gray eyes searching his face. He knew then that it was her polite way of disagreeing with Her Grace. He cleared his throat.

"Why, you are right, of course, madam. I was put on this earth to plague all of the weaker sex," he said, and smiled at Miss Kittridge.

"Lord Huntington, Her Grace described the portrait gallery to me and my grandmother earlier," Lady Susan said, redirecting the conversation. "She mentioned that I was the Veriest Picture of the first Duchess of Cavendish, and I am most curious to view her likeness."

He toyed with the idea of resistance. This lady was dispensing with as many stages of courtship as humanly possible. He moved his gaze to Miss Kittridge, who signaled her disapproval with an almost imperceptible shake of the head. The triumvirate of the doctor, his daughter, and Charley had become quite the gaol-keepers.

"Why, Lady Susan, I am sure *Edwin* would enjoy above all else giving you this small pleasure. He is much more familiar with our family's ancestors and very capable of leading you about properly." His stepmother's dark eyes dared Nicholas to interfere.

Little did the duchess know that it was the first time their thoughts had ever coincided, albeit for opposite reasons. She thought Nicholas would try to steal the silly heiress away from Edwin. He would have smiled if it had not been such a preposterous idea.

When the young lady's pout appeared, Dr. Kittridge cleared his throat. "Lady Susan, I am sure your tender nature will comprehend the necessity of Lord Huntington returning to his apartments at the conclusion of this repast. The gravity of his injury forces me to insist."

Oh, better and better. Nicholas did not have to rack his brain for an excuse.

Lady Susan's demure smile did not hide the angry frustration evident in her eyes.

Nicholas turned to his sister to see if she would chime in too, but instead saw, not for the first time, Rosamunde's timid glances toward the handsome young man seated beside her.

"You are to enter the clergy, sir? A most admirable profession," Rosamunde said with a shy expression.

"There is not much choice in the matter. I've not the head for science, and though I would vastly prefer to take up arms with my countrymen—" Mr. Kittridge was stopped by the sound of his father clearing his throat. "I have been convinced that the clergy is the soundest profession for me," he said with some gloom.

The two grandmothers, seated opposite each other, forgotten at the other end of the table, began to cackle and preen their feathers in competition.

"I have always said that I prefer a vicar's blacks to the ostentatious gold braid of an officer," said the Dowager Countess of Elltrope, Lady Susan's grandmother, as she simpered and looked toward the debonair vicar.

Nicholas's grandmother, the Dowager Duchess of Cavendish, pricked up her ears. "Good heavens, Hortense, then why ever did you marry Elltrope? Was he not an officer in the 33rd Foot before he was called home to carry on the title? His elder brother had perished, no?"

"You know the story very well, Margarita. We have known each other this age," the Dowager Countess replied stiffly.

"I am honored by your sentiments, Lady Elltrope," said the vicar. "It is not often a vicar's craven dress is prized over colorful regimentals," he said, his faded blue eyes twinkling.

The Dowager Duchess harrumphed in disgust.

Nicholas was amused. Some things never changed. His grandmother still fancied the vicar—the handsome old devil. A man whose sermons had always been mercifully short, and his kindnesses within the parish correspondingly generous. It gladdened the heart.

It was too bad he would not find much amusement the rest of the evening. Miss Kittridge, still mortally embarrassed by his chaste kiss, would tend to his father. Obviously, she was innocent of a man's kisses despite her intimate knowledge of a male's anatomy. He looked at the serene expression on the lady opposite him. She was plain, it was true, but she had an intelligent mind and a kind heart. And he had a notion that if she were allowed more gaiety in her life and pretty gowns instead of the prim gray frock she wore at every occasion, she would blossom into a beautiful woman.

If he were not the sort of man he was, he would enjoy deepening the acquaintance and giving her these things. But ladies of her ilk, or of any ilk, for that matter, were not part of the future allotted to him. He looked down at the heavy almond cheesecake Her Grace prized. One bite later, he placed the heavy silverware on the plate.

Charlotte was mortified. She had never found herself so tongue-tied in all her life. She was behaving like a milksop debutante incapable of muttering the most insignificant trivialities. It was absurd.

It was those mysterious green eyes of his. Or the combination of the somber green uniform and his eyes. She gripped her hands beneath the table and tried to take hold of herself. She would not be one of those young ladies whose heads were turned at the sight of a uniform.

At first, he had been like any other patient, although more distrustful than most, to be sure. Then when the fever had lifted, his humor and generosity of spirit had filled every hour of the time spent in his chambers—all culminating in that kiss. It was insane. It was as though she was a lovestruck schoolgirl.

And how had she dared to tap his foot? She almost

thought her threadbare slipper had moved on its own volition . . . if she had not known better.

She'd felt her appetite flee as the meal progressed, and the young ladies of the *ton* flanking either side of him flirted and charmed him throughout each passing course and remove.

And just as she'd chosen a topic to engage his views, she looked up to see his gaze resting on her. Her thoughts died, and she was sure she looked like a beached fish, mouth agape. She snapped it shut and returned her attention to the revolting dessert. Yes, she decided, it most certainly had something to do with those all-knowing eyes.

She was going to have to give up reading those poems of Byron. They were worse still than that novel she blamed for her embarrassing feminine feelings, which had heretofore remained blissfully dormant. She had put all romantical nonsense behind her years ago. *Yes, she was going to have to leave off all reading of Byron and the mysterious "Lady" now.*

Chapter Four

*"She had been forced into prudence in her youth,
she learned romance as she grew older—the
natural sequence of an unnatural beginning."*

—Persuasion

*B*egging your pardon, your lordship, but I canna read."
The stocky, red-haired stable hand held a thick tome in
his weather-beaten mitts. Nicholas glanced, unseeing, at the
man who stood in front of a small group in a large box stall.
He tried to move his leg to a less painful position as he lay
half sitting, half sprawled next to a dark horse on a thick bed
of straw. Her extended belly was streaked with sweat.

"Hand the book to Stevens, will you?" Nicholas asked,
not bothering to lift his gaze from the mare. She was struggling less now, which worried him greatly. Her eyes were
half-closed, and she flailed weakly at the air from time to
time with her forelegs. He knew what was happening, and
he knew what he would have to do. But he was willing to
grab at any other recourse. Where was the damn stable master? Even Stevens, who usually knew where every blasted
servant was at any time of day, had not been able to locate
him.

"My lord, it says that 'a maiden mare whose known foaling time exceeds two hours and who exhibits diminished
strength and heartbeat should be considered beyond salvation. All efforts should be performed to save the foal. Extended time in the birthing canal may lead to suffocation.
Preferred methods involve forcibly removing the fetus from
the . . . ' "

"Enough, Stevens," said Nicholas, resting his head on the

mare's flanks, "I know the conclusion." His large hands stroked the mare's muzzle as he whispered calming words to her now and again. He pondered if he should ask for the pistol now, and then he wondered for just the merest fraction of a second who would benefit from it more—he or the mare. The sound of someone coming distracted him.

Miss Kittridge poked her head around the stall door. "Pardon me, sir," she said, as she kept her eyes trained on the straw just inside the stall. "This is the mare, I assume then, that is experiencing a difficult foaling, is it?"

"Yes. Why do you ask?" He lifted his head to get a better view of her.

"Our maid mentioned there was a great to-do going on here. I thought I would offer my help before relieving my father this afternoon." She looked at the semicircle of rugged men. "Would you prefer . . . that is, do you want me to go away, Lord Huntington?"

Nicholas arched an eyebrow and considered the awkwardness of the situation. He was uncomfortable inviting Miss Kittridge into this crude, dark stall filled with men. He noticed a slight blush had reached the roots of the knot of wavy brown hair that threatened to become dislodged.

She was so delicate and little, almost birdlike in her dove-gray gown. Her arms were thin; he was sure they would snap in two with the merest yank. She ought to be more familiar with vinaigrettes than the two tons of prime breeding stock before her. But she had displayed her mettle in the sickroom. The least he could do, if she was indeed going to try to help his sister's favorite horse, was to save her the embarrassment of a rough-and-tumble audience.

"Gentlemen," he said with exaggerated politeness, "will you please leave us now? Miss Kittridge, I humbly beg your aid." There was a disgruntled murmur from the assembled group that indicated that they did not take kindly to the invasion of a female in their domain. They stared at her in disbelief until one dark look from Nicholas dispersed the ranks.

Stevens left the reference book in the stall and herded the group outside.

Miss Kittridge trod across the straw and kneeled behind the animal's haunches, stroking the horse's sides to signal her presence. A ripple of movement captured their attention.

"Well, at least the foal is still kicking," she said, reaching for some clean rags nearby. She pushed her short sleeve over the curve of her slim shoulder.

"Have you ever done this before?" he asked.

"With a cow. Once."

"I see," he said, with a hint of doubt. "I haven't been able to locate our stable master," he said.

She lowered her ear to the animal's side. "How long has she been laboring?"

"She has been pacing for at least one hour and a half," he said, stroking the horse's flanks. "She stopped trying to stand about twenty minutes ago."

"That is too long for a horse, I think. Yes?"

"Most are delivered of their foals within a half hour."

With one hand on the flank, she inserted the other into the birth passage slowly. The feeble horse raised her head and whinnied for a moment before lying still once again. Miss Kittridge looked lost in concentration on her task.

"Ah, there it is," she whispered as she closed her eyes. Blood seeped onto her sleeve. "I almost have it. Yes, wait," she said, as she seemed to be tugging with all her strength. "No, it's not working. I need a brace, please. Come sit beside me."

He crawled next to her, ignoring the sharp pain in his thigh.

"That's it. Now, please, I need to brace my feet to gain more strength." Her feminine voice clashed with the intense seriousness of her purpose.

"Perhaps I should do this," he said.

"No," she said. "It is better I do it. My hands are smaller, and I can already feel the cord stuck high up the foreleg."

"Yes, but I have more strength."

Her gray eyes appeared huge in her small face. He was so close he noticed the smallest freckle—or was it a mole?—under her right eye. He paused. He longed to tell her that she was the most admirable woman of his acquaintance, but he was sure gallantries held little value in her intellectual turn of mind.

"Please, I think I can save her." She stroked the mare's side. "But if I can't move the cord over the leg, I will sever it and then we will have to pull the foal out immediately. I can't promise to save either one of them. But, it is the only way, I think."

"I would not be putting added pressure on you if I told you that this is the best mare in all of Wiltshire if not all of Christendom, would I?" he asked, dryly. "We must try to save her, first and foremost." He grasped Miss Kittridge's small, booted foot as she scrunched up her leg in preparation for pushing against him.

"I'll try my very best." She closed her eyes and pulled. He felt with surprise her great reserve of strength as she levered herself against his hands.

"Oh, I don't know. The cord seems too short to come around. It must be tangled in several places. All right, so," she said with effort, "I'll need the smallest knife you have." She removed her arm and looked down at her ruined gown.

Nicholas reached into his pocket and retrieved a small pocketknife. He unsheathed the blade and placed the handle in her small palm.

"This is perfect," she said as she examined the tool. "All right. I'll cut the birth cord and then try to pull the foal out. But I don't think your mare has the strength or any natural contractions at this point to help at all, and I'm not sure I can do it alone, so you might need to help me."

"Of course," he said as she began the procedure.

Several long minutes passed before Miss Kittridge's arm became slack. "Can't quite hold onto it," she murmured with eyes closed. "There. It's done." She removed the tool and returned to the work of pulling out the foal. She shook her head. "It's not budging. It must be hung up somewhere else too. You try, now."

Nicholas reached for the tiny foreleg and felt the soft nose right behind it. The second tiny hoof was not far behind. He pulled with all his strength and revealed the two small hooves and wet, shiny nose. Miss Kittridge grabbed one foreleg in a rag and pulled alongside Nicholas. With a sudden whooshing sound they both fell back as the entire head appeared with the cord wrapped twice around the neck. Miss Kittridge untangled the cord. They then struggled to free the shoulders before pulling out the foal.

The mare made a great effort for a few moments as if she wanted to stand, but could only lay her head back down. Miss Kittridge rubbed the foal with rags, felt for the pulse, and checked the forelegs. She laughed suddenly.

"Look, he has a blaze in the shape of a question mark! It's almost as if he knew there was a question as to whether he would make it into this world or not." She laughed in pent-up relief.

Nicholas looked up into her radiant smile. She looked pretty—like a whimsical fairie. Her hair had fallen from its precarious perch and a sudden beam of sunlight weaved rays through its luxurious waves. He was dumbstruck. She was not simply pretty. She was breathtakingly beautiful.

Charlotte looked away when he did not return her smile.

"I fear for your horse," she said. "I fear she might not last. I wonder . . . is that a reference book?" She motioned toward the volume Stevens had left in the straw.

A familiar sick feeling snaked up his spine. "Yes."

"Would you mind seeing if it says anything about what to do after a difficult foaling?" She lifted up her blood-stained hands. "I don't want to dirty the book."

He swallowed and remained rooted to the spot. He had Stevens's name on the tip of his tongue.

"I'm sorry, does it pain your leg?" She continued when he did not respond, "Why, of course it does."

"No. I shall retrieve it," he said slowly. And suddenly he

knew he would not call out to Stevens. He made his way painfully to the entrance and picked up the book. He thumbed through the pages, stopping as he came upon the diagram of a horse. A large "H" was on the top, followed by an "O," but the rest of the letters danced a jig on the page. The well-remembered cold ring of sweat laced his neck cloth. It had been a long time since he had last tried to make sense of the letters on a page.

"What does it advise, my lord?" she asked while wiping her hands on one of the cloths.

He could not force himself to look toward her. He stared at the letter that looked like an "S" and remembered "*Ssssss* as in snake.*" He looked below the diagram to see hundreds of letters and words. Oh, he knew the names of most, but not how to string them together. He could feel the icy fingers of dread grip his forehead.

Finally, he looked up to face her—to encounter the familiar disgust, he was sure.

"Shall I take a peek? I've cleaned my hands now." She moved to sit beside him, settled the book on her legs, and began studying it.

She knew. He was sure of it, although she did a good job of hiding her shock at his ignorance. "I cannot . . . read."

She continued to concentrate on the page. "Yes."

Her small voice made the hairs on the back of his neck prickle. She was so calm. He wanted to provoke her.

"I am an ignorant."

She looked up, her dark eyes huge in her shadowed face. "No, never that."

"Then what do you call a stupid fellow too slow ever to acquire the ability to read?"

"I don't know, but certainly not an ignorant. An ignorant would never be able to converse on world history, estate management, and law as you did with me while you were confined to the sickroom."

"I had a patient servant willing to read aloud to me in my youth—just as you did while I was confined."

"Well, I have the ability to read, but not the memory to store facts as you have done."

He leaned closer to pick several strands of straw from her hair. Nicholas had a great desire to touch the smooth skin of her cheek. He had a greater desire to lay his head in her lap. But he knew, from experience, that it would scare her away. Perhaps the seeds of a great disgust of him had already germinated in her. It was amazing she had not found an excuse to take her leave of him straight away, given his sordid revelation. It pained him to think she might stay out of pity for him. Even disgust was better than pity. Why did he care what she thought? He had thought he had learned how to steel himself against those emotions long ago.

At last, he spoke. "I forced myself to memorize everything. It is an easy trick, I think, when one does not have the luxury of rereading facts."

"Well, you must be quite clever to have secured a commission as an officer. My brother spouts the requirements of becoming an officer regularly, and I am aware that a knowledge of the written word is necessary."

"So it is—unless one's father is a duke, with money to bypass protocol. I, of course, secured a loyal batman willing to serve as my 'eyes' around the clock."

"I had assumed your family had been opposed to the heir deserting his future responsibilities."

"Oh, no. I rather think the circumstance was quite the opposite." He stopped himself. What on earth was he doing, telling this girl these unsavory facts? He had no idea why he was offering any of these startling revelations, facts he had not pondered in many a year.

"Surely you jest. For I know that is your favored style, humor to avoid serious conversation." She lowered her gaze to the book and turned the page.

He couldn't understand why he was unable to shock her. He was uttering the most unsavory observations. Most ladies of his acquaintance would have been blubbering a bit by now or at least rendered speechless by his candor. He just wanted to turn the subject desperately now. His usual wit had deserted him.

A long silence intruded. The sound of Miss Kittridge turning the pages in the old book filled the void. He looked at her intelligent brow and wondered at the direct funnel of knowledge she could obtain from the printed word.

"It offers little information, just suggestions of care for the new foal," she said, closing the volume. "Is there another mare nursing now? May we transfer the foal when he stands?"

Nicholas called out for Stevens, who returned in moments along with the small group of stable hands. The group gawked at the prone mare and her foal, who was trying out his legs for the first time. In a moment, Nicholas arranged for the foal to be removed to another brood mare who was with milk.

"Be she dead, yer lordship?" asked the carrot topped Scottish lad, nodding to the dam.

"No. But it is probable she is soon to be. I'll stay with her now. Until . . . " The words stuck in his throat.

"I'm very sorry we could not save her," Miss Kittridge whispered.

He would have bowed down to her as a peasant to his queen for her efforts if not for his infernal leg. He looked at her blood-splattered person. "I'm sorry about your gown. Of course, we will see to its replacement. It is the very least I can do to thank you for your efforts," he said, as he looked to the group behind her. "I'm afraid I was about to end our exertions and forsake the possibility of new life when you came upon us."

"Please, my lord, let us not talk about the gown. It doesn't matter," she said, as she walked to the stall's doorway. "I'll bring some warm compresses to comfort her in a short while. I don't know what else to do to ease her discomfort. But I shall do a bit of research and ask my father."

Nicholas looked down at the horse. "I don't know how to thank you."

He looked up to see her bow her head and walk away. No one uttered a word until she was gone.

The Scottish stable hand shook his head. "An' me Da, he would be a sayin' that pigs would sooner fly than a pip of a girl would no' faint clear dead away to be performin' the likes of what tha' mere slip of a female jus' did!"

A young man who looked like the other, although shorter, responded. "Yes, and Da would clobber us o'er the head if he knew we stood by like a pack of fools and did naught to 'elp her!" That brought a round of laughter, which lightened the mood.

Stevens raised the book he held clutched in his hands. "Well, a fat lot this helped us. Thank the Lord for Miss Kittridge."

"Yes, store that book with all the others will you, Stevens?"

Nicholas closed his eyes as he remembered Miss Kittridge's lovely, smiling countenance. Yes, they should all say a prayer of thanks for Miss Kittridge tonight.

He was so very handsome. A slight shiver ran down her back. The three riders in the distance were just coming over the last hill before the deep valley, and she could finally discern that it was, indeed, he along with James and Lord Edwin Knightly. His shoulders were broader and his posture more commanding than that of the other two gentlemen. Her vision blurred as Charlotte put down the delicately enameled theater glasses. She hastened to shake the wrinkles from her gown and smooth back her mussed hair in the off chance the threesome turned in her direction.

It had been two days since she had seen him last. Two days of longing for even a mere glimpse of him. She was behaving like a silly goose. She refused to do so. She *would* behave in a normal fashion. She *would* converse naturally. Yes, she *would* return to her previous pursuit of gazing at birds. She moved back to the prickly hedgerow. The familiar scent of hawthorn and dog rose teased her nostrils. She refused the urge to look toward the riders again. Instead, she closed her eyes and picked up the distinctive call of the cuckoo. *Cu-ckoo-cu-rico.* And then the pounding sound of hoofbeats muffled out the birdcall. She opened her eyes.

"What's this? Charlotte! I thought you were with His Grace." James and the other two riders came to an abrupt stop in front of her.

"I was earlier, but Father ordered me to take some air."

"You were looking a little green about the gills after nun- cheon," James replied. "But then, perhaps it is just the re- flection of your gown."

She looked down at her green gown with embarrassment. It was a very ugly shade now that it was faded.

She turned toward Lord Edwin. "Good afternoon, my lord."

"It is a lovely day, is it not? I hope you have not taken your brother's unkind remark seriously, Miss Kittridge." He turned and gave a sweeping glance toward Lord Huntington. "Brothers can never be counted on to behave properly, you know."

She could not think of a way to contradict his mean sen- timent without appearing as abominably rude as the younger brother. Charlotte dared to look fully at Lord Huntington. "And how is the mare today, sir?"

"She lives. But I am uncertain whether she will ever re- cover. She has a dazed look in the eye, still."

"I will stop in again to look at her then," she said.

"Are you out bird-watching, dearest?" asked James, mo- tioning to her theater glasses. "Find any unusual feathered friends?"

"It is the first chance I've had since arriving." Charlotte's senses heightened under Lord Huntington's serious gaze. "I was searching out a cuckoo. He is hiding somewhere in the hedge, as they are wont to do."

"Ah, the infamous cuckoo. The usurper of the nesting an- imal kingdom," said James.

"Do tell, Miss Kittridge," said Edwin Knightly, after a small yawn.

"Oh, I would not presume to keep you from your afternoon ride."

"No, no. We are all agog," he insisted with a charming smile.

"I am afraid it is an ugly story. The mother cuckoo's modus operandi is to find another bird's nest, wherein she places one of her small eggs." She motioned toward a nest barely visible in the hedgerow. "And the mother cuckoo—"

"Or the hatchling nudges the other bird's eggs or baby birds from the nest, thereby ensuring the young cuckoo's complete care and protection by the host mother bird," finished Lord Huntington as he removed his beaver hat and ran a hand through his sweat-streaked hair. "I did not know you were fond of bird-watching, Miss Kittridge."

She watched the beautiful layers of his hair rustle in the slight breeze. There were so many different shades of brown ranging from sun-streaked to the darkest end of the spectrum. She had dared to stroke his hair several times when he had been asleep or delirious in the sickroom. She knew exactly where the fine strands became coarse below his temples.

Before she could find her tongue, her brother interrupted. "Actually, Charlotte is more interested in sculpting the bird forms she studies in the field."

Charlotte could feel her cheeks warming. She detested being made to stand center stage. She moved the small sketch pad she held to behind her back, and felt the knot in her stomach tighten.

"Miss Kittridge, you amaze us all every day. Your talents are boundless," replied Lord Edwin, laughing. "Where do you find the time for all these wonderful pursuits?"

"They are just that, pleasurable pursuits that I engage in whenever an hour or two of liberty presents itself. I fear my efforts are not in the talented realm as you suggest."

"Perhaps we could take a lesson from you one afternoon,

my dear. It would be a wonderful diversion for a dreary day. Or at least my brother and sister should join you, as they seem to be the more artistic members of the family tree. Never an interest in the written word had you, Nicholas?" Lord Edwin said before turning the subject. "But always the willing hero. Much more important that."

Charlotte turned to catch the granitelike expression on Lord Huntington's face.

"I daresay we are interrupting Miss Kittridge's solitary pursuit. Let us ride on," replied Lord Huntington. "If we dally any further, we won't have the chance to inspect the planting in the far fields and the herd of cattle."

"Well, I for one, have had enough of a ride to last me a fortnight. And I suspect Kittridge is of the same mind." Lord Edwin looked toward James. "Care to ride back to join the ladies for afternoon refreshments? My brother will keep us out here until nightfall with his infernal interest in all things agricultural."

James looked indecisive. "Well, all right, I suppose. That is if you don't mind, Lord Huntington?"

"Not at all," Lord Huntington replied, looking relieved by the promise of solitude.

She wanted to ask about his leg, as she could see him rubbing it. But she did not want to embarrass him. She could tell by the taut skin of his cheek and the beads of sweat on his brow that he was in serious pain. It was far too early for him to be riding. It had been only four weeks since his arrival, and he had broken his leg a month before that time. At least he still wore the stiffened bandage.

The threesome began to move off. "Charlotte, dearest, best retrieve your bonnet, lest a freckle or two appear," her brother said in mock playfulness.

"The air has only brought a pleasing color to your sister's cheeks, Mr. Kittridge," said Lord Huntington. He looked at her for a moment before turning away from the others to canter off through the valley.

She waved her hand, a silent good-bye on her lips. A

pleasing color. He thought she had *a pleasing color* on her
cheeks. She touched her face in wonder. She would not replace her bonnet now for her life.

Her brother and Lord Edwin made their good-byes, and
she was left to ponder the meeting in the afternoon's glori-
ous sunshine.

She placed the sketch pad at the bottom of a nearby
shaded stile and clattered to the top. Seating herself on the
old timber, she retrieved a small volume from her pocket.
Lady Rosamunde had lent it to her one evening as she sat
watch over the ailing duke. She ran her fingers over the gilt
lettering, *Pride and Prejudice*. She couldn't wait to read it.
So much for her vow to stop nurturing her newly formed romantic turn of mind. The devil with it. If she would never
have her heart's desire, at least she could live vicariously
through the mysterious "Lady's" characters. Ah yes, the
Devil was very clever in providing excuses for her behavior.

Chapter Five

*"I do not want people to be very agreeable, as it
saves me the trouble of liking them a great deal."*
—Letters of Jane Austen

*H*e would accomplish two goals, Nicholas decided the
next morning, his leg stiff from evening's slumber. He
would exercise his leg again, despite the pain, and he would
contemplate a solution to the sorry state of affairs he had
witnessed yesterday afternoon in this little corner of Christendom. Nicholas also rode out, he admitted to himself, to
escape the hours of dreary conversation at the abbey with
people whose only contentment in life could be found in discussing other people and events instead of ideas that could
improve the mind.

He had risen at his customary hour before dawn and hastened below to the kitchens, hidden away from all of the upstairs household's eyes save his. The scullery maid, there
early to stoke the fires, spied him and returned to her work
with a blush. Nicholas took the bits and pieces that would
make up his breakfast and left before Cook discovered him.

He saddled his own horse with the help of a sleepy stable
boy intent on impressing the heir. Nicholas worked the
aching muscles in his mending leg as he rode past the acres
planted with hay, wheat, and other crops for future fodder.
After touring the pastures and village the day before, an idea
had simmered in his brain. He had noticed that many of the
fields lay fallow.

He had also observed a steady trickle of returning soldiers flowing through the village. The honorable, worn, and
wearied soldiers had a certain bleakness in the eyes he had

not encountered while they faced the French army's guns. This was hopelessness. Each had a similar story to tell, one of farms lost to the enclosure acts, displaced families, and abject poverty dogging their trail home.

Nicholas had stopped one haggard fellow wearing his regiment's rifleman green and bought him a meal at the inn. The soldier told a sorry tale about how the parish had done everything possible to deny honorable men a supplement, humiliating and challenging each soldier's qualifications to be on the roll. It was a disgrace. Some of these disheartened souls he had seen in his childhood, some he had seen on the battlefield, and some he had never seen before as they were wandering without a place to call home. Something needed to be done before desperation turned to looting and looting turned to gaol or worse.

He must speak to Edwin and the steward about the idea of planting barley and hop vines. This was the beginning of a solution, he was convinced. From that, it was just a harvest away from a brewer's dream. The valley would be an ideal place for a brewery. The water from the spring flowing through the estate had long been declared the best in the county. It would take a while for the hop vines to produce pistillate catkins of the same high quality as those found in nearby Kent, but they could be purchased until then. And a brewery could provide employment for these men as well as the others living on the edge of poverty.

Nicholas rode by a series of laborers' dwellings in deplorable conditions. Edwin would condemn the idea of any lowering sort of industry on the estate. Perhaps the inducement of a steady flow of ready blunt would soften the blow to his brother's pride. He doubted it. But before he returned to his regiment, something must be done for these poor people who were barely scratching out an existence. As he passed a small cottage, a scrawny child of three or four years of age, dressed in rags, tossed a tiny handful of grain to two of the sorriest-looking chickens Nicholas had ever seen.

He shook his head and continued on past the far acres to

an untouched parcel of land his maternal grandparents had deeded to him a long, long time ago. This, perhaps, might prove to be the true answer. The land, adjoining Wyndhurst Abbey's acres, had been purchased by his maternal grandfather who had loved him. He'd given the parcel to Nicholas at age ten because as he had put it, "It has everything a boy could like; fields for riding, roaming and hunting, a very good, clear stream for bathing and fishing. I find nothing wanting, and everything good in nature."

Nicholas surveyed the vast acres with a critical eye. This land would have to be the solution if Edwin could not be convinced to aid the poor people of Wiltshire.

The dew had burned off the bracken bordering the small path when Nicholas rode toward Dr. Kittridge's cottage an hour later. If only the sharp thread of pain emanating from the point of the break in his leg would ease. But he had made a promise to the doctor, and he would keep it.

He knocked on the small wooden door and looked up at the uneven patches on the thatched roof. It looked greenish and moldy in places. He must speak to the steward about the upkeep. Several of the laborers had complained to him of similar conditions at their families' cottages. He shook his head as he entered.

The maid-of-all-work, Doro, bobbed a curtsy and bade him to wait in the small sitting room. The eastward window allowed the sunny day to invade the blue room filled with books from floor to ceiling along one long wall. A few volumes had escaped their cramped quarters and lay in small stacks near the base. The sight of them always brought a deep sense of longing coupled with fear. The secrets encoded between the covers fascinated him, yet he dreaded being around the printed page lest someone call on him to read aloud.

While he waited, Nicholas moved to the window to peer outside. His hand nudged an object in the window box. It was a little brown spotted wren made of fired clay, no doubt one of Miss Kittridge's creations. Its little mates, posed in different positions, were clustered all around a real nest with three speckled clay eggs inside. The sight reminded him of all the joys of boyhood in the spring when he had been able to escape the confines of a housebound winter to look for signs of new life.

He heard the greedy screeching of a blue jay beyond the open window as Dr. Kittridge entered the room.

"Ah, my lord. I am delighted to see you," the small man said, bowing. "I was just about to hasten to Wyndhurst to examine you and His Grace. You have saved me half a trip," he said, rubbing his tired-looking eyes and replacing his spectacles. He paused and peered over the rim of his eyeglasses. "You have not decided to forgo the examination, have you?"

Nicholas waved the doctor's doubts away. "No, no." He moved to the chaise the doctor motioned to him. "I rode here for the exercise." Nicholas extended his leg at the doctor's approach.

Dr. Kittridge ran his hand over the contours of Nicholas's bandaged thigh. "And how is the pain, my lord? Has it abated at all?"

"The wound has healed, as you know. There is still some pain from inside."

Dr. Kittridge unwrapped the outer bandage and pressed deep into the sides of his leg. Nicholas forced himself to breathe slowly and not flinch.

"Hmmm," murmured the doctor. "The bone splinter seems to be less prominent. I do think it will indeed heal itself without having to rebreak the bone. I must caution you, though, to take more care. If you overuse your limb more than the prudent amount, you might find yourself bedridden once again. I had suggested mild activities such as a short turn in your garden, not riding."

"Consider the admonishment complete, sir." Nicholas smiled. The doctor rebandaged the leg and Nicholas got to his feet awkwardly, before limping toward the window.

"I shall want to examine the leg again in another two weeks—for a final decision."

"Agreed," said Nicholas, as he pushed aside the frayed edge of the muslin curtain. Miss Kittridge was coming up the walk, carrying a basketful of greenery in her delicate arms. He swallowed as he remembered her gentle touch.

"And my father, sir? How do you find him? I must soon make plans to return to my regiment when I am well enough and if he rebounds." As he spoke, he gazed at Charlotte. She was almost childlike as she hastened up the flagged stones. There were grass stains on the front of her plain gray gown, and a smudge of dirt on her cheek. He felt old and unworthy in the face of such sweet innocence. Nicholas turned to the doctor when there was no reply.

"I would advise an unhasty departure, my lord," Dr. Kittridge said, as he walked to stand beside him. "It is doubtful His Grace will survive the spring if he continues in this fashion. But I think you are aware of that." Dr. Kittridge peered around to engage Nicholas's attention. "If you will pardon me for saying so, I would make arrangements to sell out soonest. You will be needed here. Your father needs you here."

"An intelligent suggestion, sir, but . . . I will be rejoining my regiment. You will be answerable to my brother. Although, I will, of course, make the recommendation that you remain here. The people of the village and the neighboring countryside are fortunate you agreed to come here," Nicholas said, then turned to face him. "I do hope you will stay."

Dr. Kittridge wrinkled his brow in confusion. Nicholas knew the older man would not condescend to ask for clarification. In any event, Nicholas had no desire to explain what long ago had been decided by all parties. If only his leg would heal faster. Blast it all.

It was past the hour she was supposed to be at the abbey, Charlotte thought, as she bustled into the cramped hallway of the cottage after her visit to a neighbor suffering from an inflamed joint. Doro buzzed around her collecting her basket, helping Charlotte untie her apron, even dusting a smudge of dirt from her hot cheeks.

"The good doctor has not yet left for the great house, miss," Doro said, as she took Charlotte's soiled gloves. "He be in the front sitting room with a gen'leman . . . with his lordship."

Doro must be mistaken. It must be another lord visiting. More and more patients arrived on their doorstep each week. Most had ailments so mild that they came on foot, on horseback, or in vehicles of varying importance. They had little patience for waiting for the doctor to call on them. She had learned a long time ago that those who complained longest and loudest were usually the least ill.

Charlotte had met so many of them in the last month. It was the standard fare—the stomach ailments, the toothaches. For the rich it was almost always the gout, or for the ladies, their nerves. Charlotte listened patiently to them all and made sure that her father saw the more serious cases between his visits to the abbey.

"Best steep two pots of the herbs this morning, Doro. Please add this willow bark to the usual other leaves." Charlotte pointed to the herbs she had picked from the expanding herb plot near the cottage.

"Yes, miss."

After straightening her gown, Charlotte knocked on the sitting room door. The faint voice of her father bade her to enter. The broad form and stark gaze of Lord Huntington made her catch her breath when she entered and curtsied. "My lord," she said.

"Miss Kittridge," he responded, nodding.

Her stomach tightened as she moved closer. She was keenly aware that she made no impression on him.

She remembered and tried to relive his kiss every day, especially each night, as she lay sleepless in her narrow bed. He was saying some inconsequential civilities to her father, and she knew without a doubt that the kiss she treasured was of no consequence to him at all.

But she yearned to help him, despite his station, and despite her embarrassment. It all seemed quite absurd and impossible. And who was she to suggest her ideas to the heir to a dukedom? She took her bold decision. She would speak to him.

"Father, the pots will be ready in a quarter hour. I shall bring them to the abbey directly."

"All right, then." Dr. Kittridge looked toward his lordship, and left after realizing Lord Huntington would not precede him out the door. He was too high in the instep for her father to insist that he leave for propriety's sake.

On the heels of her father's departure, Charlotte was tongue-tied. What had she been thinking?

"You have something to say to me?" he asked quietly.

"Yes, my lord," she murmured, desperate for another topic. "The mare. I have not had a chance to see her in many days. How does she fare?"

"Very well, considering."

"I shall have to stop into the stable again to see her."

"Hmmm," he replied.

Silence. Loud, oppressive silence. She looked up from the floor to see him gazing at her in expectation, not a smile in sight. She was a coward. How could she have ever thought to impose her views on this man? He would order her out of the cottage with great fury and pride. And he would be right to do so. She looked toward the door and planned her escape. He took one step toward her, using his shiny black cane.

"Is there nothing else, then? I had the distinct impression you wanted a word." He hesitated. "We have never discussed my bold actions of more than a fortnight ago. I fear I embarrassed you. I must apologize."

"Oh, no, my lord. I . . . I am sure I have quite forgotten it."

"It was unpardonable. I was out of line taking advantage

of you after all the long hours you spent nursing me with such gentleness and care."

The seeds of an idea took root. "It is not that," she continued, "I knew it meant nothing. It is just that . . . of course, I would not presume to . . . But, I thought," she rushed through the words, then stopped abruptly.

"Yes, my dear? What may I do for you to show regret for my actions? Name it and it shall be yours."

"No. No, sir, it will not do. Forgive my interference. It is not my place to—"

"Come, come, Miss Kittridge. This is unlike you. There is no need to fear me. You have seen me at my very worst, I do assure you. You have never failed to tell me what is on your mind, nor to listen to my ramblings. A refreshing attribute here in Wiltshire, if I do say so," he said with a slow smile.

He smiled so little. She hated knowing it would fade if she told him her idea. She closed her eyes. "Lord Huntington . . . it occurred to me that I could perhaps offer, or rather give, you a book I was looking at yesterday."

His smile disappeared. He looked away from her, out the window. The loss of his intense gaze allowed her to breathe again. "Let me explain—"

"No, I thought I had explained it to you," he interrupted in his deep, mellow baritone. "Miss Kittridge, I have no use for books, as you know." He moved toward the door behind her.

Charlotte presumed to stop him with her hand on his sleeve and he looked down at her, his green eyes filled with furious anger. "I must return to the abbey, Miss Kittridge. Please remove your hand." He snatched his arm away.

"No, please wait. Allow me to—"

"No."

"Please," she said in a low tone.

He was looking at her, waiting, she realized when she dared to raise her gaze to his. "Well?" he said, his irritation thinly veiled.

"Well, I thought you might enjoy looking at a book I have about birds. You were well-informed of the cuckoo's nature. You could look at the exquisite engravings and I could read the descriptions to you. And perhaps, just perhaps you could try—"

"Are you proposing to teach me how to read, Miss Kittridge?" he interrupted again.

"Well . . . Yes."

"And do you not think that every known method has been applied during my youth? Do you not think that over the course of the years five scholars were brought in to attempt the impossible?"

"No, you misunder—" she jumped in.

"Do not interrupt me, Miss Kittridge," he said, and continued above her plea. "Do you not think that I was sent off to Eton at the age of seven, returned at nine, along with a note saying that I was without doubt an 'ignorant, incapable of reading the written word, incapable of learning, incapable of anything save bashing the heads of those who mocked me'? Do you not now think that I and my father have tried everything in the power of a dukedom to try to learn how to read? It is impossible," he said, his dark green eyes flashing. "And you have the audacity and presumption to think that you will find a solution? Do you believe that one of your miraculous potions will cure me of a tendency toward stupidity, a nodding toward the nod-cock, a, a, a . . . Ah, there, you have forced me to betray my weakness in vocabulary, Miss Kittridge. Enough said."

She wanted to sink into the floor. She would really be grateful if she could just have one good swoon, say like Mrs. Bennett in *Pride and Prejudice*. But she had never swooned in her life.

"I believe you would enjoy the book, my lord." She looked him in the eye, determined to disarm him with her resolve. "And I believe you owe me, my lord."

Oppressive silence again permeated the walls of the room. It was emotional blackmail, it was. And she was sure

Nicholas knew it as well. He had probably not thought her capable of it. But then, he had underestimated her spirit.

"Are you blackmailing me because I had the audacity to kiss you or because you have nursed me back to health?"

She wouldn't blink. She wouldn't blush. She would gain her point in whatever fashion necessary. "Which reason would force you to take the book, my lord?"

"You are playing most unfairly, my dear."

"Playing fair did not seem to be working very well in this case, Lord Huntington."

"Ah, the old 'ends justify the means' tactic," he said, with just the hint of a smile. "Blackmailer."

"Coward," she said, bracing for a barrage of curses.

He almost laughed.

"You would like me very much to look at it," he said, not committing himself.

"Yes."

"For what purpose?"

What could she say? Nay, what would she dare to admit? That she loved him? Not in a lifetime of repressed longing.

"The engravings are exquisite. We could—we could discuss any of the birds that are not familiar to you."

He said nothing for a long moment.

"Where might this paragon of information on the beaked and feathered world be found?"

She rushed to the nearest stack of books behind the settee and retrieved a volume. Charlotte placed it into his outstretched hand. "It is precious to me."

"I shall endeavor not to tear it to shreds in frustration, Miss Kittridge."

"I did not mean to suggest—"

"I understood you very well. Have no fear."

The male sex. She would never understand them. This one in particular. His mood changed from anger to teasing in a moment. It was very hard to follow along. On the one hand she felt she must be deferential to his station, but on the other, she had seen him for an entire month—in his bed, in his nightshirt, in a fever, in a temper when awake, in blind terror when he slept. She did not feel at all deferential to this man, she felt protective. And so much more . . . A feeling she dared not decipher. A feeling she dared not nurture.

"Thank you, Miss Kittridge, for your kindness—your many kindnesses," he said dryly, fingering the title on the book's cover. "Shall we meet again then the day after tomorrow? To discuss the book, my dear Miss Blackmailer?"

"That would be pleasant, my lord."

"So be it," he said, tipping his head and walking to the door.

She held her breath as she listened to the muffled voice of Lord Huntington on the other side of the door asking Doro to arrange for his horse to be returned to the abbey's stables. She exhaled all at once as she moved to the side of the window. She watched his powerful broad back covered by his worn green Rifleman's uniform move away from the cottage. Something about the way he held erect his wide shoulders which then narrowed down to his slim hips and muscled legs made her shiver. He was limping badly, leaning on a cane rather than the crutch she had brought to the abbey. But she knew better than to have argued the point. Charlotte knew to choose her battles wisely with the stronger sex. She was amazed he had capitulated earlier.

He stopped just before coming to the end of the walkway and turned, looking toward something in the distance. Charlotte studied his noble profile. He looked like the statues found within the pages of her art and sculpture books. The proud brow, the strong nose, the full lips, and noble chin. A breeze ruffled his hair before he set his hat on his head. Suddenly, he turned and looked at her in the window. She did not have time to duck into the folds of the curtain. He stared at her for the longest moment, and she could not look away. And then he was gone, without a smile or a tilt of the head.

He did not know what to make of it, he thought, as he limped up the slope, moving at a snail's pace, away from the cottage. Why had she forced a book on him? He had long ago given up any hopes of reading, and had been grateful when his very last tutor of a string of them had convinced his father to stop torturing him. He had been fifteen then.

Henceforth, he had spent twelve hours of every four and twenty in the outdoor world, longer in the summer months. He had loved the camaraderie of working alongside the laborers, the shepherds, and the horses, and also the hours spent surrounded by nature's tranquility.

Those two years had been the sole period of any sort of true happiness until the day Her Grace had insisted he'd grown too wild. That day he had asked his father to buy him a commission and falsify his abilities. After listening to Nicholas's plea, his father had consented without argument or pause. His family had been glad to be rid of him—except Rosamunde, of course. And Nicholas had been glad to go.

He cursed his ill fortune as the grade of the hill increased in time to the ache in his thigh. He would be damned if he would restrict himself to a "turn about the garden." He had a hankering for a long walk. And a long walk it would be— to the lake. Nicholas stuffed the cursed volume into his breast pocket and forced himself to increase his pace.

He made his way through the woodlands of birch and oak, over the decaying fence, to the vast lake past the crumbling folly. The sun's rays burned through his many layers of clothing. Out of breath, Nicholas stopped at the water's edge, threw down his cane, and shrugged out of his uniform. He didn't even stop to think, just peeled off all of it after unwinding the bandages and shucking off his boots. The lake appeared dark green and cool, the sun bouncing off the little wavelets.

He made a shallow dive, avoiding the murky algae of the deeper water. The shock of the cold made his stroke quicken through the water. He felt powerful again, for the first time in a long while, as he let his upper body do almost all the work of propelling him forward. He swam all the way to the center of the lake, to the small island where he once collected duck eggs in the summer months. Cook had always spoiled him with omelettes when he had managed not to crack any on his return. A few geese honked their displeasure at his intrusion. Nicholas searched the favorite nesting areas and found caches of eggs.

"Have no fear, I shall not rob you of your treasure," he said to the ducks. And then with mock severity, "This time."

The opposite shore looked twice as far from this vantage point, and he was tired. He lay down on the grassy bank, under the dappled sunlight of a small tree, and dozed with one arm flung over his eyes.

Why had she forced the book on him? He understood little of the female mind. During his thirteen years as an officer with the 95th Rifleman, he'd had little opportunity to converse with gently bred females other than the bighearted wives, of military men, who refused to be left behind. Oh, he was no saint, he had slaked his thirst with one or two very willing women who followed the drum, but the acts had not banished his loneliness, and he'd taken a private oath of abstinence.

Why was she trying to help him? He feared she might have taken a liking to him, the complete idiot that he was. Perhaps that gentle kiss had been her first. He would have to take care not to encourage her. In the past, it had been so easy. His days in the army had kept him from all matrimonially minded ladies.

Miss Kittridge did not know he would never search the marriage mart. He must be careful not to bruise her heart. She had been kind to him and he was grateful. He liked her. She was a heady combination of childlike vulnerability and high intelligence that he found hard to resist. But he could never forget that his supreme failings were her strengths and her passion.

Remembering her dazed expression and open and full lips the morning he had dared to kiss her, he closed his eyes and cursed. What had possessed him to complicate matters? He knew very well that Charlotte Kittridge was the type of female ripe for heartbreak. He must take care to rein in his appetite. He was unworthy of her and would not hurt her for the world.

The sun was halfway into its descent to the west when he opened his eyes. Nicholas took the coward's way this time, inching into the chilly lake water, feeling the mud and moss between his toes before plunging in. Pulling himself up on the outer bank, he tripped over an imbedded rock, the same rock that had caused countless skinned knees in childhood. Without warning a great surge of anger and frustration over all things that could not be named took hold. Nicholas grasped the prominent edge of the dark rock and pulled using all his back muscles. His wounded leg pounding, knees shaking, he triumphantly pulled the offending element from its niche. A conquering yell surged past his lips, and he felt like one of those naked Indians he had heard inhabited the colonies. Nicholas laughed out loud at his absurd behavior, then hurried into his uniform.

Chapter Six

"I do not pretend to set people right, but I do see that they are often wrong."

—Mansfield Park

*T*he sun had pierced the darkness of early morning and bore down on Nicholas's head and shoulders. It was a perfect day to make hay. A group of laborers, using the new scythes Nicholas had brought back with him from Spain, were already halfway through the first field.

As he dismounted, he spotted Owen, who was not as hale and hearty now as he had been at fifteen. They had met up as often as Nicholas's elder friend had been allowed to quit the fields early. Owen's blond hair had thinned, and he looked older than his years.

"What do you think, man?" asked Nicholas.

"Methinks this is a damn dangerous tool, it is." Owen clapped his hand on Nicholas's shoulder. "I'm guessing the blood flowed freely in Spanish fields with this nasty weapon."

Nicholas studied the apparatus and waited for Owen to say more.

"I must admit, with its added length and moving hinge, it does cut more hay. O' course, the younger lads and old men can't take on the extra weight all day."

"It sounds as if it won't work, then," Nicholas surmised.

"Well, you'll have to take away mine at the point of a pistol." Owen gave a broad grin.

"You old bag of wind," Nicholas retorted. "Never could trust you."

"Now, I resent the implication, my lord," Owen said with puffed-up fakery.

"Now, don't you go 'my lording' me." Nicholas laughed. "That's when I know I can trust you least of all. And where is my erstwhile batman-in-training?"

"O'er there," replied Owen, pointing to where Charley was, holding a scythe much too large for his small frame. "He's taking to the farmin' life like a duck to water."

Charley ran up to him. "Lord Nick, we've been at it for hours," he exaggerated. "Thought you'd be here afore now."

"Owen tells me haying agrees with you."

"Well, in some ways yes and in some ways no."

"Well?"

"Well, 'tis pleasanter—"

"More pleasant." Nicholas corrected him.

"More pleasant to be outside singing and working with the other boys and men. But then 'tis damp and cold in their cottages. I think I prefer livin' in the abbey, even though I have to watch that Cook doesn't clobber me with her spoon. And His Grace's valet is nice enough when he chooses to lower himself." Charley sniffed.

Nicholas glanced at Owen. "Looks like you'll be losing a hand in the long run then. But what is this about the cottages? Is it the thatching? I've noticed it looks in poor condition."

"That it is. Mr. Coburn, your dear steward, says there's not time or blunt available to fix them up. Perhaps you would like to see one for yourself."

"Is that an invitation for a midday meal?" Nicholas asked, with a smile.

Owen looked embarrassed and blustered a little. "Why, of course. Sally will be pleased to see you. Mind you, we dine simply, not like them fancy dishes in the abbey."

"I haven't seen little Sally Peterson since she was following you around like a hound on a scent, all those years ago. I should have guessed she would have been the one to tame you," Nicholas said, laughing.

"Caught me under the horse chestnut tree on Guy Fawkes Day, she did," Owen admitted.

"I guess I'll have to earn Sally's fare. Shall we?" he said, motioning toward the field.

Nicholas joined the communal effort that continued throughout the hot day, taking short breaks to quench the great thirst the work churned. When they broke for the short midday meal, Nicholas and Charley walked the short distance to Owen Roberts's small dwelling.

The rushes on the roof were in the same deplorable condition as others he had seen all over the valley. Inside, it was a sadder story. Oh, Sally kept the small two-room cottage as clean as a dirt floor would allow. Whitewash was peeling off the damp walls, and a baby cried in the next room. A small loaf of bread sat in the center of the simple wooden table, where three pairs of eyes looked at it with hunger. Two meager slices of dried ham sat on a plate at the head of the table.

Sally's welcome was marred by her embarrassment. "I am afraid you have caught us with our larder a bit short, my lord. Owen was to kill a hen this eve."

He hadn't seen any sign of a chicken in the yard, however. The people of Wiltshire were a proud lot. Too proud to admit to hunger to a childhood friend. The two men sat next to each other, surrounded by the three silent Roberts children and Charley. Sally brought a bowl of boiled potatoes to the table and sliced the bread, handing a portion of each to everyone. One slice of ham was given to each of the two men.

Nicholas could hardly stop himself from forcing portions of his slice to Sally and the children. But he would never dare to deprive her of her pride. She excused herself and disappeared to attend to the baby, without consuming a bite. Nicholas was already envisioning the brimming basket of foodstuff he would have delivered here each week. But if Owen's family was reduced to this squalor, what of the other families?

The valley had been reduced to this?

During the sad little meal, Nicholas told Owen about his idea for a brewery. Owen's eyes lit up, and he spent all of ten minutes expostulating on the brilliance of the plan.

"It is a fine idea, Lord Nick. Seeing as how you're the heir, that good-for-noth— . . . I mean, your brother and the steward can't say nay to you. And the water is the best in all of five counties. Men will be lining up for the work."

Nicholas gave a small shake of his head to Charley, who was reaching for a second slice of bread. Charley withdrew his hand and glanced at Owen. Out of the corner of his eye, Nicholas saw his friend's face turn beet-red. The rest of the meal was consumed in silence, a vast change from the excitement his idea of a brewery had conjured up.

At the end of the day Nicholas rode back to the abbey, Charley riding pillion. Wyndhurst was in a disgraceful state of affairs. He was ashamed. Why had his family not provided better for its laborers and tenant farmers?

It had never been like this when he was a boy. The war and his father's ill health were poor excuses for the poverty he had witnessed. He was amazed the Robertses and others like them could survive on so little. But then they were not surviving, if the truth were known. He had not failed to notice two tiny headstones near Owen's cottage.

Meanwhile, the inhabitants of the abbey dined well no less than three times a day, including tea with enough sweetmeats to keep a tooth drawerer in high demand.

He would have a visit with Edwin, his father, and the new steward. Yes, it would jolly well be a long visit with the threesome. Life could not continue as it was.

The next day, a light rain pattered on the windows, forming tiny crystalline droplets. Charlotte dipped her hands into a water bowl and continued to smooth the small clay bird form before her. It had been foolish of her to wait for Lord Huntington in the front room. He wouldn't come. Her stomach clenched in nervousness. If she didn't keep her hands busy, thoughts of him would drive her mad.

She rubbed her eyes in exhaustion. His Grace had been up half the night with a fever and a series of coughing fits that had left him overcome. At last, he had fallen into slumber at half past three in the morning, and her father had relieved her at seven o'clock, allowing her two hours of sleep and half an hour to dress and prepare a possible lesson for his lordship—if he allowed her to teach him.

Lord Huntington had promised to meet her. Surely he would come, rain or not. She reshaped the head of the little clay wren she cupped in one hand and rehearsed her lesson plan, almost missing the faint knock at the cottage's outer door. She threw a damp cloth over the clay figure and plunged her hands into the bowl of water. Quickly drying her hands on her apron, she pulled it over her head and tossed it in the corner. Doro called to her. Charlotte ran a hand over her hair to smooth down any stray locks as she entered the narrow hall, almost knocking the maid down.

"Oh, Miss, his lordship be in the front room waiting on you." The maid straightened Charlotte's gown. "Shall I bring you some refreshments, deary?" she asked with an inquisitive gleam in her eye.

"Oh, no, Doro. We shall not require anything, thank you." Charlotte could see the disapproval in the maid's eyes. She felt a slight blush in the making, but hurried to the front room as the maid muttered something behind her.

He stood looking out the window the same as yesterday, except that a flawlessly fitted dark blue coat stretched between his broad shoulders, tapering down to his narrow hips. Buff-colored breeches and top boots finished the elegant picture he presented. It was the first time she had seen him dressed in anything except his uniform or nightshirt. The crisp white cravat was tied in many intricate folds and emphasized the tanned color of his face, the face of a man who obviously spent most of his time out of doors. Lord Huntington turned to her and smiled, revealing straight teeth that rivaled the shade of his starched white cravat. It was all quite dazzling. Charlotte again found herself without words.

"It seems you do not recognize me, Miss Kittridge," he said, bowing. "I am afraid this is the first time I have been forced out of uniform in many a year. My father's valet has been displaying paroxysms of delight while he attempted the newest way to tie a cravat—almost more so Charley, who has decided that he will learn every version by day's end. I left the two of them with a boxful of stocks next to a much more willing victim—my bedpost."

He was trying to set her at her ease, she knew. It was almost working. She did not know how to compliment his attire without appearing foolish. "Your appearance . . . You appear lov-lovely, Lord Huntington," she said, cursing inwardly at her ridiculous words.

He threw back his head and laughed. "Ah, Miss Kittridge, I thank you. It has been many a day since I have been complimented thusly," he said. "If I had known you would approve, I would have asked the tailor my stepmother insisted I employ to work much more quickly. It seems Her Grace had insisted that my battered Rifleman's uniform was no longer presentable to her elegant eye. Actually, I am hounding the poor man to finish a new uniform. I don't feel I am myself without one on—much like a hermit crab between two shells."

"Yes, of course. It would be natural to feel that way." She looked down at her modest dove-gray morning gown. The muslin had been washed so many times that it appeared to be half its original weight. She must talk to Father about new dresses.

He took a step closer and pulled out a starched new handkerchief from his breast pocket. "Miss Kittridge, will you allow me to offer you the use of my handkerchief? You seem to have a few spots of something—something powdery on your nose." He peered at the offending feature.

She was utterly mortified as she accepted the cloth. She swiped at her nose and looked up at him after several seconds. "I am afraid it is some clay. I was—I was in my workroom before you arrived."

"Ah, that explains it. Allow me," he said, taking the cloth from her fingers.

She closed her eyes and held her breath as he gently touched her nose and cheek with the delicate handkerchief. She inhaled his warm, sandalwood scent, and for a moment she was floating. The rubbing stopped and she fluttered her eyes open. His mesmerizing, half-closed green eyes were very close to hers.

She was paralyzed with longing. Longing for him, for a return of her . . . her deep affection? No, she must be honest—it was more than that, much more. Dangerously more.

She swayed toward him before noticing a painful reflection in his eyes. He stepped back and she almost lost her balance. How mortifying. She covered her cheeks with her hands and closed her eyes.

"Thank you for your assistance, my lord." With those seven words, spoken without the hint of a quiver, she recovered her grace and her pride, and swore never to behave so foolishly again. She would not. "I—I took the liberty of visiting your sister's horse and the foal yesterday. Your stable master said he thought she would make a full recovery although it is doubtful the horse should continue her role of broodmare. But he did say Lady Rosamunde will probably be able to ride her once again in a few months."

"Yes, and it is all due to your actions, *Miss Kittridge*. I cannot thank you enough. You have won the respect of every last man and boy in the stable yard with your quick thinking."

"It was my pleasure and my duty, sir." Charlotte walked over to the window well and picked up the familiar slim volume Lord Huntington had placed there.

"I have dutifully looked over the wonderful engravings. I was quite taken by two species that I had not seen before," he said, as he motioned Charlotte toward the settee before joining her there. He took the book from her hands and skimmed through a few pages before pausing at one.

She touched the page. "Oh, yes, that is the grey wagtail.

A bird I have never seen in England either, although I did see one, once, in France."

"A wagtail? What a curious name," he said, grinning.

Charlotte refused to comment. "Let me see, yes . . . It says here that it gained its name by wagging its long tail up and down while perched atop long willows or on the ground."

"Fascinating," he replied.

Charlotte noticed that he was not looking at the book, but focusing on her face. She feared he could see more clay on her nose. "Yes, isn't it?" she said. "And the other bird?"

He turned several pages and stopped at one, smoothing the sheet then handing it to her. "I believe it says 'water rail'?" he said, with some self-consciousness in his voice. "Although I have never seen this one in my travels either."

"Why, Lord Huntington," she said with wonder, "that is precisely what is written in the book." She hesitated. "You were able to read it?"

"Well, yes and no, to be honest. I made out 'rail' and concluded it said 'water' before it as I spied the water in the engraving and the word began with 'wa.' I remembered the word begins with those two letters."

She hesitated, steeling herself. "Would you be insulted if I showed you a primer I found at the abbey? I am curious to know where your difficulties in reading lie."

This was the crucial moment. She bit her lower lip and crossed her fingers under the bird book. Crossed fingers had only ever failed her once. She looked up at him with the most innocent expression she could endeavor to form on her face.

"Was there ever any doubt that that was where all of this was leading, Miss Kittridge?" he asked.

She would take that for permission. Charlotte jumped up and picked up the primer she had tucked below the top few books of the nearby stack.

"Your certainty of a positive response to your request leaves me almost deflated, Miss Kittridge," he drawled.

She leaned over the book stack, then glanced at him from her bent position to find him staring at her . . . her posterior. "What, sir?"

"Please forgive me. Actually, I was thinking of . . . " and here he began a deep rumbling laugh. "As we have always been ever honest with each other, I was thinking of a grey wagtail, Miss Kittridge."

Charlotte bumped her nose on the stack in front of her as she straightened quickly. She was sure she was blushing. The fine light of humor sparkled in his eyes, and she could not stop herself from laughing with him.

"I see you are trying to disarm me with your candor." She came around the settee with the primer. "Perhaps in an effort to escape your lesson, sir," she said, attempting a stern stare. "But it cannot be done. I refuse to be put off."

"An admirable and necessary trait in a teacher, I do assure you," he admitted ruefully.

She opened the primer to the first page, which had the alphabet printed in large letters stretched across several lines. "What do you see?"

She watched as he looked to the side and began reciting the alphabet by memory.

"No. What do you *see*?"

"Ah. You are observant, Miss Kittridge," he said, staring at her. He lowered his gaze to the primer, his face now pale. "I see the letters of the alphabet. It is just that some are dancing around on the page and moving around in a way that will give me the headache if I stare too long at them." He gripped his forehead in aggravation.

"Which ones can you make out?"

"*A*—and the next I realize is a *B*—but it sometimes looks like a *D*. Then *C*, and *E* or *F* and *G*. Later I see *M*'s and *N*'s, which look the same, and *S*'s and *Z*'s, which also look similar. But worst of all is trying to string together the sounds of letters."

He gazed with intensity at the page. A small vein at his temple pulsed near the surface. He looked up at her with frustration. "Shall I tell you what I think of all *I*'s and J's, which annoy me with their dots?"

"Which letters are clear?"

"*A*'s and *O*'s and *G*'s are quite straightforward letters, don't you think?" he said with a wry smile.

"Humor serves you well, does it not?" she asked.

"Come, come, Miss Kittridge, let us get on with the lesson. We have much to cover if you intend to have me reading within the hour."

Charlotte sighed. She hadn't the faintest clue how to begin. For the next hour and a half she forced herself into the role of patient teacher, reading aloud then listening to Lord Huntington stumble over page after page of childish nonsense.

His endurance was staggering, but the task seemed impossible.

Well past the time she would have suggested a rest, he plodded along, with errors and stops aplenty. After one particularly challenging passage where he had tripped over many words, he came to a full stop.

"I think we have had enough, don't you? I daresay I have demonstrated my superior skills to you, Miss Kittridge," he said, a cynical expression on his face.

"I believe we both need a rest from the page. I am exhausted, and I can tell that you have the headache."

"Your fatigue must be due to your superior ability to bite your tongue, Miss Kittridge. I have never been fortunate enough to have a teacher willing to let me fail alone. Instead they could not stop themselves from telling me the word I was trying to decipher. You are a veritable fountain of patience and kindness."

Well! That was praise indeed. "I am quite sure I would not have tried so hard as you have done. You are a relentless student, sir," she replied with feeling.

"We shall have to form a mutual admiration society with a membership limited to two, I daresay," he said, giving her a glimpse of his dazzling smile.

He was so very beautiful, she thought for the hundredth time this past hour or more. She could not come up with a more appropriate description. How she longed for Byron's turn of phrase, or Shelley's brilliant talents, displayed in the volumes she had borrowed from the abbey. How could she describe the way his brown hair fell forward onto his forehead when he bent over the page? Or the evenness of his profile and his sonorous voice? Or the feeling she had when his knees, fabric pulled taut over muscle, had touched her own?

She smiled, finding herself unable to form a lighthearted retort.

"Has my limited ability frightened you, Miss Kittridge? Are you going to refuse me another lesson?"

"Of course not. I am gratified you are willing to return for more torture, my lord," she said, before moving her gaze from his neck cloth to his eyes, the color of the fast rise of grass in the fields.

"I am willing because *you* will be my teacher." His intense gaze made her breath quicken.

He stood up from their cramped position offering his hand to aid her from her seat. She felt her stomach clench as she watched him bring her hand to his mouth. Warm, full lips pressed onto the sensitive back of her hand. She felt the slightest wisp of heated breath on her skin before gooseflesh covered her arms. He peered down at her and winked beneath half shuttered eyes.

"Thank you, Miss Kittridge. May I return then in two days time?"

"I would be honored, my lord," she said, as he released her hand. She curtsied to his brief nod.

Charlotte watched him depart from the room, but would not allow herself to spy on him from the window. Turning, she noticed he had forgotten his handkerchief. She pressed it to her face and breathed deeply his masculine scent. At least she would have this little memento until her conscience would force her to return it.

She shook her head in annoyance. She would not play the tragic, longing heroine. The hero would have to return a measure of feeling other than gratitude for her to justify such passionate sensibility. And the idea of unrequited love went against the grain of her practical nature. He had no feeling for her in the least save for appreciation of her teaching and nursing abilities. A poor substitute for love, indeed.

She would talk herself out of any tender feelings she harbored, if it was the last thing she did.

Chapter Seven

"For what do we live, but to make sport for our neighbors, and laugh at them in our turn?"

—Pride and Prejudice

*F*ather, I am so happy you have been able to join us," said Rosamunde.

"Not such a grand feat, my dear, when one considers I have merely moved a sixteenth of a mile from Wyndhurst at most, and all of it by way of two very capable footmen," the Duke of Cavendish replied with a wan smile. "But I am very glad to be a part of your picnic."

"I think it is most foolish of you, Richard. I shall not forgive you if you become weaker from the exertion. You are looking too pale by half. But no one consulted me," Her Grace said, looking at Nicholas.

"Octavia, I shall be fine—" the duke said.

"I am, indeed, to blame," Nicholas interrupted.

"Nonsense, my son." The duke patted Nicholas's hand.

Nicholas surveyed the gathering on the manicured middle level of the parterre garden flanking the stone abbey. The entire family and three houseguests, supplemented by the Kittridges and the vicar, Mr. Llewellyn, were happily ensconced on the lengths of cloth laid out under an old oak tree that bordered the view of the magnificent formal gardens. The scent of roses and jasmine permeated the air.

Dr. Kittridge fussed about his frail patient while the two grandmothers had begun a fevered battle to claim the attentions of the amused and flattered vicar. If his father had had more vitality, he would have put a stop to the old ladies' nattering and coy preening of withered flesh. Years ago the duke had forbidden his mother to have anything further to do with the vicar, save Sunday sermons. For while the aging Mr. Llewellyn was the third son of an impoverished earl, he was not to be ever encouraged to take the place of the much beloved—and long dead—Duke of Cavendish, Nicholas's grandfather.

It was a lovely early summer day on one of the most beautiful estates in all of Christendom, thought Nicholas. Yet, a distinct feeling of unease filled his mind as well.

"I am certain the young ladies would like a turn about the garden, Nicholas," said the duke.

"Oh, my, yes. It would be a Fate Worse than Death to neglect to exercise our limbs on a day such as this." Lady Susan moved to Nicholas's side and linked her arm with his with admirable haste.

Rosamunde jumped to his aid. "I think I will take a turn as well, Brother," she said with a shrewd smile. "I am sure Louisa will lend me her arm as yours will be full," she said to tease him.

"Miss Kittridge would you and your brother care to join us too? Edwin?" asked Nicholas.

"Thank you, yes, Lord—" Miss Kittridge began.

"Oh, yes, Miss Kittridge, you must join us," Lady Susan interrupted, her nose held high. "It is only fair that you be given the chance to rub elbows with us occasionally. Edwin, do condescend to squire about Nurse Kittridge." She tightened her grasp on Nicholas's arm.

"This will not do. Miss Kittridge, I would be honored if you would join Lady Susan and me," Nicholas said.

"I am capable of walking along unaided, but thank you." Miss Kittridge turned and hurried away. Lady Susan tugged his arm, urging Nicholas toward the gardens.

Nicholas shook his head. "That was unkind."

"Yes, it was very rude of her."

"I was not referring to Miss Kittridge."

"I don't understand, my lord," she replied.

Nicholas looked down at the aura of petite femininity that

graced his arm. Wide, cornflower-blue eyes looked back at him and fluttered. The white flowers entwined in her pale blond hair together with her white muslin dress painted a pretty picture, indeed. She was a very fetching little *devil* in disguise.

"It is such a lovely time of year to take the air, is it not, my lord?" she asked.

Ah, they would embark on the safe topic of the weather—a skill taught to well-bred young ladies early in life. "If one doesn't mind the irritating little insects that plague us all," he said, swiping at one of the offending gnats.

"Yes, of course, my lord," she said, crestfallen.

How Nicholas longed to drop back to take part in the intelligent conversation behind him. He could hear Rosamunde engaged in a conversation with Miss Kittridge about the rapid recovery of her mare Phoenix. Lady Susan propelled him along despite his injury.

"Do you not think that a folly would look beautiful at the center of the garden? Just here, surrounded by rosebushes." Lady Susan indicated a spot in front of them.

"It might be difficult to enter without getting a thorn or two." He looked over his shoulder to find Miss Kittridge.

When he returned his attention to Lady Susan, she appeared on the verge of tears. He had to try to be polite, lest the creature dared to create a scene. "But there is a folly a mile or so from here, overlooking a lake. It has fallen into disrepair, however, as it is not a walk that is favored by most of the family," he admitted.

"Do you favor it?" she asked tremulously.

"Actually, yes. It was a favorite haunt of mine in my youth."

"I should like to see it then Above All Things," she said, with a look of rapture.

Nicholas had not failed to note her disturbing tendency toward the cliché. He glanced once again toward Miss Kittridge. "I am afraid the shrubbery has grown a bit wild and difficult to navigate in delicate footwear such as yours," he said.

They both looked down at the tiny white satin tips of her slippers. He looked at her and could almost see the calculating nature of her mind at work. Would she sacrifice her shoes in an effort to win him over?

A gleam appeared in her eye. "Perhaps you could help me over the small stretches of rugged terrain?"

He had underestimated her talents.

"Lady Susan, I could not bear to mar a single flounce on your gown. I will not hear of it. We must not leave our guests at any rate," he said, smiling at her. "I could not steal the brightest flower from their midst now, could I?" He looked into her eyes and forced himself not to wince at the ridiculous sentiment.

"No, I suppose you are right. I would not want the others to be deprived of our superior conversation."

He bit his tongue to stop from laughing or making an unsporting remark. "Shall we return to the party, my dear? You must be quite famished."

She looked happy to return. The conversation had been altogether too taxing on her bird-sized brain.

Despite the pain in his leg, he helped all the ladies, along with the other males in evidence, to the shade of the ancient tree. He maneuvered a seat between Rosamunde and Miss Kittridge as the liveried footmen and maid servants brought forth the picnic fare—cold roast beef and pigeon pie alongside early artichokes and cheeses of Wiltshire. Conversation lulled during the consumption of the excellent foodstuff. A few oohs and aahs were heard at the arrival of the tarts and custard dessert trays.

Miss Kittridge was quiet, as he had noticed was her way with a group of people. She sat with a graceful curve to her arched back. Her gray silk dress had been allowed out of its confinement, he could see, as it was on important occasions such as this. He smiled, happy to see his sister conversing with her.

James Kittridge soon captured the attention of Rosamunde, and Miss Kittridge withdrew a bit from the group, taking a slim volume from her pocket. He focused on her beautiful lips—the upper crescent so full and inviting. His interest moved to the little dark freckle under one eye and her chestnut hair falling a bit from its perch.

For the merest moment, Charlotte looked up from the page to glimpse at him, then returned her wise gray eyes to the parchment. He shook his head and moved his glass of wine away. He must stop staring at her heady features lest he embarrass her. "And what are you reading, Miss Kittridge?" he asked.

She blushed prettily. "Miss Nichols was kind enough to lend me a new book she brought down from London—*Mansfield Park*. It is a—novel," she said, appearing self-conscious of her admission. "It is by the same author as *Sense and Sensibility* and *Pride and Prejudice*."

"Ah, you are taken with this writer?"

"Yes, her works are very amusing and entertaining," she said softly. "But, my father would not agree. He does not approve of exposing the mind to the nonsense of novels."

"I promise not to reveal your secret, Miss Kittridge," he said with a smile. "We all must have our secrets. And now that I know yours, I will feel more secure in mine's safety."

She arched her fair eyebrow. "You are stooping to blackmail, I see, sir," she said, turning a page and ignoring his gaze. "It is beneath you."

He threw back his head and laughed. "Ah, Miss Kittridge, you are delightful."

Edwin moved to sit next to Miss Kittridge and offered a glass of lemonade to her. "What is this? Did I hear rightly the mention of blackmail? Do not tell me that my brother has used you ill in any way, my dear. I could not let that stand," he said, smiling to both parties. "Shall I slay the beast for you?"

Miss Kittridge smiled. "I think not. For then I would be called to nurse the dragon back to good health. An unwelcome task, I do assure you, for he is a most uncooperative patient, as you know." She turned her gaze on Nicholas. "But there is a fortitude that is unmatched. I don't believe I have ever seen anyone heal so quickly in my life. But I fear he doesn't reveal the pain all his vigorous activities cause him."

Nicholas detested when someone could see through him.

"Ah, but my brother has never complained about anything in his entire life," Edwin offered. "He made it very difficult for a younger brother to follow in his footsteps." Edwin smiled. "And never a false step. He always played by the rule book, always followed the straight and narrow, and all that—a difficult act to follow."

Nicholas sat up straighter, ignoring the pain in his thigh. "You are jesting, Edwin. It was you who brought all the fine marks from university. We were all so proud of you."

Edwin smiled and preened just the smallest amount. "It was a jolly time there, I do admit. I was lucky how easy it all came to me. Barely had to study. How could I, with all the other sport . . . er, rather, fun there was to be found." He appeared to enjoy flustering Miss Kittridge. "Knowing your scholarly pursuits, Miss Kittridge, you would have enjoyed the academic life. It is too bad the female mind is not capable of expanding to a male's superior limits." He looked first at her and then to Nicholas. "Or at least, those of most men. I must admit there are some gentlemen whose abilities are of a . . . lesser quality."

Miss Kittridge's eyes appeared very large in her face. "Lord Edwin, but I must beg to differ."

"I am not surprised, my dear, not surprised at all." Edwin looked between the two of them knowingly and winked at her. "I understand my brother has taken to haunting your cottage as of late. Have you been showing him your sculpture? Or maybe other matters occupy his time there. Perhaps I should make an effort to pay my respects more often as well, my dear."

He would fry Edwin's kidneys for breakfast. His brother

had never crossed the thin line of courtesy before. Oh, he had toyed with insults toward him in the past, skirting the issue of Nicholas's ignorance on occasion, but he had never seen him behave this badly.

"Perhaps the sun has gone to your head, Edwin. Apologize to Miss Kittridge, and take yourself away, before I do something we will both come to regret later," Nicholas said.

Edwin jumped to his feet. "Miss Kittridge, I do beg your pardon. I had no idea my words could be construed in a way to offend. Perhaps it is my brother who misunderstood, as he sometimes is wont to do," he said, then continued after taking one look at Nicholas, "But please do accept my apology." He finished with an exaggerated bow.

The entire party of young people had become aware of the conversation, and had one by one stopped their discussions to hear the interesting exchange.

"Charlotte, what did he say to you?" inquired James. "I shall not stand for him to insult my sister, even if his family provides our bread and butter."

"No, James, I shall not hear of it. It was nothing, nothing at all. Do let us talk of something else." Miss Kittridge rose. "I must go and speak with Father. He might need something for His Grace."

Rosamunde stood up and offered Miss Kittridge her hand. "Oh, please, Miss Kittridge, will you do me the honor of allowing me to go with you? I am so sorry for anything my brother might have said. I am mortified by his behavior," Rosamunde said, with contrition written across her fine features.

James Kittridge had jumped up to accompany the ladies, who were joined by Louisa Nichols.

Miss Kittridge, her face still colorless from the exchange, looked at Nicholas for a moment, and then the group was gone.

Nicholas was obliged by courtesy to remain behind with Lady Susan. He was forced to endure the calculating little smile decorating her porcelain face and her cloying perfume fouling the air—and another half hour of wretched words that could not be mistaken for any sort of clever conversation.

After, he would think how best to make certain that his brother would never consider making insidious insults to Miss Kittridge ever again, if Edwin treasured the idea of saving his neck for further displays of frothy cravats.

It was the heat that had done it. That was the conclusion drawn by Dr. Kittridge and his daughter in private. They could not go against Her Grace, who was convinced that it was the very nature of the *air outside* that had brought on the duke's relapse.

Charlotte hastened outside the duke's vast chambers, daring to leave His Grace alone for a few moments to communicate the necessary ingredients—cinchona bark and licorice—to make a tea to soothe the duke's cough and reduce his fever. She could hear him still coughing violently as Lord Huntington appeared on the stair's landing.

"How does he fare?" Nicholas asked, hope and fear vacillating in his expression.

Charlotte frowned. She despised this part of her position, that of imparting bad tidings. "He has worsened with each passing hour, my lord. Perhaps you could bring a measure of comfort to him now. Let us go in."

His father lay motionless on the bed, eyes closed. The duke's flesh was stretched over bone, showing the all too apparent skeleton that loomed beneath. His prominent forehead was as still and white as marble.

"Father," exclaimed Nicholas as he grasped his hand.

"Nicholas, my son—so glad you came back. Wanted you to know this before I am gone," he rasped, his eyes opening a crack.

"I am glad I came back as well, Father. I missed you over the years," Lord Huntington admitted.

"I am sorry you went away, even if we all agreed it was for the best," the duke said hoarsely. "But I missed you . . . I missed you more than I can say." On the last words, he began to cough. The effort required to do so seemed to rob the old gentleman of an energy he did not possess.

Charlotte supported the man's frame as he continued in a long spasm, advising him to talk less. The duke lay back upon the many pillows she then arranged to his liking.

"Is there nothing to ease his discomfort?" Lord Huntington gave her a haunted look.

She took his hand to comfort him. "Yes, my lord. There is a soothing tea for the throat that is being prepared." He did not surrender her hand.

The duke was looking at them through half-shuttered eyes.

"Miss Kittridge, how can I thank you?" Lord Huntington asked, covering their clasped hands with his free one.

"There is no need." She felt embarrassed under the old gentleman's gaze, and excused herself without delay. "I must see about the tea. My father should arrive any moment, Your Grace." She gave a quick curtsy and removed herself from the room.

Running down the stairs, she held her flaming cheeks in her hands. It had been mortifying to face the perceptive glance of the Duke of Cavendish. Despite his age and condition, his knowing, eagle eyes had pierced her composure. And she had fled like a poacher caught with a tangle of game over one shoulder.

She met Charley coming the other direction, carrying a heavy book. "Miss? The doctor said you might be needin' this. Said sumpin' about a book you've been lookin' for."

"Oh, yes. Thank you, Charley. Is he coming then to relieve me?"

"Yes, miss. He be waitin' on the medicine you asked to be brewed. He said for you to wait until he comes."

Charlotte took the large volume and returned to her post, outside the duke's door, after thanking the lad.

The door was ajar, and she could hear the voices of the son and father clearly. Charlotte, desperate for a distraction, opened the tome and refused to eavesdrop. But the temptation was too great, once she heard her name mentioned, and her resolution too weak. The voices floated from the sickroom.

"My son," the duke said. "Don't think I haven't seen the look in her eye."

There was a long silence.

"Miss Kittridge is not for you." Again a coughing fit overwhelmed the father. "No, let me continue. I must . . . it cannot be left unsaid."

She could hear the bed creaking and the whisper of the satin-ticked bedcovers being arranged. He must be sitting on the grand bed.

"Yes, Father?"

"She would not be happy living the life of a duchess. And our acquaintances, even the servants, would snicker behind her back, as some do even now, guessing her roots, questioning her French lineage and physician father. And you well know she would never suit you. You, you," he paused, "are not suited for one another in any way, my son. It would be disastrous for you and for the continuation of our line."

"Father, I gave you my word, many years ago, that I would follow a certain course. Do you doubt my promise? I have never given you cause to worry. I do not plan to marry Miss Kittridge," he said.

Seated just outside the doorway, Charlotte pressed her tired fingers against her throbbing temples. She didn't want to hear anymore. A chill had fallen through her as she had listened to the conversation.

Her exhaustion had weakened her control, and she felt a sob threaten to escape her tight throat. She couldn't bear to hear any more. She had to leave, and she would do it on cat's feet. Her ancient slippers would not give her away, she thought. And they would have done their duty, save for the crash of the forgotten tome on her lap. She stopped to pick it up, half hoping he would come out and confront her.

But, he did not. There was to be no enlightenment, no feelings to swell the heart. No denials. Nothing at all. But of course there would not. She knew with all her being that there never would be. Not for her. But then eavesdroppers deserve every poisonous word they hear as their just desserts.

Her father appeared at the top of the stair, and walked with purpose toward her. He whispered, "Charlotte, my dear. You are exhausted. Go and rest. I insist you spend the whole of this evening and tomorrow at our cottage. I'll have Hetty sit up with His Grace tonight."

Charlotte felt like protesting. But in the end, her sadness and ill ease made her accept her father's prescription.

The duke's voice grew weaker. "Are you sure, my son? Quite, quite sure? I never liked the idea of holding you from a wife," he said gruffly. "Perhaps I could ask your stepmother to find a suitable young lady. Someone who is unable to produce children."

"With your permission, sir, I will continue on with the original plan. It is much more to my liking. And I shall take better care not to elevate Miss Kittridge's expectations."

"I am glad to hear it, for Miss Kittridge has become very dear to me of late—almost like another daughter. She reads to me, and nurses me with the most gentle spirit. I would hate to see her hurt in any way. Her intelligence is vast—even surpassing her father's, I believe, at times. I would not see you overpowered by her wisdom, and her cowed into hiding it to boost your own confidence."

"I believe you have the right of it, sir."

"You hold her in very high regard, do you not, my son?"

A long silence ensued.

"It is as I thought. Do not answer."

"I gave you my word."

"Nick, my son, I believe you. I promise not to question you again. I know you will stand by your promise."

"Thank you, Father."

"I began giving Edwin authority over Wyndhurst and the other estates several years ago when I began ailing and he was of age. The war has been a great blow to the estates—our profits are shrinking and our expenses increasing. It would not do to take any chances with everything in such a precarious state. Edwin is doing an admirable job despite the economic downfalls. I trust you will allow him to continue."

"Of course, Father. It has been agreed long ago. I shall have the title, in name and by law only. I will not meddle with anything he puts into place." Nicholas bit his tongue. He could not burden his father on his deathbed with his ideas to help ease the poverty in the parish.

"You will be tempted when I am gone, I will hazard a guess. And the tenants and laborers will all come clamoring to you, the new duke, with their lists of grievances when I am gone. They seem to come more and more these last few months. . . . But I don't want you to worry about any of it. You chose your course a long time ago." His father began to cough again.

Nicholas willed himself not to leave his father's bedside to find out where in blazes the blasted tea was. He poured a glass of water from the pitcher nearby and forced his father to take a sip.

"Yes, I know, Father. You must rest now. Please, put your mind at ease. We made the arrangements long ago, and I will stand by them. I will not be swayed by the power of the title. And besides, I have decided to return to my regiment very soon."

"I had guessed as much. But you will wait, then, until I am . . . gone?"

"Let us not talk of these matters. I will stay with you for as long as you need me."

"Then you will stay as long as it takes to see me on my final journey."

"Yes, sir." Nicholas leaned down to kiss his father on his forehead. He had the sudden thought that they had exchanged roles. Unlike many heirs, he loved his father. And yet, he had never spent that much time with him: very few hours in his youth, and almost none in his adulthood. But he loved him. He dearly, dearly loved him. And he would honor his promises to him, without wavering.

Chapter Eight

"A woman especially, if she have the misfortune of knowing anything, should conceal it as well as she can."

—Northanger Abbey

*H*aving spent an agitated night with little slumber and even less happy thoughts, Charlotte rose from her bed exhausted. At least she would not have to face *him* today. He would not come for the promised lesson when his sire lay so close to his final moments. It was close to the end now; she had seen it in the old gentleman's eyes. And he knew it too. She hoped he would be out of his pain soon, now that he had had a chance to say his good-byes and make his peace with the world.

He would not come, she thought as she sat in the simple dining room, nibbling on the corner of her toast. And it was for the best. She had been overcome by the duke's keen observation of the state of her heart, and humiliated by their discussion. She was certain that her poor acting skills would not stand up to her next audience with Lord Huntington or his father.

Suddenly, the door to the room opened and in walked her father. He appeared haggard from the long night spent at the duke's bedside.

"Ah, there you are, Charlotte. Here's one more burden to add to our dish." Her father waved a letter before Charlotte as James walked in and joined them. "We are to expect a visit from your cousin, Alexandre Barclay, the Friday after next."

"Not, dear old Alex? After all these years?" James asked. Charlotte's hand stopped for just the merest second in midair as she poured herself another cup of tea. One drop escaped onto the pale green tablecloth.

"It seems your half French cousin on your mother's side has ascended to his English father's viscountcy. He is now Lord Gaston and he has a desire to visit our little family circle in whom one member in particular"—her father paused to look pointedly at Charlotte—"was destined to become a part of his own twice over many years ago."

"Many years ago," echoed Charlotte.

"He has a very pretty way of turning a phrase, he does," said her father, as he continued reading the letter. "Will he be able to turn my dearest daughter's intelligent head as well?" He peered over his spectacles at her.

"Father!"

"I am but teasing you, child. The viscount must possess lofty ambitions far superior to a physician's daughter, no doubt. And you are practical enough to admit it." Her father returned to scanning the page. "We have no way to warn him of our vast descent from the *ton*. I cannot like this visit. It portends nothing but trouble, if I remember this young gentleman's character very well. However, we do owe his parents much," he concluded, shuffling the pages.

"The way I understood it, Grandmamma had selected him with care for her favorite and only granddaughter," James said with a grin. "Wonder what the chap looks like. Do you think he is short and portly, or thin and mean-tempered?"

"I would not care to guess." Charlotte concentrated on spreading some jam on her toast.

"Oh, come, Charlotte, do not tell me you are not curious about the man you were to marry?"

"Not in the slightest," Charlotte replied, using her napkin.

"Remember you are speaking to a future man of the cloth. Falsehoods require serious penance."

"James, this was all arranged when I was but four years old—a mere child. I barely remember him, I assure you," she said, lying through her teeth. She had never been able to forget the tall, dark-haired boy who had been much more inter-

ested in horses and fishing than meeting the girl for whom he
was intended. When she had been a child, Charlotte had
thought of him as her handsome prince. "None of us ever expected him to carry through with both families' intentions
after the revolution." Charlotte gave her brother an angry
glare.

"Forgive me, dearest," James said, trying to swallow a
smile but failing. "I for one would like to meet the man who
callously jilted my sister, fairly broke her heart with sorrow
for long-lost dreams."

"James . . ." warned the father. "Enough poppycock.
Charlotte has never had any intention to marry," her father
said, as he speared several sausages and transferred them to
his plate. "We shall see how the viscount conducts himself.
And we will learn the purpose of his visit. I for one hope his
stay is short and without incident. Once he sees that we are
unable to supply him with any interesting forms of entertain-
ment, as we are always required at the abbey, I am sure his
visit and any curiosity he holds will wane quickly," he said,
before turning his attention to the breakfast before him.

Charlotte tried to ignore her brother's teasing grin as she
considered the viscount's forthcoming stay. She finished her
meal in a pensive state. The visit would bring nothing but
embarrassment and a continuous stream of annoying remarks
from her brother. She must find an especially large tome of
sermons at the abbey to recommend to her father, thereby ensuring a premature retribution for James's unbrotherly behavior.

With gratitude, she acceded to her father's request that she
take some air this morning and visit Mrs. Burnsides, one of
the tenant farmers' wives, who was lying in after the birth of
her eighth child. Yes, that would take her mind off her embarrassing situation. Then she would return to the abbey to
confer with her father, who had hastened there soon after the
sparse morning repast.

Her plans in place, Charlotte ignored the grayish clouds in
the distance and the short rushes of breeze that assaulted her

body when she departed the cottage. Head down, and
equipped with a basket full of supplies and muffins, Charlotte headed toward the valley. It was but two miles to the
rundown Burnside cottage.

The first fat raindrop struck her arm a little more than half
the distance to her destination. It had been folly to think she
could have returned from her jaunt before the storm began.
And she had misjudged the direction of the wind. Those were
her last thoughts before the heavens let loose their fury. She
turned back and ran as fast as her skirts would allow. The wet
grass tickled her cold ankles, and more and more mud began
to fly as she ran. She slid to a stop upon the sudden appearance of a horse and rider—Lord Huntington, to be precise.

Her heart lurched. Before she could say a word, he spoke.

"Miss Kittridge, give me your hand, and use the stirrup to
step up," he ordered, kicking free from the object in question.
"I will have you at your cottage in five minutes, if you will
allow."

Charlotte very much wished she had the courage to refuse
his offer because of the humiliation of the last evening. But
looking into his kind eyes and handsome face, she found she
could not, and obeyed without a word, finding herself seated
sideways atop his "good" leg in a moment. Wordlessly, he
opened his greatcoat and wound her arms around his waist.
He covered her with the front of his coat almost completely.
She tucked her head under his broad chin and allowed herself to absorb the lovely warmth of his body. Had Marianne
in *Sense and Sensibility* felt thusly with Willoughby when he
had carried her home? Charlotte's experience far surpassed
anything she remembered reading. Just the smell of him in-
toxicated her senses, making it difficult to speak.

"His Grace? Is he—"

"He has turned the corner," he interrupted. "Your father
said to tell you that my father is resting comfortably now—
not a cough for the last hour. Perhaps he has turned a corner."
He gave her a warm smile despite the rain pouring off his hat.

"I thought to keep our appointment. Your maid sent me out after you in fear of the storm."

"I have made you all wet and dirty." She glanced down to where her boots had muddied his new high-topped boot.

"Save your breath, my dear. It is Charley who will come after you, boot brush in hand. He has become quite the dandy's keeper."

His happy exuberance was contagious. He was obviously relieved by his father's turn for the better. And she was glad the old gentleman had been made comfortable once more.

With that, they were off. It was a very uncomfortable perch despite the smooth, rolling gait of his horse. The pommel dug into her body, forcing her to move closer to him. But she would not have had the ride end if she had had a choice. For several minutes they rode without words, and she tried to imprint the experience in her memory.

She breathed in the heated, masculine smell of shaving lather and his overall scent, feeling dizzy from his closeness. And she hugged his muscled torso closer to her, marveling at its broadness. She heard a deep rumble of laughter when he finally brought the horse down to a fast walk. The drenching shower changed to a light patter.

"I would not have let you fall, Miss Kittridge, fear not."

"I trust you, my lord."

"Do you, now? Is that wise?"

"I trust you to deliver us back to the cottage, at least," she said, joining him in laughter. Sunlight broke through the clouds and bounced off the wildflowers, glittering in the now light mist of rain. She looked up at him. The sunlight had turned his eyes a clear green.

"Ah, Miss Kittridge, I warned you I cannot be trusted around dimples," he said, as she experienced the full intensity of his expression.

She tried to wipe the smile from her face and force her lips over her teeth.

"You are failing miserably, you know."

A giggle escaped her.

"Ah, Miss Kittridge, did you know that you have two sets of dimples when you attempt to erase the first pair?"

"You are an out-and-out bounder, sir," she said, conceding a full smile.

His eyes crinkled at the corners. And then, suddenly, his gaze moved to her mouth.

"Are you going to kiss me again, Lord Huntington?" she whispered before she could stop herself. She cringed privately with embarrassment.

"Are you flirting with me, Miss Kittridge?"

"Oh—that was very wrong of me." She shifted and tried to regain her composure.

"More's the pity, my dear. But never let it be said that I allow an opportunity to pass." He had transferred the reins to one hand and lifted her chin with the other while halting the horse.

Did he speak in jest or in earnest? She had never had any experience to sharpen her wordplay—whereas he was a master in the trenches of human dialogue. Perhaps he was excessively gay because of his father's improvement. Joy overtook many a person with news of good health. She was very unsure of herself, not knowing that her very timidity would add fuel to the fire.

Oh, God, what was he doing? What was he thinking? Her eyes looked so large in that virginal face of hers. And he could not embarrass her now by not following through, could he? She expected a kiss, so he must oblige. *He must.*

His lips touched her beautiful mouth and he was lost. She tasted of honey toast and roses and rain all bundled into one small pretty parcel. She opened her mouth tentatively to his gentle prodding, and he had a great desire to crush her to him. He felt overwhelmed by her trust in him.

Her skin was so soft and her lips so inviting and sweet. He lightly nipped her upper lip and touched her slick hair, with waves more pronounced from the rain. Ah, he wanted just a little more. Just a very little more.

Without a word, he disentangled her arms from around his neck, and lowered her to the ground. She said naught as he dismounted and pulled her back into his arms. Ah, she felt so very small, but perfect there. He could almost span her tiny waist with his hands. But she was no child. His palms traveled slowly up her frame to find perfectly formed breasts filling his hands.

He felt her catch her breath, and looked down at her up-turned face. He saw surprise, and trust, and a great longing in her expression. He leaned down and kissed her on her milk-and-roses cheek then moved to trace her ear with his tongue. She again inhaled quickly, and he moved his attention to her mouth.

"You have the most enticing lips I have ever seen, Miss Kittridge," he said quietly.

"As do you, Lord Huntington," she said, looking at his mouth.

Her bold response augmented his desire, and he leaned in to taste her again, but not as tenderly as before. He kissed her long and deep while stroking her tightened nipples through the drab-colored wet gown.

A light moan escaped her. He looked at her half-shut, passion-filled eyes, and felt the greatest desire he had ever known to take her right there. He stiffened his arms and rested his forehead on her soaked hair, breathing deeply, try-ing to regain a measure of control. What on earth had he been thinking? This was not the way to keep his word to his father. This was the path toward broken promises. And his lack of control would hurt her, the one person he would not harm for the world. The mood was broken more thoroughly than a giggle in church.

"Miss Kittridge . . . I am sor—," he began.

She interrupted. "No, oh, please no. Please don't say you are sorry. I am not," she said, looking to one side. "But I am aware we are breaking a goodly number of proprieties. I shall endeavor to avoid smiling at you in future—" she continued and dropped her voice to a whisper—"although I am sure your comments about my physiognomy are all made in kind-hearted jest."

"Miss Kittridge, this is a poor way of showing my gratitude toward you and your father's care. I had not thought I was the sort of man to engage in such unbecoming behavior toward a young lady."

"We have discussed this before. I am not a 'young' milk-and-water miss, although I am well aware that I appear so. I have never been taken seriously by anyone except my family my entire life. You will kindly stop inferring that I am a young innocent, or, or—"

"Or what, Miss Kittridge?" he said, with a smile.

"Or I will be forced to demonstrate that I am not as you think."

"Perhaps you are not young, I concede" he said, unable to resist moving a lock of tumbled, wet hair from her cheek. "But you are an innocent. Are you not?"

She refused to answer him, and turned away, walking past the stand of birch trees in front of the cottage.

"I take it that you would prefer we postpone our lessons until tomorrow," he called out to her retreating form.

She did not even pause or turn around. She waved an acquiescent hand and continued walking.

Nicholas watched her stomp away, her delightful small, round posterior clearly visible through the wet muslin. She was correct, she was not a girl, but a mature woman at the peak of her prime, he thought, rubbing his chin. And she exhibited spunk when he was able to goad her out of her natural shyness.

Nicholas remounted his horse and eased the animal into a canter.

Charlotte paused at the top of the hill to watch his elegant form fly toward the abbey. She sighed.

"Charlotte! Wait a moment," called a deep voice behind her.

She turned to find her brother, James, coming toward her.

His clenched hands were pumping as he trudged up the wet hill behind her.

She shivered and felt like a cold, doused cat. She guessed by James's angry expression that he had witnessed her encounter with Lord Huntington. At least he had not interrupted them—that would have been embarrassing in the extreme.

"Charlotte, what are you thinking to encourage Huntington in that fashion?" he asked. "Have you no shame? No notion of what is proper and decorous for a lady of your standing?"

"Oh, I have a very good notion what is right and proper for a woman of my standing, James. I am a lowly daughter of a physician, a nurse and the sister of a soon-to-be clergyman."

"Charlotte," he said, all anger leaving his face. "My dearest, you are the granddaughter of a marquis, do not underestimate your standing in the world."

"So you think I am acting unladylike do you?"

"No. I think you are making a gross mistake. And I would hate to have to challenge our dear employer's son to a duel because he was leading my sister to ruin."

"Really, James, how ridiculous you are. Lord Huntington and I were flirting," she said, then turned fully to face him. "Just as you have done on every occasion you have found yourself in the company of his sister."

He had the grace to flush. "I have not been caught kissing Lady Rosamunde, however."

"Ah, so you have kissed her then?"

He was silent.

She sighed and looked down at her drenched gown. "Ah, so then we are both going to wrack and ruin. Well, if it is any consolation, I suppose we will have each other's shoulders to cry on when they leave us brokenhearted," she offered. "Or I shall find myself nursing my brother or Lord Huntington's wounds of honor."

"Charlotte, he will not have you," he said quietly.

"I know."

"He is the heir to a dukedom. My guess is that he will return to his regiment if Lady Susan does not entice him away altogether."

"I am well aware that her beauty far outshines any shallow amount of femininity I might claim."

"Charlotte, I do not mean to degrade your own charms. You have many, and you are very dear to me, you know that. I would not choose another sister for all the world," he said, looking at her drenched form.

"High praise, indeed," she said, feeling like a pathetic half-drowned mouse. But then she had no need for her brother to confirm her meager ability to attract the other sex. She had had seven and twenty years of disinterested and disinclined gentlemen to demonstrate the truth. She shook her head.

"I would not see you hurt again," he said.

"I have never been hurt!"

"You do not think I did not see how unhappy you were when our dear cousin never answered our father's letters? When you were refused a voucher for Almack's? When Mr. Cox never paid us a third social call? And what about Mr. Reed, who never appeared to take you on the promised carriage ride? Charlotte?"

"Please, please stop. Enough!" she said, turning to walk away.

"Charlotte, have a care. Do not see him alone again—if only to guard your heart."

She stopped to face him again. "I promise to heed your advice when you choose the same course."

Males. They were impossible. The whole lot of them, she thought, while walking toward the cottage. She would not spend one more minute with a brother who knew better than anyone how to reduce her to feeling like a drenched rodent.

Nicholas smiled to himself. Miss Kittridge had left him in her workroom to fetch a covering for his clothes. She had insisted they take a rest from the page when she had caught him clenching his head.

The second and third lessons had proceeded better than he had expected, although Miss Kittridge had been reserved. He had not been able to tease a single half-smile from her grave countenance. But she had continued to prove herself to be a formidable teacher. She had a calming way of listening and not hurrying him, and not destroying his concentration and renewed desire to overcome his affliction.

It was the first time he had ever made any kind of progress. But it was infinitesimal—and frustrating. The letters still swam all over the page, and he always walked away with his head aching from the effort. And to make matters worse, he was having a hard time keeping his hands off her modest form.

Her patience and her kindness, and the sweet innocence she refused to acknowledge, were like aphrodisiacs. If he were a whole man, an intelligent man, he would make an offer for her because he was so attracted to her gentle goodness. Yes, it was going to be difficult to leave her behind when he returned to his regiment.

If only his regiment could see him now, about to dabble in clay, they would be certain he had taken leave of his senses. He did not feel like the battle-hardened officer; he felt the fool.

The smoke, mud, and cannon shot seemed a long way away. And in fact, the battles were over. With Bonaparte on Elba and the wild celebrations in London and Paris, he wondered what role he would be able to play in the postwar effort. Certainly not any diplomatic post. Perhaps he would have to seek a commission fighting the Americans. He shook his head. He had little desire to fight the scrappy colonists. Nicholas felt much like an outmoded chariot: too old to fix, too young to throw on the debris pile, yet of little use to anyone.

He had had Charley write a letter, in his neat hand, to Wellington's aide de camp. Nicholas was anxious to receive a reply. It would determine his future. In the meantime, he would better the lives of the people in the parish.

He had spent a maddening morning with his brother and
Mr. Coburn, the steward Edwin had hired three years ago.
They had met every single one of his suggestions concerning
the brewery, the need to improve the cottages, and the growing ranks of the poor, even the rampant lack of food, with
haughty disinterest. Mr. Coburn had brought forth the
ledgers and indicated that there was not enough money to
start expensive, ill-advised ventures without proof of future
income. However, Mr. Coburn had many ideas on how to fil-
ter Nicholas's monies into the dukedom, starting with Her
Grace's plans to redecorate the town house in London.

Edwin's pleas were difficult to ignore. "Our sister will
need to go to London to snare herself a husband. Do you
really think our ramshackle pile in Mayfair will entice a rich
man to offer for Rosamunde? I think not. Best hand over
your blunt to help our dear sister."

"Her Grace has also mentioned a tour for Lord Edwin,"
Mr. Coburn threw in for good measure. "And for herself, of
course."

"Oh, you must help us, for what will you do with it fighting a war? Rethatching cottages is a complete waste. It will
just have to be redone again and again. Furthering the lot of
Rosamunde is a far better investment. Come now, you have
not the head for all this."

He had withstood the barrage with stoic fortitude as always. Even his ideas on improving the breeding stock of the
sheep and cows had been met with negative response.

Well, he would not go back on his word to his father. But,
he had not promised that he would not use his own funds to
improve the lot of the people in the dukedom's realm. And he
had a considerable amount left to him from his mother's family, as well as his conserved officer's pay, meager though it
was.

Nicholas was equally sure that the land deeded to him by
his maternal grandparents would prove to be as fertile as
needed to raise the hops and barley crops necessary for a

brewery. And the spring, which provided water for his father's needs, also ran through Nicholas's acres.

If Edwin was unwilling to start a venture, Nicholas would do it on his own parcel of land. He could also open a portion of those three hundred acres as common land for those who had been hard hit by the Enclosure Acts. There would be plenty of room for the crops, the common land, and space for the actual brewery as well.

Miss Kittridge's voice beyond the door, calling out to the maid, brought him back to the situation at hand. He grasped one of the dried bird forms and studied it.

He knew her sculpture meant a great deal to her, and he would show a measure of his gratitude by pleasing her with his interest. He must find a place to have these fired for her. The figures were even better formed than the ones displayed in the front sitting room. She had refined her technique.

The sound of her light steps preceded her return to the workroom.

"I found one of my brother's shirts—after realizing you would never fit into my father's," she said, a little out of breath. A slight flush was in her cheeks as enthusiasm beamed from her face.

"Your brother will not delight in finding his collar ruined."

"Ah, but there you are wrong. Anything to sway him from his future would please him, I assure you," she said.

"Then we are alike in one way, I see."

"My lord?"

"I am being obtuse, Miss Kittridge. A favorite pastime of mine."

Intent on her art, she did not acknowledge his comment. She cut a square of clay, using a fine wire, and handed it to him after he had removed his coat and donned the second shirt, which proved to be too small after all. She cut a similar block for herself. Engravings of sculpture adorned the walls, and a small marble bust was in the corner. Walking over to it, he noticed that the beautiful bust of a young woman resembled Miss Kittridge in some ways, despite the old-fashioned, high-on-the-crown hair arrangement.

"Who is this?"

She turned to him. "Oh, I had forgotten it was in here," she said, then paused. "It is of my mother when she was four and twenty."

"The eyes are so unusual, the pupils and irises complete in form."

"It is the technique of Monsieur Houdin. Is it not perfection?" she asked with some awe. "He is the artist I most admire, I believe."

"Most unusual," he replied, then turned to compare her face with that of the bust. "You favor her."

"Perhaps I have something of her eyes and mouth, I suppose. But I did not inherit her inherent wit, and loveliness, and charm. My character is all my father's doing," she said with a sigh.

"I fear you have been misled somewhere along your life's path, Miss Kittridge. You have never failed to show me, at one time or another, all of the characteristics you attribute to your mother."

"Your memory is not as good as I had surmised, my lord," she said. "I am not sure you found me charming and graceful when I forced ministrations on you and helped deliver a certain large foal several weeks ago."

"You are incorrect again, Miss Kittridge. I found you most lovely when you were covered in blood and straw while saving the mare and foal. And most charming when you wheedled me into your way of thinking while I was half-delirious."

He had silenced her. Miss Kittridge's shyness forbade further comment.

She guided him to a high stool beside her own, and they sat side by side in the sunlit workroom, which looked out into the shrubbery and vibrant green of summer in the Wiltshires. After a comment or two on forming clay, she left him to his thoughts and solitude. From time to time he looked at her fine-boned profile as she concentrated on sculpting the round, diminutive form of a nuthatch. Where had she ever formed the opinion that she exhibited less than a perfect display of charm and grace?

He looked toward her mother's bust again. The sole variation was in the regal, aristocratic tilt of the cold marble head and chin. Who was her mother that such a sculpture was commissioned of her? He had encountered a distinct silence on the subject, which he had then abandoned out of politeness to the émigrés. Without a doubt, she had been French, and the father thoroughly English—from his ruddy cheeks to his London accent. Nicholas would have questioned Miss Kittridge further but sensed her discomfort on the topic.

The clay would not take the shape of any sort of winged creature. His attempts were childlike and he had no doubt that he had no talent for the medium, unlike his love of music and the pianoforte, an instrument forbidden to him from the age of sixteen, when he had infuriated his stepmother outrageously one final time.

Nicholas rolled the hard clay between his hands and formed a thin, long column and laid it on the table littered with clay dust. He coiled it into a fat snake, pinching a diamond-shaped head at the end. He unrolled it and formed it into the letter S with the head at the top. He took a larger piece of clay and formed a solid N, and finally an A. He had no idea what else was needed to write "snake."

She looked at his effort and immediately formed the rest of the word. "Take a closer look at this N and see how it is formed from all angles," she said, placing the letter in his hand. "Perhaps it will help unlock the mysteries of the difference between N and the M and W."

A certain stillness invaded his being as he studied the letter from every angle. The solid figure did not dance, nor did it seem confusing in any way, shape, or form. She handed him an M she had formed. It was as if someone had handed him a key that unlocked a thick door in his brain. The M was very solid, immobile, clear. He turned the letter upside down and could see the *W* quite clearly. The key was looking at the letters in three dimensions.

Nicholas looked toward Charlotte and saw wordless comprehension. He couldn't speak, afraid to break the spell of sudden understanding. They each turned to the mound of clay and formed crude letters of the alphabet, rushing their efforts in their excitement. In ten minutes time, the forms were complete. He picked up each one and turned them at all angles. After the first ten or so, he stopped and shuddered as he inhaled deeply. He felt overwhelming emotion—a great weight lifting from his shoulders.

"Perhaps we should hold off a bit," she said.

"No. I want to look at all of them."

"All right."

She handed each one to him, and rearranged them carefully when he was done. Only the sound of the raspy crickets and an insistent blue jay could be heard from the open window. A small but profound transformation had begun in the recesses of his mind. He closed his eyes and breathed deeply again after laying aside the *Z*.

When he reopened his eyes, Miss Kittridge had arranged a line of letters on the table. "Can you read this?" she asked.

Slowly, he spelled the word, "r-e-m-e-m-b-e-r, re- remember," he said in wonder, the word he had ironically always failed to read or remember.

She formed a few more letters and made a sentence.

He stared at the words. "You-can-read," he said without pause. His hands were shaking.

She took his hands in her own and gave them a little squeeze.

"I don't understand it," he said. "I don't even want to question why. All I know is that something has changed by looking at these figures. I am afraid to walk away from here and lose this feeling."

He closed his eyes and willed himself not to show the emotion welling up in his throat and threatening to escape from his eyes. Most unmanly, these emotions were. He gave a shaky laugh and stood up, pushing back his stool. She stood in front of him, holding both his hands and staring up at him, her eyes filled with tears.

"Ah, Miss Kittridge, do not say a word. You will force me to behave disgracefully, and you would not like that." He could see she was trying to smile with great effort. And suddenly, it didn't matter. He felt a tear escape the far corner of his eye and he pulled her roughly in his arms, squeezing the breath from her, he feared.

"I daresay I have put clay all over your gown, Miss Kittridge," he whispered into her ear as he continued to embrace her. "That is two dresses I owe you."

He could feel her smile as he rested his cheek on hers. "That is quite all right, Lord Huntington, as I owe you at least one pair of boots from our recent escapade in the rain, and one coat made of the finest cloth," she said, dusting off a place high on his shoulder. "We are even."

"No, I owe you, Miss Kittridge. How I will repay you, I know not, but I always attend to my debts."

She leaned back from him, a hint of tears still residing in her gray eyes. Her lashes were very long, he noticed. Nicholas leaned down without thinking, and brushed a soft kiss on her cheek. "Thank you, my dear. Thank you . . ." He looked deep into her eyes.

A knock sounded, forcing him to release her. Miss Kittridge hastily rearranged her gown and called out, "Yes?"

The maid said through the closed door. "There's a gen'leman come to call, miss. I told him the doctor was with His Grace, but he insisted on waitin'," Doro said.

The door opened and a figure loomed large behind the maid. "Now see here, I told you, I am a relative of the family. Lady Charlotte would want to see me *immediatement*!" a deep baritone intoned behind the maid. He pushed past Doro, a quizzing glass firmly planted on his aristocratic face. His haughty countenance looked amused. Only the smallest trace of a French accent marred his perfect English. The gentleman looked the two of them over from a high tilt of his nose, assessing the situation. He looked back to the maid. "But I thought you said your mistress was in this—" he looked at the room again, "this atelier."

"This be Miss Kittridge, sir," Doro said, trying to imitate his puffed-up air. Clearly the maid did not take well to glorified French dandies.

Again the eyepiece was brought up to his face, making his eye look unnaturally large and quite amusing.

Nicholas's exuberance had been doused with all the thoroughness of a bell in a chaotic schoolyard. He wanted to yell at the stranger to get the bloody hell out of the room. He needed to be alone with Miss Kittridge—to keep reading and to make sure this newfound ability would crystallize in his brain and not disappear, only to leave him frustrated and tortured all over again.

"I believe you were invited to wait for Miss Kittridge in the front sitting room, sir. I suggest you do not compromise your welcome." He looked toward Miss Kittridge and tried to regain his composure. "I am sure the lady will join you there momentarily."

The gentleman executed a slight bow and departed, mumbling something in French as the maid closed the door.

Miss Kittridge stared after them without saying a word. Nicholas came up behind her and rested his hands on her shoulders.

"Who is he? Are you acquainted with him?" Not waiting for her answer, he continued, "I will be happy to toss him out on his pompous derriere, if you would like," he said with a cultured intonation of the Gallic word.

"You speak French?"

"A fair amount, and Spanish too, given the necessities of war."

"Any other language, you fraud?"

"Fraud? I am most insulted, Miss Kittridge."

"You call yourself an ignorant."

"Ah, that. Yes. Well, to return to the original question,

which I believe you are very skillfully attempting to avoid. The name of the gentleman in question?"

"He is a guest. Actually a distant—very distant relation who will be visiting us, probably for a very short period," she said, looking up to him. "He is Viscount Gaston, to answer your question. We have been expecting him. But—"

"But what, Miss Kittridge?"

"But, I do not think he recognized me, nor do I think he was expecting us to be living in this—this fashion," she said, indicating the room with her sweeping hand.

"In that case, you should count yourself lucky, for given the gentleman's obvious lack of manners, perhaps a curtailed visit would be far preferable." He dusted off the dried bits of clay on her shoulder. "Well, I shall leave you to your distinguished guest." Nicholas looked toward the clay letters on the worktable. He hated to leave them behind.

She followed his gaze. "Lord Huntington, I shall wrap these for you once they are dry."

He kissed her hand without another word and left the room.

My God, he could read. No, he could *possibly* read, his more rational self insisted. He fought to hold hope at bay. He had hoped too many times in his life and failed. He must get inside that miraculous workroom again—alone with her as soon as possible. This first taste of comprehension had been like tiny sips of ambrosia to a man dying of thirst.

His mind raced, thinking about the dueling topics of where he could have fired the clay letters, the winsome Miss Kittridge, and the absurd visitor at the doctor's cottage, as he walked down the hall.

Nicholas hoped the gentleman's visit would indeed be short, perhaps a week's duration would be most preferable. No, two days would be better, two hours best of all. But it was not to be, he decided, when he saw three large trunks blocking the door.

Chapter Nine

*C*harlotte changed her gown and hastened down to greet their distant cousin, all the while wishing that her brother or father would appear to relieve her of the task.

Viscount Gaston was as handsome as ever. He still possessed those dark, flashing eyes that matched his longish hair. And his arrogant posture always had exaggerated his already tall height. As she entered the front salon she noticed he was dressed in the height of London fashions from his polished, white-tasseled Hessians to the elegant beaver hat he bore in his hand. Charlotte's eyes widened when she noticed the vibrant plum-colored waistcoat that topped the tightest pair of breeches she had ever seen. A very large bulge was clearly outlined. Charlotte knew enough of the male anatomy to wonder if it could possibly be real or stuffing. She stifled a giggle. Was this a new fashion in London? She knew gentlemen stuffed their stockings to give the appearance of a well-developed calf, but this was taking it too far.

"Is that really you, Charlotte? You have been rusticating from civilized society far too long, I see. No proper mademoiselle would dare to stare at a gentleman of the *ton* in that fashion, *ma cherie*," he said, looking down his nose at her.

She gulped and tried to collect herself. "Cousin, I am happy to see you again. It has been an age." She motioned to the blue settee and armchair next to it.

Charlotte chose the settee and faced the armchair he was

sure to use. She was forced to change the direction of her knees when she found him sitting next to her on the settee.

"I asked the footman at the abbey to direct me to you, but I think he must have misunderstood. It will be a trial to move my trunks to the family's actual great house. But," he sighed, "that is for the servants to worry about, is it not, *mon chou*?"

"Alexandre, these *are* our living quarters."

"What? This cannot be. The greatest physician in the court of Louis XVI has been reduced to living in a, a cottage with not a thought to keeping up appearances? *Mon Dieu*, your grandparents and mother would turn in their graves if they could see how you live," he said, showing more feeling than his usual languid self.

"I am sorry you do not approve," she said. "However, this is indeed where we reside. But I would not dare to suggest you stay in such unrefined quarters," she continued, an idea forming in her head. "Perhaps you would be more comfortable staying at The Quill & Dove? It is quite charming, and even boasts some of the finest suites of rooms in all of Wiltshire."

Alexandre looked around the small room with distaste. "But, my dear cousin, I would not consider it. I have come to sample country life and to visit my dearest family in the world," he said, removing his gloves and looking with distaste at the threadbare furnishings.

Ah, that explained it. He must be desperately short on funds to allow his polished perfection to be diminished by simple countrified living.

Doro arrived carrying a heavy tray of tea and scones with all the trimmings. She had a sour look on her face when Charlotte regarded her. Her bulky form was heaving a bit under the burden as she placed it before Charlotte.

"It be his fine lordship, here, who *ordered* the tea and goodies," she said in a disgusted tone before flouncing away.

"What a charming idea," Charlotte said in a deflated

voice. Where was James, anyway? She poured the honey-colored liquid from the delicate teapot into the cup.

"But where is the tea strainer? This is intolerable," he said.

"Doro must have neglected it. It is not often she is called on to prepare such a display," Charlotte said, looking over the vast array of confections and even sliced cold ham with bread and butter. "You must forgive us. We live quite simply here."

"This will not do," he said, rising from his chair and looking for a bell cord.

"There is no cord, you must call out to her from the hall," she said, then added, "It would help considerably if you tacked on the word 'please' to your request, Alexandre."

"Impossible!" he muttered prior to performing the necessary requirements for requesting the aforementioned article.

Tea in hand, properly strained, with no less than three lumps of precious sugar added, he tasted it and finally formed a pleasant expression. He turned over the spoon on his saucer.

Out of the corner of her eye, Charlotte noticed him examining the silversmith's mark on the silverware.

"Harrumph," he muttered, then caught her glance. "Ah, Charlotte, my dear. I find you looking very well. Very well, indeed in spite of your descent in the world. Rusticating has proved beneficial to your health. We shall see if it does the same for me," he said, grimacing.

"It is pleasant to see you again. It has been a long time; almost two decades, I believe. I thought never to see you again, if the truth be known." She could feel his slow perusal of her form as she concentrated on breaking off a corner of her scone.

"Charlotte, *mon chou*, how could you say such a thing? I adore you," he said languidly, while examining his fingernails. "I could not survive without seeing my dearest cousin as often as possible. Ah, but I have always said that a man's sensibilities run much deeper than a lady's emotions, which the fairer sex allows to run too close to the surface."

"Perhaps you are right."

He looked quite pleased that she had agreed with him. "Of course I am right," he said, assessing the paintings on the wall. Charlotte felt like a piece of merchandise in a store when his gaze returned to her. "Now, tell me, how is your family faring? Surely, you can do much better than this little . . . hut? I myself have a divine set of rooms off of St. James's Street."

"I cannot imagine what could have tempted you away from London, Alexandre, to visit us here. You could have saved yourself the trouble of a trip if you had visited us while we were in London."

"I was determined to see you, *cherie*. I kept assuring myself we would run into one another at one of the many soirees and routes, but you never cared enough to come," he said, with a practiced look of sadness in his expression.

It was lucky that many long years of waiting for his call had thoroughly erased any of her doubts concerning the true nature of his character. He was not to be trusted in any sense of the word, but he was an amusing charmer. There was no need to burst the illusion.

"I worry about the state of your heart. Were you not just now dabbling with the heir to the Duke of Cavendish? But, I must warn you, *cherie*, even a girl such as yourself, who is beyond question, with every virtue intact, should take care to obey the strictures of society. It would not do to be caught unchaperoned with his lordship." Then he smiled and arched one eyebrow, "Unless, of course, you have a plan to secure him."

He held up his hand when she was about to burst into a denial. "No, no, I see that is not your style. But, you know that your happiness is my only motivation. I would, of course, release you from any sort of understanding we have."

Charlotte could not hold back any longer. "*Understand-*

ing? I thought it was quite clear that the 'understanding' you refer to became a *misunderstanding* when my family's fortune was reduced to ash and worse," she said with some emotion. "Although it was my 'understanding' that your branch of the family fared better— which made a connection with the now less fortunate side, *id est*, ME less attractive."

"Charlotte, Charlotte, my dearest, please no Latin, it gives me the headache. You are in a royal tizzy—over nothing, I assure you. I had intended to apologize. Ah, here I shall get down on one knee, if I must," he said, sliding off the settee in as elegant a fashion as his tight clothes would allow. "I see I must beg absolution from my sweet cousin, for I cannot live another day knowing you do not care for me as I have always cherished you," he said with perfect, languid aristocratic charm. His request had been performed quite expertly, except for the moment he reached beyond her to help himself to another scone.

Charlotte laughed.

"Oh, my Charlotte, you are quite delightful when you smile," he said in amazement. "You look very much like your mother, in fact. I must convince you to smile more often. It will become my mission in life," he said, licking the crumbs off his fingers.

The squeak of the door announced a newcomer. James, in all his newly made religious finery, entered. The picture he presented made Charlotte want to burst into laughter. James looked uncomfortable and embarrassed in unrelieved black.

"What in heavens are you doing pawing at my sister?" James said in shocked tones. "Oh . . . is that you, Alexandre? I didn't recognize you."

"*Bonjour,* James." Alexandre rose to his feet and bowed. "And I would have not recognized you dressed like a . . . shall we say, a puffin?"

It was the worst possible insult. Everyone knew James was irritated enough by the role forced on him by his father.

"You shall be required to perform penance if you continue to insult a man of the cloth, Cousin," said James with a scowl. "At least I don't look like a *damned peacock*!" he concluded, while eyeing the Frenchman's waistcoat.

"A fine welcome I am receiving," he said, taking a minute snuffbox from his pocket. He leaned his head back and breathed in a generous pinch before offering the enameled box to James, who shook his head with repressed desire in his face. "Perhaps you and your sister would prefer I not stay?" He waited a moment as if expecting a flood of denials. "Ah, but I cannot deprive your dear father of a visit. He wrote in such a kind manner of his great desire to reclaim our past familial ties."

James snorted.

"Where is the good doctor?" Alexandre asked.

"Attending the duke. His Grace is in very ill health," responded Charlotte.

"I must go there then to receive my welcome."

"No, Alexandre, I beg of you to wait here for my father. It would not do to intrude on the sickroom of the duke at present," Charlotte said.

He smiled, exposing his wonderful bright smile. "You are of course correct, *ma cherie*. I am a patient man, and we have so much cousinly news to discuss between us."

Charlotte sighed and looked toward James, who rolled his eyes. It was going to be as difficult as she had imagined. But, she thought with relief, her heart was fully mended. She had worried that his visit would provoke a painful reoccurrence of the sad days in London when Alexandre had refused to call on her, destroying her last shred of hope for a husband. Oh, he was charming and everything handsome and elegant to be sure, but his wit could not overcome his deficit in character. The veil had been removed from her eyes. And she was grateful.

A fortnight passed, and as Nicholas toured the activity in the far corner of his property, he realized he had been correct in his guess. That poppycock of a Frenchman had shown every intention of settling in till Michaelmas, if not longer. It was not surprising the alacrity with which Viscount Gaston had inveigled himself into his family's inner circle. The man was as cunning as a snake charmer, his features handsome enough to deflect questions about his actual station in life.

Within three days of his arrival, he had become a great favorite with all the ladies at Wyndhurst. At least he did provide welcome relief to Nicholas by distracting the females of the household, his stepmother and Lady Susan being the prime examples, from focusing their efforts on filling Nicholas's hours with frivolity and idleness.

Oh, the viscount was very accomplished in those arts. To be fair, the man had filled the abbey's walls with more laughter than there had been for a very long time, given his father's illness. Nicholas should be grateful. But he did not like the way *the frog* looked at the abbey's inhabitants, or rather, the way he looked at a particular resident of the cottage beyond the downs. And the man had had the audacity to embarrass the doctor by revealing Charlotte and her brother's French ancestry— something Nicholas knew the distinguished doctor had taken great pains to hide.

As he rode past, Nicholas acknowledged the shy nods and grins of the group of men he had hired to dig the brewery's ponds. The pits were growing bigger every day. Soon they would be able to unleash the spring water held at bay by the strong dam the men had also built.

The skeleton of the sluice house stood on the small rise in front of him. Owen Roberts walked up as Nicholas's horse began to paw the ground.

"We're on schedule, actually ahead of plan, Lord Nick."

"Thanks to your oversight, Owen." Nicholas knew from experience that praise always worked wonders with men, contrary to the popular opinion of officers in most regiments, where daily abuse reigned supreme.

"Begging your pardon, but it's the men. They're a hard-working lot, desperate to keep their pride and put more food on their tables," Owen said, squinting toward the men.

"I'm sorry Wyndhurst failed you, and them."

"But you won't fail us," Owen said, reaching up to pat Nicholas's hand. "I have no doubt at all about that."

"Well, that makes one of us, at least," Nicholas responded with a self-deprecating laugh. "I am counting on you to continue my plans and maintain the running of all this when I leave."

Owen scratched his head. "I still don't understand it. Why're you leaving when your father is so sick? The war is over."

"I'll explain it all before I leave," Nicholas said, skirting the subject. "Tell me, did you find the old orchard I remember from my youth? Made myself sick many a day from eating all those apples. . . ."

Chapter Ten

*". . . it requires uncommon steadiness of reason to
resist the attraction of being called the most
charming girl in the world."*

—Northanger Abbey

*T*he sweet cacophony of birdsong filled Charlotte's bedroom. The vibrant symphony stopped long enough for
a thrush to mock the nightingale's beautiful song. But it was
the comforting sound of the ringdove that beckoned Charlotte out of her warm bed.

"Good morning, Miss Dove. I wish I could stay here and
listen to your song all day," she said, fully opening the sash.
"But I must spend the day cooing at Father's patients."

A cool morning greeted her senses and brushed the last of
the dream cobwebs from her mind. If only she could fly to the
highest trees and do nothing but stretch her wings and chirp all
day. The thought of worms for breakfast dampened her zeal.

Breakfast . . . she must go down straight away to intercede
between the daily machinations of Doro and Alexandre. Yesterday's morning ritual had seen new heights, with voices at
such a level as would have blown off the roof of a lesser
dwelling. Before tearing herself away from her window rever-
ies, she spied a liveried footman's approach. Perhaps she was
needed at the abbey . . . but he carried a large parcel of some
sort.

Charlotte dressed with haste and descended below stairs to
find Doro flustered, package in hand. A French curse describ-
ing the maid's undergarments floated from the direction of the
small dining salon. Thank God Doro could not understand
French.

"This be for you, miss." Doro shoved the parcel into her hands and reentered the fray with the Frenchman. Charlotte took the package to the front salon, curiosity adding a quickness to her step.

She unwrapped the parcel with care, saving the soft, fine paper for reuse. A bright ray of sunshine seemed to emanate from the last piece of tissue. She sucked in her breath when a beautiful dress was revealed in all its yellow glory. A cornflower and burgundy braided ribbon decorated the middle of the low neckline, while a hint of white lace provided some security for a modest female. It was altogether the most beautiful gown Charlotte had ever seen. She plucked out a card from the paper.

"My dear Miss Kittridge,

It is my great pleasure to gift you with this small token of my family's esteem. Your gown was ruined beyond salvation while attending to my horse, Phoenix, and it has been many weeks since I have promised my family to provide restitution.

I do hope you approve of the color. My brother suggested you might enjoy borrowing the hues of a goldfinch. His reasoning is beyond my understanding, but I do agree that it will suit your graceful form. But, I would not press this upon you. If you had rather a different pattern or material, please do not hesitate to return it with ideas for its replacement . . ."

Charlotte glanced at the gown. Replacement? *Replacement? Why, she would cherish this gift to the end of her days. It was perfection.*

"If you are partial to the gown, I would beg of you to wear it tonight. We would be most obliged if you and your family, as well as your guest, would join us for dinner this evening.

Thank you again for all your gentle ministrations to
my father, my brother, and to my beloved Phoenix.
With fondness,
Rosamunde Knightly"

Charlotte lowered the card and reached for the soft silk,
crushing it to her body. Her heart raced as she again glanced at
the letter. This was the best, most wonderful present she had
ever received.

As she whisked herself back upstairs, she wondered if it
was quite proper to accept such an extravagant gift. One *es-
sayage* of the beautiful golden gown was enough to force the
small grain of vanity that Charlotte possessed into a veritable
pebble. And instead of finding herself agreeing to her father's
stubborn insistence to return the object of her struggling shoot
of pride, she found herself arguing with her father for the first
time in her life.

"But, Papa—"

"There will be no further discussion about this unsuitable
gift. We are not peasants in need of finery. It is inconceivable."

When Alexandre took her part, she was even more sure that
she had chosen the evil course.

"But, my dear sir, you will not find it out of place for me to
tell you that it is not at all out of the common way for your
daughter to accept this gown. In fact, it would be considered
the height of rudeness, *très imprudent aussi,* to reject this simple act of kindness." Alexandre ruined the softening she could
see in her father's eyes by continuing, "And besides, I cannot
deny myself the joy in seeing her dressed prettily. Those rags
she wears are pure torture on the cultivated eye," he said, using
a toothpick discreetly after nuncheon.

"Papa, you must see that Lady Rosamunde will be very
hurt if I return her present. It is far better to accept it with
grace," she said as forcefully as she dared.

"And as I see it, it is Lord Huntington who had a hand in it.
I'll not have a daughter of mine accepting gowns from a gentleman. It smells of, of, of . . . well, of actions unbecoming a

lady," he said, turning beet-red. "And furthermore, I wish to understand these newfound attentions he is paying you. I understand that his lordship has been known to skulk about this residence while I have been at His Grace's bedside. What is the meaning of this?" he asked. "Charlotte?"

Charlotte noticed a smile Alexandre was trying to hide behind a napkin without success. He found vastly amusing the idea of his lordship finding any interest in a plain little nurse with little conversation.

"Charlotte, *cherie,* you have not given your heart to this man, have you? He will undoubtedly dash all your hopes without the smallest hesitation. And what is to become of my sensibilities for my dearest *cousine?*" Alexandre displayed the dimples that seemed to have been inherited by every branch of her family. But they looked so attractive on his bronzed cheeks that set off his white teeth to perfection.

"We'll have enough of that, Alexandre. Charlotte is a sensible female. She is beyond all nonsense of love. She has long cherished the joys of duty and science."

Charlotte was close enough to catch Alexandre's sigh and whisper, "Ah, yes, a pity that."

The subject had run its course with no firm conclusion, and therefore she approached her appearance before everyone that evening with not a little trepidation. Charlotte had no way to judge her overall appearance as she had only a small mirror that reflected her form above her bosom. But she could see that the delicate lace, ribbon, and yellow hue made her appear glowing and bright-eyed. She ran down the stairs when she heard her father's insistent call, stopping long enough to accept the shawl from Doro, who looked well pleased. Her father just stared at her, saying not another word about the gift.

To Charlotte's embarrassment, all eyes were upon her as the group from the cottage entered the duchess's magnificent drawing room filled with more gold leaf–encrusted surfaces than Versailles. She was acutely aware of his presence, but dared not glance in his direction until she knew without looking that he was in front of her. She glimpsed at Lord Huntington for the briefest moment, during which he tipped his head silently, acknowledging her presence.

"Miss Kittridge."

"My lord." Charlotte curtsied.

He had an unreadable expression, neither approving nor the opposite.

Charlotte stopped herself from tugging at the low bodice. She was very much on display, a feeling she had avoided her entire life. She retained her faculties enough to speak to the lady responsible for her present happiness.

"Lady Rosamunde, how can I thank you for this gift?" Charlotte accepted a glass of ratafia from a servant. "It is the most beautiful gown I have ever possessed." Charlotte felt Lord Huntington's shadow fall away from beside her and shivered.

"You must call me Rosamunde. I would be honored by your friendship," the striking young lady replied. "But, I wish I deserved your heartfelt appreciation. It is my brother who merits your gratitude. He is the one who insisted that you must have a new dress. He requested that my modiste work on the design he specified before commencing my long list of needs."

Charlotte turned to glance at Lord Huntington again when Rosamunde nodded in his direction. She found herself staring into unfathomable green eyes that made her long to escape to the wilderness beyond the winding gardens of Wyndhurst and feel his broad shoulders and long arms cover her with an overpowering embrace.

She was intensely aware of him. An aura of natural dominance and integrity radiated from him. Charlotte was powerless to look away.

The touch of Lady Rosamunde's hand broke the moment. "*Mother* is looking your way. I think we are to go in now." Rosamunde tugged Charlotte away to the group gathering before the massive oak doors.

Her Grace was pursing her lips in disapproval.

It was obvious that Rosamunde changed the subject to distract her. "Your brother is to take orders very soon, no?"

Charlotte tried to recover her equilibrium. "Yes, I am afraid that despite all his dillydallying and attempts to dissuade our father, his days as a gentleman in white stock and colored coat will soon be history. Although," she continued, "he would much prefer the army life, as you must know. He would . . . how do those young gentlemen in town describe it? 'Boil his lobster' is the term, I think, at a moment's notice if ever a military opportunity presented itself."

Charlotte dared not look at Lord Huntington again. She would not make a cake of herself. The dress was a mere pittance to a man like Lord Huntington, a simple gift because she had helped him on several occasions. He was staring at her because he had only ever seen her with dirt, blood, straw, or clay covering her.

Charlotte wondered if she was asked to go in to dinner on the arm of the vicar as punishment, or if Her Grace had decided that the best method to keep both of the elderly ladies' claws sheathed was to remove the so-called mouse, or rather vicar, from play. Due to the low status of the Kittridge family, Her Grace indicated to Charlotte a chair at the remote end of the table next to one of the grandmothers. As far away from Lord Huntington as was possible. At least she could be thankful that it was not Lady Susan's grandmother, whose constant screeching could produce the headache within minutes.

Delicate porcelain platters and bowls arrived by many liveried servants dressed in the finest satin. The chef displayed the enormity of his talents with quail eggs in aspic followed by fish, pheasant, and lamb prepared à la francaise. But the pièce de résistance was the turtle steaks served with butter and Seville oranges.

Unfortunately, Charlotte's appetite had left her the few precious minutes she had been in Lord Huntington's presence. She doubted his stepmother would allow her to speak to him at all. And she was right. He had been seated between Lady Rosamunde and the duchess.

The vast display of extravagant food sickened her. Did not

the family realize that there were entire families starving within a five-mile radius of the estate? It was shameful.

"Miss Kittridge, may I be allowed to compliment you on your beautiful gown this evening?" The vicar regarded her with kind eyes. "The color becomes your perpetually sunny disposition."

Before she could offer her thanks, the dowager duchess took up the bait. "Yes, yes, my dear. So nice to see you in bright colors for a change. When I was younger, I had a particular yellow gown that was my favorite. I do believe there was a time that Mr. Llewellyn thought it rather pretty too." She gave as coy a look as possible for a lady with eighty-two years on her dish.

"My dearest Margarita, that color would look ghastly on you. It would bring out the sallow tones of your complexion," said Lady Elltrope. "What can you be thinking? I am sure the vicar prefers more refined color such as this purple I am wearing . . . truly a royal color, do you not agree, Mr. Llewellyn?" Lady Elltrope batted her eyes at the vicar.

"Well, I am, I am—" stuttered the vicar.

"Do you have something in your eye, Hortense?" inquired Her Grace Margarita before the poor beleaguered man could finish.

"Why, you have the audacity . . ." Lady Elltrope began and then stopped, as if unwilling to stoop to unladylike behavior. Both women looked fit to cast off their jewels for the catfight of a lifetime.

For once in his life the vicar seemed unable to resolve the situation in a pious manner befitting his station without chastising the ladies and causing more damage.

Charlotte felt sorry for him. "You are quite right, Lady Elltrope. Purple suits you very well, especially with the lovely gray of your beautiful hair." She turned to the dowager duchess. "And this beautiful dress, for which I owe your family much gratitude, I believe, is very similar in color to the exquisite portrait I spied of you in the gallery. Was it not by Jean-Honore Fragonard? Perhaps the style and fashion has changed, but the colors are very much the same. I could only wish to be half as well-looking as Your Grace is in that portrait of you reading."

Both ladies looked well pleased. However, her long speech had interrupted the various pockets of conversation at the table. What had she been thinking? This gown must have empowering properties, she thought with mischief.

"I say, we must have some dancing after supper to see the superior qualities of Miss Kittridge's gown," said Lord Edwin, "and of course those of the other charming ladies."

"A brilliant idea," seconded the viscount with a twinkle in his eye. "I have it on good authority that all the ladies are dying for a romp."

Lady Susan tittered. Louisa Nichols looked hopeful. Her Grace, the Duchess of Cavendish, remained silent.

"I am sorry to suggest otherwise," Lord Huntington said in his deep voice. "However, while my father lies ill, I cannot think of dancing."

His sister looked pale.

"Oh, my dear brother," replied Lord Edwin. "Father would want us to make merry. It has been nothing but gloom and doom for weeks. I'm afraid your nature has not allowed for the necessity of entertaining our guests."

"Perhaps you are right, Edwin. But I still do not like it."

"Perhaps you would prefer that we sit about the fire and read? That is a favorite pastime of yours, is it not?"

Charlotte sucked in her breath and couldn't bear to hear a retort.

James, ignorant of the situation, and always ready to smooth over any awkwardness, stepped in. "I would enjoy that a great deal. I have just finished reading last year's *Annual Register* to fill in the gaps of my knowledge of events. I suppose you have already read it, Lord Huntington?"

He shook his head, and Charlotte grabbed her hands under the table to control the shaking.

Edwin chortled. "Why ever not, Nicholas?"

All the eyes at the table were focused on Lord Huntington—most perplexed, some knowing, all waiting. Lady Rosamunde committed the unpardonable act of excusing herself from the room, and left, tears in her eyes.

Charlotte forced the full powers of the gown into action. She had to raise her voice to be noticed by the other end of the table. "Lord Huntington, did you, by chance, read more of the novel you were reading to me this afternoon?" She was not lying, precisely. He had made remarkable progress ever since they had unlocked a door in his mind with the clay letters. He had been reading longer passages, of more complex words each day with fewer faults and less rest for head pains, though she doubted he had attempted *Mansfield Park* on his own.

"I confess to reading ahead a few pages, Miss Kittridge," he said, staring at his brother.

Her heart swelled with vicarious pride.

"What? You dare to tell falsehoods with a vicar in the room, Brother? You go too far," said Lord Edwin, slapping his napkin down at the side of his plate. "We all know you cannot read. You are an ignorant."

A chorus of shocked sounds filled the room.

"Perhaps, I am," Lord Huntington said, his face like granite. "But that is not to the point. What is relevant is that no revelry should occur until our good father has recovered his health."

Charlotte shivered. He'd sounded as if he were addressing soldiers under his command. She did not doubt the troops in the 95th Rifleman would have instantly obeyed and respected such a man.

"However, Edwin, fear not, you will not have me to force you to attend to social strictures much longer. I have promised Father I would stay only as long as is necessary for his peace of mind. I have had a letter from headquarters requiring me in Paris as soon as it is convenient."

Charlotte could keep silent no longer. "But, you have not recovered. . . ."

Her heart lurched when she encountered his piercing gaze. He had turned into the battle-hardened warrior.

"I thank you for your observation, Miss Kittridge. I assure you that I will be capable of resuming whatever position Wellington's coattails assign me. So far, I am sure there is nothing to do but attend every sort of military parade and social gaiety given in the Ambassador's honor." He smiled at his brother. "Actually, I do believe you would enjoy it."

Lord Huntington turned to his stepmother. "It is time for a glass of something a bit more fortifying than this wine, is it not, *Your Grace*?"

The duchess jumped up from the table. With glacial cordiality she invited the ladies to withdraw to the salon.

Lord Edwin looked very much as if he would like to follow them.

The ladies were reduced to fortifying themselves with coffee. Charlotte wished she could hear whatever the gentlemen were discussing behind the august doors of the former room, whose servants were no doubt longing to decamp the dining hall to tell their colleagues below stairs the story of how Lord Huntington had finally taken his brother to task.

Charlotte took the exquisite porcelain cup and saucer from the cold hands of the duchess and walked to the distant window alcove. She was exhausted by the events of the evening. But her hopes of a moment of tranquility evaporated with the appearance of Louisa Nichols before her.

"Was it not brilliant?" Miss Nichols asked, giggling.

"To what do you refer?"

"Why to the most excellent set down by Lord Huntington."

Charlotte had no desire to hear this lady's gossip, but did not know how to extricate herself.

"You know," Miss Nichols continued, lowering her voice, "I was witness to this family's machinations for many years. Each time I came on holiday, I watched as he was taunted by cruel remarks regarding his inability to learn. He never said a word to defend himself, although it was quite obvious how it tortured him. And Rosamunde was never allowed to defend him either. Lord Huntington forbade her after the duchess punished Rosamunde once for 'interfering.'" Louisa ran out of steam and recollected herself all at the same moment. She appeared discomfited to have revealed her private remembrances.

"What are you two talking about?" asked Lady Susan, her familiar tinkling laugh signaling her approach. "I must take part in your conversation. I cannot stand another moment with the old biddies. The dowager duchess is about to make my grandmother expire in a fit of the vapors."

Louisa giggled. "I think I just heard the dowager infer that Lady Elltrope was a harridan looking to play the trollop!"

Lady Susan sniffed. "I cannot fathom why those two old ladies cannot act with more propriety. It is utterly Beyond the Pale. I would never act in such a fashion."

"Oh, no, Susan. You would *never* flirt," Louisa said.

"I take great offence, Louisa. You must explain yourself," Lady Susan replied in a high-pitched voice.

"Why, I mean your behavior toward Viscount Gaston, of course. Do you think we are blind to your fawning ways?"

"He is quite magnificent, *n'est-ce pas?*" said Lady Susan in the worst French accent Charlotte had ever heard. "But you have all been entranced too."

"I do believe you are going to have to practice your irregular verb conjugation and your accent before making your conquest," replied Louisa.

"Do I detect a hint of jealousy? You seem to be always underfoot whenever we converse."

"Just trying to help you follow the rules of chaperonage that your mother, with her merchant background, might not have taught you," Louisa said, looking furious. "Besides, I thought you were here to snare Lord Edwin. Although the heir seems to have captured your fancy ever since he arrived."

"How dare you!" Lady Susan did not look nearly as embarrassed as she should. "Honestly, this place is as boring as two sticks. Mayn't I have a bit of fun before tying myself to a Man who Dislikes Frivolity? I am being forced to consider a life devoid of all gaiety in a future marriage to the heir."

Charlotte's eyes narrowed.

"The viscount is marvelous, is he not?" Lady Susan continued her ebullient quest to reveal all. "He has such bearing and presence and, of course, wit. Did you not notice the way his shoulders are molded by the cut of his coat, and the way he fills out his, well, *his unmentionables*?"

With that, Louisa Nichols almost spilled her coffee. But Lady Susan was not ready to relieve her conspiratorial role. She gathered her listeners and continued in a whisper. "I have it on the greatest authority that he is the sort of man who could make a lady want to experience the Obligations of a Wife."

"Lady Susan!" Charlotte said in hushed horror.

"And . . . ?" Louisa's curiosity was not to be disappointed. "There must be more." The group gathered tighter together. Charlotte was swept along in the shock of it.

"And, my French maid told me all about it," said Susan, whispering. "She said that the viscount performs in such an exemplary fashion in Matters of the Bedchamber, that it would be well worth taking him as an immediate lover after my marriage to Lord Huntington."

"Lady Susan, I insist—" began Charlotte.

"Oh, hush," Lady Susan said, ignoring Charlotte. "I just wish I could first experience the Pleasures of the Flesh by the viscount on my wedding night."

Charlotte turned in time to see Louisa's shocked expression.

"Actually, it is a difficult decision—trying to decide if becoming a duchess is worth tying myself to an ignorant sobersides or settling for being a gay viscountess in all respects. If I decide on the former, you, dear Louisa, must promise to come to every house party I form. I daresay I will have to have at least one every fortnight if I hope to partake in a modicum of fun," she said with a tinkling laugh.

"You will, of course, excuse me, Susan, for saying that not only is your proposal alarming, but it is an impossibility," Louisa said with a satisfied smile. "I can assure you that Lord Huntington has no intention ever to marry anyone. Even a lady of many charms such as yours could not sway him from his decision made years ago. In short, he shall not have you."

What?! Could Louisa's words have an ounce of truth? *He had promised not to marry any lady?* Not just Charlotte? Not that it mattered. He had told his father that he would never choose her for a wife. He had promised his father. But for some perverse reason, she could at least take comfort in the idea that she would not have to witness his marriage to another.

"Oh, phooey, Louisa. You just want the title for yourself. No heir to a dukedom takes a vow such as the one you have described," Lady Susan said.

"Perhaps you should consider more the idea of a marriage with the viscount. Surely he can provide your inflamed desires with an additional measure or two of persuasion to shake you from your original designs on the heir. If not, I am afraid you will have to be satisfied living vicariously through your maid."

"Yes, well, it is too bad the younger brother could not switch places with the elder. At least I could be assured a steady stream of entertainments with that gentleman in his sire's seat—although no one could possibly be as charming as your cousin, Miss Kittridge," she said with a pitiful sigh.

Charlotte felt the cold anger that had been flowing through her veins move to the very tips of her fingers. She curled her hands in rage. If this was not the most embarrassing conversation she had ever heard, it was certainly the most absurd. If this was what young ladies discussed, she had her doubts as to whether she would continue to cultivate any friendships save Rosamunde's. "Perhaps you could measure the three gentlemen's physical attributes and ask for a formal examination of their formidable wits before choosing a life's partner. But if expensive amusements are your primary concern, then I would go with Lord Edwin. He has far more to offer."

She could tell by her expression that Lady Susan's pea-sized brain could not discern if Charlotte's words were said in jest or in seriousness. In her mind it was all Too Complicated.

Chapter Eleven

"One has got all the goodness, and the other all the appearance of it."

—Pride and Prejudice

The next morning, Nicholas exited the arched doorway of the abbey, forcing himself not to limp. His leg only cramped a little now as he walked down the stone stairs toward the stables.

He had just had a satisfying meeting with Owen Roberts, who had agreed to oversee the building of a large kiln for Miss Kittridge's clay figures. He had also informed Owen of his decision to place it all—the brewery, the kiln, and the farmlands—in Owen's capable hands. He was a man whose honesty and integrity could be counted on without question. Nicholas was at the point of wondering if there would be enough land to start a better flock of sheep when he heard a voice call out to him.

"May I have a word with you, my lord?" James Kittridge asked.

"Of course." They walked into the stables, and Nicholas stopped in front of Phoenix's stall to check the remarkable recovery of the horse. "I am going for a ride beyond the valley to look at progress on some land. Would you care to join me?" Nicholas knew full well that Kittridge would accept with alacrity the chance to try one of Wyndhurst's superior hunters.

"Why yes, my lord. I would be honored!"

After feeling Phoenix's legs and looking into her eyes, Nicholas arranged for a second horse to be saddled. Once they were both mounted on feisty geldings, Nicholas proposed a good gallop before anything else and was met with a broad grin that nearly split the younger man's face in two.

As they reached the valley's roiling spring, and turned to follow it upstream at a more sedate pace, James Kittridge spoke. "First, I must apologize for the discussion last night," he began. "I would never have continued that miserable subject of reading had I known of your, of your . . . " He had turned beet-red, and Nicholas relieved him of his misery as they road side by side.

"There is no need to feel any embarrassment. I accepted my deficiencies long ago. While I might prefer to have them remain unknown to others, I have finally learned not to fear the unveiling of any truths."

"I shall have to remember that as a seed for a future sermon," he said.

Nicholas threw back his head and chuckled. "Sermonmaking does not appear to be a task you will take up with any real zeal."

Kittridge snorted. "You have the right of it. I think everyone is aware that I would prefer the military. In fact, I want to be just like you—a decorated officer in the 95th Rifleman. But I shall not disappoint my father."

"You and I are alike in many ways . . ."

For a few moments, neither said another word. Nicholas was glad that Kittridge did not choose to pry the meaning of his words from him.

"You mentioned that you wanted to discuss something— was it just about last evening?" asked Nicholas.

"No," Kittridge said, and paused. "There was something more . . . It is about my sister."

"Yes?"

"She is very kindhearted, and practical, and of course very intelligent . . ."

"I agree." Nicholas wondered where this was all leading.

"Well, sir, I would not want to see her hurt. She might appear very strong, but after all, she is a female, and has had her emotions toyed with in the past. And I, and of course my father, would not want to witness a reoccurrence."

Nicholas stopped his horse, forcing young Kittridge to do the same. "Do I understand you? Is she in expectation of a proposal of marriage from me?"

Kittridge flinched. "No. It is rather that you might not know her as I do. And I feel I must warn you," he said, before continuing in a rush. "She is quite delighted by *your family's* gift of the dress. And, well, you see, I saw you both returning after the rain shower."

Nicholas closed his eyes for a few moments and shook his head. "She said nothing to you on the occasion?"

"No," he replied. "Well, actually she reprimanded me and told me to go to the devil . . . Well, not exactly in those words. But that was the gist of it."

"While you do not know me well, I can assure you I have no intention of ruining your sister. She has been of immense help to me. I would not hurt her," he said, then urged his horse forward again. He looked over his shoulder toward Miss Kittridge's brother. "I would look no further than the viscount, if you desire a proposal of marriage. He seems to have captured more hearts than the post on St. Valentine's Day. A veritable Romeo Shakespeare would approve of. Is he not here to woo her?"

"He seems to want to lead my sister to the altar 'ere long, although my father is not altogether desirous of the match. But they have been long promised to each other—since childhood. And Charlotte—"

"And your sister desires the match?" Nicholas interrupted.

"If I could figure out the maneuverings of the female mind, I would not be talking to you now. I have never understood my sister—or any other female for that matter."

"And why does your father seem to be disinclined to approve of the viscount?"

"He considers the man to be frivolous in his pursuits. They would not suit. Although, I think a bit of gaiety in

Charlotte's life would do her a world of good. She has been deprived of far too much. She has not been exposed to the entertainments enjoyed by most young women. Instead she immersed herself in my father's books, and helped to nurse the ill and infirm for the last decade. Perhaps, the viscount will have her after all, although why he wants her I cannot fathom. Her dowry is modest, to be sure." Kittridge paused. "But it will not happen without my father's blessing."

"Why would your father reject his suit?" Nicholas asked, unsure of why he was persistent in the matter.

"Well, there is the matter of our heritage. As you might have noticed, my father suppresses as much as possible our French ancestry."

"I daresay they are thousands of French émigrés in England today. What does he fear? The guillotine has long been sheathed."

The young man's face had become white and drawn, Nicholas discovered when he turned around to see why his comment had met with no response. He stopped his horse again and caught at Kittridge's reins as he drew beside him. "It is my turn to apologize. Did you know many who died?"

"Yes," he said. "My mother and grandparents, during Thermidor."

"They were declared 'enemies of the people'?"

"Yes. It was their wealth and titles that killed them," he said. Then added, "My sister witnessed the worst of it."

Nicholas knew enough to keep silent.

"I was with my father in Paris. We shared a small town house with my cousin and his mother's family, who were prudent enough to hide their wealth. My maternal grandparents were proud and defiant and refused to heed their warnings. They remained on their estate, and Charlotte refused to be parted from our mother. Her governess managed to rescue Charlotte, who was just seven years old then. She dressed her in rags, and hid in the woods until it was safe enough to walk to Paris under the cloak of darkness." Kittridge refocused his eyes and looked toward Nicholas. "Do you wish to hear the rest? I must warn you it is ghastly."

"Tell me."

The faraway look in his expression returned. "My mother, her sister, and my grandparents were taken before the tribunal and sent to Les Carmes prison. They watched their friends led away by the cartful each morning. Soon it was their own turn. Charlotte only ever spoke of it once to me. She had slipped away from the town house to catch a glimpse of our mother when Charlotte had overheard they were to be guillotined that day. She managed to touch our mother's hand before the crowd swelled and broke them apart. She tried to crawl out but was unable to press through. Charlotte did not see our mother guillotined, but she heard the sound of the blade drop and the cheers of the crowd."

James stopped, and tried to collect himself. "When we lived in London, my sister would not enter any crowded place. And she refused to be out of my father's or my sight. My father or I had to stay with her every moment—even while she slept. She has a great fear of being left alone in the world."

Nicholas felt sick to his stomach.

"I am not surprised," Nicholas replied. "I do not know what to say, except that I am very sorry. At least I was a grown man of seventeen when I first witnessed the gruesome realities of a battlefield. I cannot imagine how a seven-year-old little girl felt upon hearing the guillotine and a crowd cheer at her mother's death."

"Well, it explains why my father refuses to acknowledge any ties to the aristocracy. Indeed, I was surprised that he allowed my flamboyantly aristocratic cousin to visit us. But, I suspect it was only because Alexandre's family supported us during those sinister days of the Terror."

"Who were your grandparents?"

"Le Marquis and Marchioness de la Palladin. But I pray you do not tell my father what I have confided to you. I have told you this so you will understand why I do not want my sister to ever have to suffer again. She has experienced enough pain for one lifetime."

"I assure you I would never hurt your sister. I owe her more than is comfortable for a man to owe a lady."

"That is all I can ask," Kittridge replied.

As the two gentlemen toured the lands the grandfather had deeded to him, Nicholas kept the conversation on topics limited to battlefield facts, to please Kittridge, and farming, to please himself. The young man approved of Nicholas's ideas for the use of the vast acres, but preferred arguing over the merits of the Brown Bess over the French musket. And all Nicholas could think of, in the corners of his mind, was how soon the viscount would convince Dr. Kittridge and charm the doctor's daughter to the altar.

It had been a frightful morning for Charlotte. First Alexandre had so insulted Doro that the poor woman had left, swearing never to return until "his French viscount's arse" was gone from the valley. Then her father had not returned from a middle-of-the-night visit to a neighboring tenant farmer too ill to be moved.

Her brother had been of no help as usual. After returning from a ride with Lord Huntington yesterday, James had lectured her all afternoon, yet again, about that gentleman's plans to return to his regiment. Early this morning Charlotte had forced him out of the cottage in the direction of the abbey to get a report on the duke's condition.

In her father's absence, a growing gaggle of patients argued amongst themselves in the front room, as to who had the most grievous illness or injury. The villager with bunions took issue with the laborer with an inflamed cut from the new scythe, while an infant, quite yellow, wailed his hunger to the entire household. Most were more than annoyed to have Charlotte to complain to instead of her father. But she had listened to them, stitched and bandaged them, and cajoled them into compliance before seeing the lot of them out of the cottage.

The pièce de résistance arrived in the petite form of Lady Susan, who had condescended to visit that Den of Disease, their cottage, to be of Service to the Less Fortunate. Charlotte doubted her lofty motive because the lady kept her gaze glued to the doorway, no doubt in high hopes of seeing a certain French gentleman and his Impressive Unmentionables. She was only able to dislodge Lady Susan when Charlotte described a bilious gastric complaint that seemed to be circulating the area. She was lucky enough to get rid of both Alexandre and Lady Susan by calling the former, when he emerged from his toilette, to offer escort to a most Willing Recipient of his Services.

Ah, peace at last. The clatter of hooves broke the momentary lull. She sighed as she rose, knowing she must attend to the visitor herself given Doro's defection and her father's absence.

A familiar deep baritone voice raised the hairs on the back of her neck. The intensity of the tone cut her to the marrow. "Charlotte! Charlotte, make haste! Your father—"

She entered the hallway to see Lord Huntington half dragging, half carrying the crumpled form of her beloved father through the doorway. "My God, what happened?" she implored as she helped carry him into the front room, laying him on the carpet. He was unconscious and muddy. She peered under his closed eyelids and felt for his pulse at his wrist.

Lord Huntington, completely out of breath, began a halting speech. "I found him at the edge of the stand . . . of trees near the lake. . . . It's his head, I'm afraid," he said, indicating a bloody patch near the back of the skull. His fingers were covered in blood when he pulled his hand away.

Charlotte rocked back onto her heels, her father's hand still in her own. There was no pulse, no breath, no—nothing. Numbness spread from her hand to the rest of her body as an immense blast of coldness invaded her being. She refused to acknowledge the scene before her, so filled with horror was she. She looked up to Lord Huntington, who was staring at her and saying something. How long had he been talking to her?

"Is he beyond all hope, then?" he asked, leaning from the other side of the body to grip her arms. He shook her.

"He is gone," she whispered.

He closed his eyes and released her, sighing heavily. Within moments she found herself being lifted from her spot. "No . . . no, I won't leave him," she insisted.

Lord Huntington settled himself behind her and tried to force her to lean back into the circle of his arms. But Charlotte felt frozen like a block of ice, all cold, hard angles that refused to yield to his embrace.

"I am so very sorry," he said. "I shall go and find your maid. Where is your brother?"

"No, they're not here." With that she crumpled, and the tears began to fall. "For God's sake, what happened?" she said through her tears, still refusing to lean on him.

"He fell from his horse, I believe. I found the horse he uses grazing nearby, the saddle askew. If I were forced to hazard a guess, I would say that in his haste he didn't retighten the girth after mounting. And that horse is known to fill his lungs to avoid a tight girth," Lord Huntington said. "I shall have the animal destroyed at once."

She covered her face with her hands and wept. "No, please don't. There is to be no more bloodshed."

He shook his head. "Let me find someone to attend to you—the vicar and a maid perhaps?"

He was leaving her? Here, with her dead father in her arms? Why did everyone always leave her *alone*? No, it was unfair, she was not being rational. Rational thought was impossible. She looked at him. He must have seen something in her expression to give pause.

"Come. You must come away with me now. I cannot leave you here, alone. At least let me take you to my sister."

"No, I must stay here," she said. "It is all right. I will stay. I cannot leave him," she said, looking down at the gray countenance of her father. The image wavered as her eyes filled with tears again. "What if my brother returns? I must be here." Her voice sounded very far away to her as the walls of her vision began to cast dark shadows toward the center.

At the last moment, she knew she was losing consciousness, and she was grateful for the surcease of pain . . . endless pain . . . endless loneliness . . . always alone.

The next hour proved to be one of the most difficult in Nicholas's life. It was a full ten minutes of trying to revive Miss Kittridge before she allowed the peaceful bonds of unconsciousness to give her up to the real world. Even then she wore a pale, expressionless mask and refused to speak, curling herself into a ball.

Cursing his leg, which he had overstrained in his exertions, Nicholas lifted her onto the settee and brought a blanket before starting water to boil for tea. Where was the blasted maid? Then, despite her mewling cries, Nicholas carried her father's lifeless body into the doctor's bedchamber and covered him with a sheet before returning to the kitchen.

With a murmur of approval, he unearthed a nearly empty bottle of good French brandy in one of the cupboards. At least the viscount had served a purpose, for surely no one else in the household imbibed. It was her turn to try it today—if there ever was a time for it, it was now, he thought, shaking his head. He poured two glasses, emptying the bottle, and carried the tray into the front room.

She was shivering on the settee when he returned but took the spirits without protest. Nicholas downed the contents of his share in one swift movement as he watched her sputter and cough after one small sip. "Keep drinking, if you can. It will offer temporary warmth."

She appeared very pale. He kneeled down in front of her, despite the stabbing pain from his thigh, and grasped her hand, rubbing it to soothe her. "Miss Kittridge . . ."

Her gaze moved to him, but there seemed no life in her. When she didn't speak, he tried again. "Charlotte, I don't want you to worry. I will take care of everything . . . of, of you, and your brother. I won't have you worry," he insisted.

"No. You are not to play the hero. No one can do anything to help me. I have feared this day, but—" she said, then burst into tears. "But, I realize now that I somehow always knew it would come. And no matter how hard I tried to protect my father and James, it was all in God's destructive hands."

He did not even try to speak. He must get her to talk as much as he could, otherwise she would retreat into the horror of it all.

"I shall survive this, have no fear," she said, looking down at her hands.

"Listen to me." Nicholas took her hands in his own and squeezed them gently. "I have no doubt of your strong constitution. It is your future with which I am concerned. I assure you that you will never want for anything. I do not want you to worry on any account."

"It is a characteristic of all gentlemen, this need to reassure females of their protection. It is unnecessary. I refuse to burden someone who will be far away in some distant place, working or fighting for the British Crown. Please do not say anything right now."

Without hesitation, he responded. "There is nothing that would bring me more happiness than assuring your protection."

Her face had taken on a blank expression. He feared she was in shock. A great sense of peace enveloped Nicholas as he took his decision. He would do what he had known he would do as soon as he found the lifeless form of Dr. Kittridge in the field.

"Miss Kittridge . . . Charlotte, would you do me the great honor of becoming my wife?"

"What?" she asked, in a daze. "It is out of the question."

He wanted desperately to envelope her within the protection of his arms, to comfort her, insist on her obedience, reassure her of his care, but he would not. He knew she would resist it.

"I am sorry, I spoke in haste. I must give you time to recover from the shock." He tucked a stray wisp of hair away from her tear-streaked face. "But, Charlotte, I will help you, no matter how much you resist."

The sound of the rusty hinge on the front door sounded, indicating someone's arrival. Nicholas rose to his feet and rearranged the blanket about her thin shoulders before beginning preparations for the rest of Charlotte's life, whether she wanted him to or not.

Chapter Twelve

"Half the sum of attraction, on either side, might have been enough, for he had nothing to do, and she had hardly anybody to love."

—Persuasion

*T*he funeral was all things bleak and mournful, occurring in a steady rain. Charlotte looked at the gathering of mourners through her black veil and thought they looked like a flock of crows. She pushed up the too-long sleeves of her borrowed black finery, grateful for Rosamunde's generosity. A robin stood on the ground nearby, singing in the pouring rain, competing with the jumble of sonorous words pouring from the lips of the good vicar, Mr. Llewellyn.

The church had been cold and somber. But she had refused to leave the coffin after. She had insisted on following the pallbearers to the graveyard. And she supposed the others had come because they pitied her.

She felt the weight of the presence of the thirty-odd people. At least she was outside now, so the crowd did not suffocate her and the promise of open fields beckoned behind her.

Was her father's spirit there? She kept wanting to turn around, sure he would be behind her shoulder. She longed to touch his shiny pate again, to feel the scratchy wool fibers of his coat on her cheek, to smell the faint herbal scent always surrounding his person.

Charlotte closed her eyes and failed miserably at concentrating on the vicar's words, the promises of heaven, and the goodness of God. She felt like screaming at them all. . . . There was no fair God, no heaven, no promises.

What God would allow the death of both her parents? She looked across the open hole in the earth to the cool, arrogant mask of the Duchess of Cavendish.

A hand gripped her arm, steadying her just as she realized she was swaying. *His* strong hand. James gripped her other arm. They must think she was about to flee. They were right.

The duchess had visited Charlotte and James two days after their father's death to inform them that they were most welcome to the use of the cottage for another fortnight or two given their father's service to the duke. James had sputtered their thanks, unsure if Her Grace had been generous or paltry in her offer. Charlotte had not enlightened her brother as to her opinion.

Had the duchess known that the heir had offered for her, Her Grace might have considered it more reasonable to offer a roof over their heads for at least two months. Or perhaps she would have chased Charlotte away with a horsewhip. Yes, that was much more likely.

The thud of the first clumps of muddy soil and rock hitting the simple pine coffin jarred her out of her reverie. Charlotte shook at the sound of the second shovel-full. She could not endure this agony further.

She shook free of her captors and forced herself past the onlookers, feeling all at once frantic at her inability to burst free from the small crowd. It was Paris all over again, without the gleeful bloodthirsty shouts of encouragement to the murderers controlling the guillotine's heavy blade.

She heard a strangled cry and realized it emanated from her own throat. Her brother appeared at her side and parted the sea of black in an instant with his words and his huge umbrella. He forced her to slow to a fast walk when he gripped her elbow.

They walked a good twenty minutes through the fields in silence before she forced herself to stop and speak. "James, I posted several letters to London yesterday. I am certain to find a good position as a lady's nurse. We both know I have had many offers in the past. And I know you prefer London.

And I will find another position whenever and wherever you find a living."

"Yes," he said.

They continued walking again, side by side. But she could feel his reluctance to speak to her. "What is it, James?"

"Would you be very sad if I didn't take orders, Charlotte?"

"What else could you do? We have not the funds for a new field of study," she said, peering anxiously into his eyes.

"Well, I am considering a very generous and kind offer. . . . Lord Huntington has suggested that using his connections, he might be able to secure a commission for me in his regiment, despite the current peace. Many are selling out."

"And who would pay for this commission? No—wait, allow me to guess," she said, with a touch of anger. "Lord Huntington? James, you cannot accept such a gross amount of money."

"He insisted. He said after all our father had done for the duke, it was the very least he could do. And the duke seconded the idea." The bright glow of excitement overspread her brother's face as he spoke.

"And I see you did not choose to argue the point. That it is impossible to accept a debt of gratitude of this magnitude."

"Charlotte, I will not go if you do not want me to," he said, with a glum expression. "I promised Father long ago that I would always watch over you."

She could not take it away from him. But letting him go meant facing her greatest fear: The fear of being left all alone had grown inside her seven-year-old form that horrible night. Thoughts of that evening's events made her inhale sharply.

She could still remember the flames of the torches surrounding the great house, her mother pushing her out the side door along with the governess, the obscenities, the hounds' barking coming from every direction, the smell of Mademoiselle Barr's hands when she covered Charlotte's mouth as they tread water among the reeds of a secluded pond. And worst of all, being left alone with a stranger when her governess had not wanted to risk going all the way to Paris with her. The terrorized woman had paid a man to take her, on the back of his dogcart, to an unknown address in the city. He had tipped back a bottle every mile or so. Halfway there, he had told her to get out "and find your own way, you little bugger." Charlotte shivered. She could not ever remember the many miles she had walked or how she had managed to find the town house.

James took her hands in his own and squeezed them. "Charlotte? I shan't desert you," he assured her.

She shook her head. "I will not withhold your fondest dream, James."

"I told him you were the most kindhearted sister in the world," James said, with a cautious degree of hope.

"Perhaps I could follow the drum. Come with you . . . There must be a great need for nurses."

James blanched.

"No, I can see that would not work," she said, doing an excellent job of controlling herself.

"Charlotte, I will make sure you are settled in an excellent position before I go."

"Do you mind if I continue on alone a bit. We can talk a little later, to sort out all the details. It has been such a horrid last four days. . . ." She would not cry in his presence, 'ere he take pity on her and not follow his heart.

He hugged Charlotte, squeezing the breath out of her as he kissed the top of her head before turning away.

There, she had done it. She had had no choice. She was certain that within a few weeks the grim reality of her future would force her to wonder if she had taken complete leave of her senses to acquiesce to her brother's plan. But, she had made a promise to herself to stop worrying about the future.

She had fine skills that would provide a room and nourishment, and with any luck, it would be in a comfortable, fine house in London.

She was more worried about Alexandre, the more she thought about it. Oh, he had borne her father's death with real grief. But he had accepted the revelation of the meager accumulation of her father's income with even greater sorrow.

It was obvious Alexandre had gambled on a notion that her father had hoarded a nice bit of income, some of which would come to her in the form of a dowry. What he had not figured was her father's staunch refusal to turn away any patient, and to often provide medicines without reimbursement. Her father was *un vrai sans culottes* of the first order. The murderous French peasants who caused the revolution should be proud to call him one of their own.

She hopped over a low stile to continue her way through the edge of an open field. One benefit of their poverty was that Alexandre had abruptly changed. In the last four days, he had become her confidante and friend—and she was pleased. He seemed to love her as a favored sister, once he had shed his false front, something he did but when they were alone.

During the plans for the hasty funeral, she had come to rely on Alexandre more so than her own brother. He was very good at giving orders. He pretended that his newfound role of dependable cousin was really a desire to show off his manly character to the ladies at Wyndhurst Abbey. Charlotte knew better.

He had agreed to move to the abbey when it was decided by the duchess that it was unseemly for the viscount to remain in a cottage with only a brother to watch over a spinster female. One positive effect of his removal had been the return of Doro, who had practically thrown Alexandre's valises out of the cottage door to the waiting arms of the beleaguered footmen of the abbey.

And given the fact that everyone seemed to have changed

their spots within the last four days, it was not surprising that Lord Huntington had followed suit by halting all visits to the cottage. This was slow torture—constant looking through the window, eager to see his figure. She had come to depend on Lord Huntington's visits. She had not realized how much she looked forward to just the sight of him, the scent of him, the comfort of his presence. He had given her the illusion that perhaps he cared for her, maybe just the slightest bit. But no. He was like all the others that had gone before him. Just when she began to believe in the impossible, they disappeared into thin air.

He obviously regretted his impetuous proposal and now was embarrassed to have to face her without the safety of others about him. Lord, he probably worried that she expected him to offer for her again now that the burial was over.

Until this morning at the church, she had not seen him since the day he had brought her father's lifeless body back to the cottage. And today he had barely said three words and only touched her when she swayed as the earth hit the coffin. She dreaded their next meeting.

A drop of rain fell on her nose, and Charlotte looked up to find that the umbrella had sprung a leak. She sighed and turned toward the direction of the cottage. There was no escaping the future.

For four days he had planned a proper proposal, then deconstructed it, and replanned it again, and again. The first time he had been too hasty and ill-prepared in the heat of the moment and the shock of death. This time it would be different.

As he walked to her cottage the morning after the funeral, he thought about his tactics one last time. He would not relent no matter what flimsy line of reasoning she offered. Nicholas had prepared rational counterarguments to her every possible hesitation. He must get past her pride, past her defenses, and he would do it in a much more facile man-

ner than if it had been any other lady. He would use logic, as
that is what it would take to win over a cerebral female such
as Charlotte.

There was not a single doubt in his mind that he must
take care of her. Her brother thought she would be able to
find a good position in London as an elderly lady's companion or nurse. Nicholas snorted in disgust. He had promised James that he would ensure Charlotte's employment
was everything good and secure. But unlike her brother, he
was not willing to desert her, whether she valiantly argued
against him or not. Oh, he would win her all right, as he had
won almost every battle during the war. And he would do it
because she had cut through his hardened shell as swiftly
and easily as a surgeon with a sharpened knife. She had
taught him how to hope again, to never give up. Perhaps he
would be able to read and write with a degree of proficiency
that would live up to an abbreviated set of expectations. He
highly doubted he would ever master enough to allow him
to oversee the Cavendish wealth and properties. And it mattered little in his role as an officer as long as Charley stood
by him. Reading was of little value in the corridors of war.

Very early in life he had, by necessity, replaced his great
desire to stretch his intellectual abilities with an ironclad
will to succeed in the profession his father and he had chosen for him—the military. And he had done it. He had become the top marksman of all the other officers in the 95th
Rifleman's. He had synchronized and carried out more am-
bushes, lost fewer men, garnered more respect and com-
mendations than others with his high rank. Yet, he had felt
little pride in these accomplishments. They were marred by
the horror and omnipresent stench of death on the battlefield.

He wanted to sustain life and help fellow beings, not kill
them. With a small smile, he realized all this soft living was
making him as weak as a child and as philosophical as a
gentleman with too much idle time on his hands.

Charlotte had given him hope, and now he must give

something back to her—security. The protection of his name. And if she would not choose to follow him to whatever far-flung post he was assigned, then he would settle her wherever she would like to reside. Anywhere except here, Wyndhurst Abbey. He would keep his promise to his family by allowing his half brother to rule the roost. By staying away he would not dilute any question of Edwin's authority.

But what of the question of possible heirs? It had been his father's primary concern. While Charlotte might be able to teach any child of theirs who might inherit his failing to read at a rudimentary level at least, Nicholas could not bear the idea of watching a son struggle through life as he had. The taunts, the pity, the destruction of the ego. He couldn't, wouldn't watch it all unfold again to his own flesh and blood. And there was a good chance the flaw would be even further pronounced in an offspring. It was often the case with deficiencies.

Would she agree to forgo the physical intimacy marriage embodied? Could he? He was very unsure of his ability to restrain himself over the course of a lifetime. Could they practice methods to ensure that their relations would not bear fruit? It was the only question that gave him pause. If she desired children, his plan would fail. But then he would argue that the long-term protection offered by marriage was far superior than the often temporary comforts provided to companions of ladies in the often short, final years of their lives.

As he crested the last small hill before the little cottage came into view, Nicholas reached down and rubbed the tight muscle in his thigh. The break was all but healed, though he still experienced an achiness upon waking and occasional clenched muscles. He remembered Dr. Kittridge's gentle ministrations and vowed to repay his kindness by marrying the daughter. The other reason he would marry her, he refused to admit to himself.

*   *   *

Charlotte had slept very little last night. The bleak truth of her future had taken hold while she had sorted through her father's personal effects last evening. James had gone to the abbey instead. It had been the first time she had had a taste of what it would be like to be entirely alone. To her surprise, she felt no terrifying waves of fright. Only the grief of loss. She would recover and she would go on—alone.

She wondered, as she performed her simple morning toilette, if she would be leaving in a fortnight to live with the Dowager Countess of Livingston, whose corpulent form suffered from gout. Or possibly Mrs. Smith-Pennington, who was hopelessly deaf. The least-pleasing scenario would entail caring for Lady Sorringham, a virago of the worst sort who suffered from excellent health, despite her constant stream of complaints. At least Charlotte would be secure in that position, as she was sure Lady Sorringham would outlive her by a decade at the very least.

Her reverie was broken by the sound of a knock on the door below. Doro was talking to the visitor—a man, by the tone of the voice. Charlotte had told Doro that she would receive no more visitors today except Alexandre, who had promised to stop by to make arrangements for her departure for London. She did not have any energy left to receive more calls from the well-intentioned inhabitants of this corner of Wiltshire. She was putting the last of the pins in her chignon when Doro knocked on the door.

"Beggin' yer pardon, it's his lordship, come to call. Says it be of an urgent nature, it is," said the maid through a crack in the door.

"Lord Huntington?"

"Yes, miss."

"Please inform him that I'll be down in a moment." A tight knot formed in her stomach. She had not even had her morning tea. Not that it mattered. She had had no appetite for anything at all since Papa's death.

He stood at the same window he always chose, wearing a new green Rifleman's uniform. His striking and familiar form made her catch her breath. He was all masculine angles and muscled planes, but his expression was unreadable when he turned to face her. He was here to bid her good-bye. He was, quite obviously, leaving for Paris.

"Miss Kittridge," he said, bowing.

Charlotte curtsied, then stood still.

Lord Huntington walked over to her and grasped her hand in his own. "I apologize for not coming earlier to formally express my sadness over the loss of your good father. He will be missed by all who knew him. I have not known anyone so willing to exert every ounce of himself in the performance of his chosen profession," he said, pausing. "I am so very sorry."

"I thank you for your formal call." She halted, unsure of how to continue.

"I am unpardonably early, but to be frank, I hoped to have a private word with you before others come to call."

She looked down at his large bronzed hand. It was so warm and comforting. She was intensely aware of his body only a pace away from hers. It would be easy to take that one step into his arms. And he would hold her close to his heart, filling her with that rush of emotion she tried to force herself not to relive every day. But it would be out of pity or gratitude only, a poor relation of the passion she felt flowing through her veins.

"Miss Kittridge . . . It has been many weeks since I have found you to be one of the most admirable women I have ever known."

Good God. His conscience had gotten the better of him. He felt impelled to do the honorable thing and propose to her once more.

"There are many, many reasons why I am here this morning, and I must be allowed the time to elaborate, for once I have explained all, it is my hope that your wishes will coincide with my own."

She looked up to find his heavy-lidded eyes studying her face. The intensity of the feelings his proximity engendered within her breast forced her to lower her gaze to a spot just below his right shoulder. She watched his powerful chest rise and fall with each breath he took.

He squeezed her hand gently. "Charlotte. I hope you will allow me to call you that now?"

She gave a very brief nod of her head, not daring to look at him again.

"Charlotte. I desire to marry you," he hesitated, then rushed on. "With your father gone, and your brother soon to leave, you will be left on your own. And a single female, all alone in the world, is easy prey for all sorts of cruel mishaps. While I am sure you would be able to secure a post, what would befall you if that person died and your services were no longer sought by another lady? Or what if you should fall ill—too ill to perform your duties, and were therefore let go without references?"

Charlotte half listened to the continuing stream of depressing scenarios he presented. How was she to find the strength to refuse him when she desired more than anything else the possibility of being by his side always? Her pride was not that strong. Perhaps she would be able to live happily with him. She would love him more than life itself, and he would admire her. *Admire her*.

He would admire her but not *love* her. She forced herself to remember that he made his proposal because her father was dead and her brother was to leave her as well.

If she married him, she would fall deeper and deeper in love with him until she would hate herself because she would be unable to gain his love. And she would end up losing the meager amount of self-worth she had worked so hard to retain. She would go to her grave desperately wishing he loved her as she loved him. She would become a grasping female.

She shook her head slightly to rid herself of the unappealing thought. "My lord, I am aware of the great honor you do me in proposing to join our lives together. But, I fear you have taken too much upon yourself in an effort to be noble. You are not responsible for my brother or me. If you must perform a service, let James's commission fulfill that need. That is much more than either of us ever expected."

"Yes, well, I was aware that in securing a commission for your brother, I would be taking him away from you. I must be allowed to right that wrong. Surely, Charlotte, you must see that it is the only logical course."

"No, my lord," she said quietly, garnering the courage to look at his earnest expression. "It would prove to be a disastrous course. I am aware that His Grace and the duchess, as well as Lord Edwin, would never approve of a union between us. And I am also aware that you promised to never marry. I would not be the impetus for you to break your word. And you would regret your actions within a month's time."

"I had taken an oath never to marry. But in fact, my father never forced this promise from me. It was I who made it voluntarily. I have decided that it is in our best interests that I reverse my decision." He tugged at her chin to bring her gaze back to his.

He looked so impossibly handsome. It was all unbearably tempting. She only had to say one word. But she could not.

"I made that promise when I was seventeen, when I had shown no aptitude for the huge responsibility that awaited me when the title and the properties would come to me. Edwin suffered none of my numerous failings. I was relieved to be unburdened by the prospect of a lifetime of tangible failures, from which my family and the families dependent on the dukedom would suffer. And so, I promised to immerse myself in military service to the Crown—or to die trying."

"And your father allowed this? Surely it was not his idea?" she asked.

"Actually, the duchess proposed it when I told them I would not live another moment within the confines of Wyndhurst. My father did not oppose the idea when I agreed to it." He paused for a moment to run the back of his hand along her cheek. "But Charlotte, so much has happened since then. Not the least of which is your doing. It is by your encouragement that I am trying to learn once again. Most likely I will never reach a plateau that would render me capable of assuming the duties of a duke. In fact, since I have yet to conquer numbers, I highly doubt it. But, at least I will never have to fear that I am unable to continue on as before, as an officer of the 95th Rifleman."

"So, I would not have to live here?" she asked with wonder.

"Correct," he said, with the glint of a smile. "I am certain that will be an added inducement. And you would have a choice as to where you would live—either in the small but quite lovely town house my maternal grandparents left to me in London, or you could follow the drum or accompany me to any postings I might receive."

Oh, he was very persuasive. Did he realize that the offer to possibly see her brother from time to time would be an enticement almost impossible to resist? She closed her eyes, searching for the strength to deny herself.

"There is one last point I must touch on," he said.

Charlotte opened her eyes and looked at his closed expression.

"Because this would be a marriage of convenience for you, I would not require you to perform any wifely duties."

What? What was he saying?

"That is . . . any activities that would result in the conception of a child."

Charlotte's hands were cold, and she could feel all the blood suddenly rushing away from her head. How utterly mortifying. He found her so lacking that he could not bring himself to desire a child by her. The tiny sliver of pride she could claim her own came roaring to life.

"So let me see if I understand your offer," she said. "If we were to marry, I would be offered the choice of living comfortably, tucked away in London, or following you about like a loyal puppy to perhaps see my brother. I would be kept away from the critical eyes of the *ton* and your family, but provided for like a, like a—well-cared for distant relative? With nothing expected of me in return?"

It was amazing how much she could not abide pity. And pity from the person she loved was the most painful hurt of all. It gave backbone to her resolve.

"Charlotte, no!" he replied. "You have twisted my words quite thoroughly."

"Have I?"

"Yes. I would never classify you as a distant relative."

"Then what would be my role?"

"You would be my wife, and as such would have the protection of my name."

"Yes, this you already mentioned. So, I suppose that after the wedding night, and required consummation, I would be free to live my life however I choose?" she asked, then rushed on, "But then, perhaps consummation would not be required?"

His short hesitation was all Charlotte needed to form another layer of protection for her fragile heart.

"I am not sure, but I believe consummation—a one-time affair—would be required to legalize our wedding vows. If we are careful, it is highly doubtful a child would be conceived."

"Ah . . ."

He pulled her into his arms. Try as she might she could not raise her arms to resist his embrace. It felt so good to be held. But she forced herself to remain stiff, her nose buried in his neck cloth. She breathed in his warm, masculine scent. Her resolve was so very weak, weaker than at any other time in her life. She wanted him so very badly. She wanted the comfort of his arms, his name, and more so, the possibility of seeing him— even if only for short periods in her life. A little voice also reminded her that she would never force him to remain by her side. It was too much. She wasn't sure she could refuse him, even when her pride screamed no.

"Charlotte, please say yes. I promise to take care of you.

And I promise everything will be all right," he said quietly into her hair.

"All right . . . yes," she whispered, desire triumphing over pride. What was she saying? She had meant to say the opposite.

He squeezed her. "I promise you will not come to regret it."

"I wish I could say the same to you, my lord."

"Do you think you might be able to call me Nicholas? The occasion calls for it," he said, pulling back to look at her.

A sudden wave of shyness engulfed her. "Yes, of course . . . Nicholas."

"Well, then, it is all settled. I am sorry your circumstances will force you to marry me before the proper amount of mourning time for your father has passed, Charlotte." His tone had changed from tender to efficient. "And of course, you will still be able to wear mourning for a year or for as long as you choose."

Charlotte felt faint. This was all too fast, too unreal. "How soon would we have to marry?"

"I am afraid it will have to be as soon as your brother accepts his commission. I would not want you to have to live alone in this cottage," he said. "I arranged everything in London a few days ago whither I went to discuss my future position with the Military Secretary at the Horse Guards. I was also able to purchase the commission, and arrange for a special license in Canterbury."

How mortifying. He had arranged for a special license, knowing she would accept his offer—so sure was he in his success. She swallowed her hurt. It was too late now. She had agreed to marry a man who did not love her.

"You will inform your family, then?"

"Yes. They will be delighted to accept you into the family," he said.

Charlotte remembered the painful scene between Nicholas and his father when he had been near death, and

felt a knot form in her stomach. "Nicholas, please let there
be a minimum of falsehoods between us. I know I will not
be welcomed. But, it does not matter. We will not be living
here. And at least Rosamunde will accept me as a sister, I believe."

"I would never tolerate any ill-behavior toward my wife.
But, forewarned is forearmed. And we will only stay as long
as my father desires me to remain near him, and to watch
over the beginnings of some agriculture and industry I have
approved on my holdings."

Charlotte's curiosity was piqued.

Nicholas told her about the adjacent land his maternal
grandparents had deeded to him and his projects. "While in
London, I hired a man, who is very knowledgeable about the
brewing process. Mr. Gunter helped to select a few key
items and made arrangements for possible future distribu-
tion points."

After listening to all his other plans, she replied, "Oh, this
will mean so much to the Roberts family and so many like
them."

"The land was going to waste. It was very easy to help
these poor people."

"Don't belittle your efforts. It will mean the difference
between slow starvation and a much better life for the few
who are involved," she said with spirit. "And if you do im-
port the sheep, even more will benefit. I cannot bear to see
such poverty."

"By opening some of the acres I own for common land,
it will also help ease this problem, I hope," he replied.

"I only wish my father was here to see the good effects
this will cause."

He squeezed her hand, his gaze warm and sincere. "I am
so sorry, Charlotte. He was the best of men. I felt honored to
know him."

He had said exactly the right thing, unlike so many others who had tried to console her. He was tugging at her chin.
Charlotte raised her head to face the deep green intensity of

his heavy-lidded eyes and prayed he would never know how much her love for him consumed her. She would never allow him to feel the heavy weight of her unrequited love. But his gaze moved to her lips, and she closed her eyes, hoping he would kiss her.

Warm lips touched hers, enveloping her in a sea of passion. She dared not breathe. He opened his mouth and his tongue reached past her lips. She curled her tongue against his and felt a spiraling sensation leap between her legs.

He would consummate the marriage. If only that one time, she would know him fully. And he would be part of her and she would be able to hold that memory with her for all time. She would have to make it enough. And perhaps if she was lucky, very lucky indeed, a force that had evaded her throughout her life, her wedding night might give her a child. And she would have a chance at reciprocated love.

She wished it would happen with Nicholas. She wanted him with every ounce of her being. Her arms had somehow found their way up around his immense shoulders, and she felt his warm hands caressing her waist.

He broke off the kiss. "Perhaps I should be on my way. I know you have much to do. Will you and your brother accept an invitation to dine with my family tonight?" he asked. "I will inform them all of our intentions before then."

Charlotte closed her eyes for a moment. "I suppose it would be best to face them all at once. Although I fear the effect the news will have on your father. If he is very angry, perhaps it would be better for me to put an end to any bedside nursing. I could give Doro the tisanes and some instructions."

"Let us take it one step at a time. This has all been very overwhelming for you. Let us say no more until tonight."

"As you wish," she replied.

He bent down and kissed her forehead one last time before releasing her.

Chapter Thirteen

*"If a woman doubts as to whether she should
accept a man or not, she certainly ought to refuse
him. If she can hesitate as to "Yes," she ought to
say "No" directly. It is not a state to be safely
entered into with doubtful feelings, with half a
heart."*

—Emma

*W*alking back to the abbey, Nicholas wondered if he
had done the right and proper thing. It was clear that
Charlotte did not really want to marry him. If the doctor had
not died, Nicholas would be planning his departure as soon
as his own father and brewery venture would allow. He
would have probably never seen her again. She had only
agreed to marry him because he had used every logical argument to force the agreement.

She had blanched when he had mentioned consummating
the marriage. And he would not soon forget her wistful questions: "I would be free to live my life however I choose? Perhaps consummation would not be required?" At least he had
not had to face the embarrassment of explaining that he and
his family had decided long ago that the risk of any of
Nicholas's progeny inheriting his great failing was too large a
risk for the successful continuation of the dukedom.

She had wanted to make sure that a coupling would only
have to occur once in their marriage. It would be as she had
suggested, a marriage of mutual respect such as one held for
a dear distant relative. That would have to be enough for him.

And she would be safe from harm, never dependent on the

whim of an employer. Perhaps in time she would grow to admire the set of skills he possessed: his organizational capabilities, his cool head under fire, the loyalty he could inspire in his men, and his willingness to give of himself.

But as his father had warned him, he would never try to live up to the high set of intellectual standards she would expect in a man she could truly respect and love, for it was an impossible task that he was sure to fail.

He had yet to attempt to tackle his greatest difficulty: the task of figuring numbers on paper. He had always had the capacity to calculate long sums in his head, just as he had been adept at music. He had confounded Rosamunde's music teacher and his stepmother by his ability to perfectly execute memorized piano concertos. Her Grace had been horrified and had denied him access to the music room, saying the playing of instruments was reserved for young, unwed ladies.

That was when he had realized that he must leave the abbey; he would never be of any value to his family. But with perseverance he had regained his self-worth through servitude to the Crown.

Nicholas was on the precipice of wishing he could alter his fate. She would be worth it. Her love would be worth it.

The consecutive private interviews she had faced with the two male relatives in her life proved more trying than expected. First Charlotte had had to endure the exuberant well wishes of her overjoyed brother, who believed that it was a love match on both sides. Then she had had to withstand the cynical musings of Alexandre, who had dissected her betrothed.

"Ah Charlotte, it is a shame that he is a cripple both mentally and well, perhaps less so, physically. You deserve a 'whole man,' not someone you will have to nurse and read to your entire life. But I suppose his title and his gold will go a long way in erasing his faults," Alexandre had said, after receiving the news.

She was infuriated. "That is most unfair. You know he is as fit as you or James. And as for—"

"Did his injury affect his ability to sire . . ." He waved his hand loftily in the air, allowing her to guess his vulgar question.

"Why, of course not. But I have not had firsthand—oh, you are just teasing me now, I know your tricks," she said in annoyance.

"Well, I suppose if I cannot have you . . ."

"You never wanted me, *mon vieux.*"

"You burst the illusion so heartlessly, my love."

"It is easy. It is too bad the ladies at the abbey are not so well-used to your illusions," she said, with a knowing smile.

"But then it would not be nearly so amusing. The petite Lady Susan, is she not deliciously delicate and feminine? Albeit not a trace of intelligence in her attic," he said, with a sly smile. "Unlike you, my little bluestocking *cousine.* It is really too bad your father was not the miser I made him out to be. I was so sure. . . . We could have returned to Paris and cut quite a dash, as the English say."

"Yes, well perhaps for a week or so. Then you would have found *une petite amie* to try your charms on, and I would have become a shrew."

"My dear Charlotte, you think me very fickle," he said with a grin. "Do you think it would be de trop to continue to bed Lady Susan's delightful maid if I marry Lady Susan and her divine ten thousand a year?"

Charlotte shook her head, and could not stop the tickle of a giggle in her throat. "Impossible. You are a rake without boundaries, Cousin. You do not deserve my notice. If you were not my cousin, I would give you the cut direct at every opportunity," she said, regaining a serious expression. "As it stands, I can only beg you to never speak unkindly of my future husband again."

"I see how it will be. No joy in your marriage, only duty and honor. How very English and boring. I would expire within a week's time. *Ma cousine,* I wish you joy, but do not expect my attentions to change toward you just because you have altered the rules somewhat. In my experience, married ladies are adventuresome and quite enchanting!"

Charlotte sighed. Alexandre used his flirtatious charm to hide the genuine familial bond he had finally developed for her since arriving in Wiltshire. At least his verbal jousting had forced her to sharpen the meager amount of wit she possessed. It was a tool she would need to survive the ordeal of facing the frosty overtures of the duke's family.

"Well I see you have not lost *all* notions of propriety, Miss Kittridge," said Her Grace, halfway through dinner that evening. She had not condescended to say one word to Charlotte before then. The duchess had refused to meet her gaze, and had given the briefest nod when she and her brother had appeared at the abbey. "I suppose we should have a mourning dress or two made up for you so you do not have to continue to wear Rosamunde's."

Charlotte would not rise to the bait. "That will be unnecessary, Your Grace. I ordered several a few days ago."

"Well, I for one find this hasty marriage business more than a little awkward. It is unheard of to marry in blacks. Not that I was consulted. People will talk. I don't understand why this cannot be put off until the proper mourning period has passed. At least a year. Indeed, I do not see why it should take place at all."

A long, awkward silence enveloped the room. Lady Susan drew all attention her way with the sound of a loud sniff and a haughty tilt of her nose.

Nicholas cleared his throat. "I am sure, madam, that you are not intentional in your insults. However, let me assure you that I will not allow my betrothed to suffer any abuse. Miss Kittridge and her family have been nothing but beneficial to us. I suggest you remember that on all future occasions. She has done me the honor of agreeing to become my wife, and as such I will insist that she be accorded the respect due her position."

"Well, of all the—" replied Her Grace before halting when faced with the steel of Nicholas's gaze.

Stone-cold silence invaded the room. Only the clacking of silverware could be heard. Charlotte forced herself to continue taking small bites of food that tasted like sawdust.

Only Rosamunde was capable of maintaining the facade of gentility. "Will you remove from the cottage, Charlotte? There is a lovely bedchamber next to my own in the south tower."

Charlotte's gaze darted to Her Grace, who was biting her tongue in anger. "No, I think not. At least not until after my brother departs for London. I must sort through all of my father's papers and books. Lord Huntington has been kind enough to suggest that I store the books and such in the Duke's great library," she said, before continuing, "And it will be easier to see those who stop by for the occasional complaint or two between my visits to your father and other patients."

"Do you intend to continue to practice your nursing skills when you are the future Duchess of Cavendish, my dear?" Lord Edwin asked in a mocking tone. "How utterly charming and provincial."

"I see nothing wrong with helping the less fortunate, my lord," she replied.

"Yes, but Miss Kittridge, you might bring some horrid disease to the abbey. We can't have that, especially when His Grace lies so ill. And we do have a respected apothecary in the village," said the duchess.

"I understand your concerns. However, my father and I tended the infirm throughout our stay in Wiltshire, and no one expressed any concern until now. I fail to see what has changed. Although I am sure the apothecary will be frequented much more now, despite his ill care of His Grace."

Charlotte glanced at Nicholas, who gave her a small smile of encouragement.

"I would be delighted to help you in any way, Miss Kittridge," said the vicar. "I for one am most impressed with your good deeds in the face of your devastating loss."

"Oh, please do not offer me compliments. They are unjustified. Really, I do not think I have had a moment to comprehend what has happened," Charlotte said in a low voice.

"My dear, we are very sorry for your loss," the Dowager Duchess of Cavendish said. "I fear we will never be able to find another physician as competent as your father. We are lucky to have you still willing to nurse my son."

The Dowager Countess Elltrope made a disgruntled noise. "Well, I still say my Susan would have made a dedicated nurse to the duke as well."

The dowager duchess snorted.

Alexandre stepped into the fray. "What? My delicate flower—Lady Susan exposed to the dangers of the sickroom? I think it would be most unwise. Her sensibilities would be overpowered."

"Thank you, sir, for understanding my wilting Feminine Nature, although I am sure I could match Miss Kittridge's abilities if I was ever to Heed the Calling," replied Lady Susan haughtily.

"My dear, perhaps it would be better for you and your grandmother to consider departing our little family gathering. We would be sad to lose your delightful presence, but I would not want to compromise your sensibilities and your delicate health," said the dowager duchess, with a comical mixture of false sadness and ill-concealed triumph. "Really, the duke's illness and now Dr. Kittridge's sudden demise must surely have left you feeling unsettled in the extreme. We would understand if you must cut your visit short."

The elderly Hortense Elltrope easily trumped her hand. "But my dearest friend, we could not leave you in your hour of sisterly need, and besides, I daresay the extensive renovations we have ordered on the country estate are not complete. I fear we must trespass on your hospitality a bit longer, Margarita," she said, directing a simpering smile to the vicar.

If Charlotte had not been feeling so vulnerable to every person's speculations, she surely would have found the exchange amusing. As it was, she was amazed to watch Lord

Edwin vying with Alexandre for Lady Susan's favors as feverishly as the two matrons fought over the patient vicar. And glad she was to have the attention of almost everyone move to other corners.

James and Rosamunde continued to glance in each other's direction. Louisa Nichols tried unsuccessfully to garner a few compliments from Lord Edwin and Alexandre, while Lady Susan preened and pouted.

Charlotte felt the weight of the duchess's disapproving stare and Nicholas's gaze in her direction throughout the rest of the lavish meal. She would count the days until she could leave these argumentative and frequently unkind personalities. She was only sorry to leave Rosamunde and perhaps even the Dowager Duchess of Cavendish, who had offered a kind word or two when she could be torn away from the fray.

All in all, the idea of her union with Nicholas had gone over as well as could be expected. And at least no one had thought to bring up the embarrassing topic of possible children the union might bring. She would not have been able to hide her sadness. Without a doubt, the duchess would place infertility at the top of her list of requests—or demands—to God in her evening prayers. Little did Her Grace realize that her prayers were unnecessary.

She kept putting off the date of their nuptials. Nicholas wondered if he would have to bundle her up and force her to face the vicar. He rested on a log, taking a brief respite from helping to finish building the brewery's sluice gatehouse. How many more days could he stand the delay of the marriage?

The commission was in her brother's eager hands, and he was panting to be off. And Nicholas very much wanted to accomplish the deed before his poor father departed this earth, and he feared the end was near. For the last three weeks he had had to withstand his stepmother's insistence that the news of his engagement had led to the current spiral downward. He had refused to listen to any of it.

And now the brewery was well on its way to completion. The ponds had been dug, the buildings almost completed, and the barley planted. The expert from Prussia had proved his weight in gold. Mr. Gunter had spent hours teaching the ragged group from the countryside all there was to know about his trade. The man had even gathered orders from several neighboring counties, and he had agreed to stay on through the first several batches.

In the upper areas, more and more neighbors were beginning to use the fields and pastures Nicholas had declared common land. The laborers and tenant farmers did not know it yet, but he had also arranged for the purchase of twelve milk cows for the most needy families.

Those animals would not be the first to munch their fill of the verdant pastures. Already, old Silas had brought in the first small flock of prize sheep he had been sent to purchase in Lancashire. Altogether, three shepherds would be required to oversee the flock once it filled out. Rough enclosures were planned to provide protection for the prime animals.

Edwin had been furious, calling Nicholas all kinds of unchivalrous names for not using his funds to support the ducal lands. Edwin had pulled out the ledgers, indicating every reason why the estate could better use his monies. Nicholas had listened patiently and promised to consider the dire situation. The steward had coughed once and asked who would be overseeing the enterprises once his lordship returned to the military life. Nicholas had a growing unease with Wyndhurst's steward, despite Edwin's assurances of the man's past successes. Mr. Coburn had shaken his head when Nicholas had mentioned Owen Roberts's name.

It was here in his own fields that Nicholas felt a glow of pride fill his being at all the productivity. He loved to see progress. It was the first time he had ever experienced it. For so many years he had seen only destruction. He had witnessed the devastation of war and had participated in it. And he had been excellent at it—too excellent in many cases.

Until now, he had not realized how much it had weighed

on his conscience and on his soul. He prayed he would not have to return to it. The fragile peace with France must hold. Nicholas would help preserve it, or better yet, help the war-ravaged countries rebuild.

The one little burr in his future was Charlotte. Would this marriage prove disastrous? She was so hesitant to go through with it. He could envision many bleak evenings with her at the hearth reading a huge tome, trying occasionally to give him false hope in his first childish workbooks.

He thought of his endless reams of blotched papers, filled with rows of ill-formed letters. At least the headaches had disappeared altogether. And he had even taken a few moments to form numbers out of clay, to put in the first firing in the kiln he had had constructed near the brewery. It was a secret. He had planned to show the kiln to Charlotte right away, but she had avoided him at every opportunity.

"Hey ho!" hailed Owen Roberts. "We're ready to unleash the last dam. . . . Come along, if you want to see it, then."

Nicholas arose from his shady perch, rubbing his aching thighbone by habit. "Go on, I'll meet you."

He smiled. Owen was someone he trusted to ensure the proper running of all Nicholas's endeavors when he returned to his duty. Owen had told him that being literate did not make a man; being a leader of men made a man. It was Owen who had insisted Nicholas was the only one who could organize the menfolk to save themselves.

Nicholas arrived below the ridge and watched a dozen men remove obstacles from the stream's flow. A series of eight interlocking reservoirs, increasing in size, would provide spring water for ale making. Another dozen men were finishing the work on the sluice gatehouse and the adjacent building containing the rudimentary elements needed to begin the brewing process. Owen and Mr. Gunter joined him at his vantage point.

"A fine sight is it not, my lord?" exclaimed Mr. Gunter in his accented English. The spring water flowed into the first pond before them.

"Yes, indeed," replied Nicholas. "The hops should arrive from Kent in two weeks time. And the barley should be ready to harvest then if the weather holds." Nicholas glanced up at the brilliant blue sky. "My father agreed to allow the dray and draft horses I purchased to be stabled at Wyndhurst. And the first of the wooden kegs should arrive tomorrow."

"We'll begin then, in two weeks time, my lord," Mr. Gunter said with a broad smile. "The water from this spring should produce one of the finest ales in all of England."

"Have you decided about the orchard?" Owen asked, reminding Nicholas of the badly overgrown grove of apple trees on the property.

"Yes. Have some of the men begin the clearing away and improvements in the soil. We'll look into purchasing a large press next year once we see profits from the brewery. We can't afford to invest in it yet, but we can distribute what meager produce the trees yield this fall," Nicholas said.

Mr. Gunter left to check the levels in the ponds, leaving Nicholas alone with Owen Roberts. A brief silence ensued.

"What is on your mind, man?" Nicholas asked.

"I was thinking I should be offering my congratulations. The missus has a sister who's a chambermaid at the abbey. She says you're to marry Miss Kittridge."

Nicholas clapped a hand on Owen's shoulder. "News travels fast."

"If you'll pardon me for sayin' so, you look none too happy about the idea," Owen said. "You havena' mentioned it once."

"Outspoken as always, that you always were."

"Marriage isna' so bad. The procreatin' business is the best part," he said with a wink.

"Hmmmm. Blunt as always, too."

"From what Sally's sister says, there's a French feller trying to do lots of procreatin' at the abbey. Better mind what's your own and send the man on his way after the weddin'." Owen wheezed, and coughed at his own humor.

"All right, old man. You've had your say."

"No, I havena'. What's this I hear about you still plannin' on leavin' for Paris? What are you thinkin'? With a missus, and your father so ill, you need to plant your roots here."

"Owen—" Nicholas breathed deeply and shook his head. "It's no good. I've only ever known the military life. Don't think I don't want to stay here, even though life with the duchess and Lord Edwin would be unpleasant at best. It is just that I made my path long ago, and I am too old and tired to change it. I know how to organize soldiers and execute skirmishes with precision, how to shoot dead on, and I know how to work through the channels of the military. I know nothing about overseeing five large ducal properties."

"You could learn."

"Actually, I'm not sure I could or would want to. Sometimes it is better to stay with what you know you can do well."

Owen indicated with a sweep of his arm the brewery and kiln in front of them. "Isna' this proof enough that you can do other things just as well? Don't be dense, man."

Nicholas paused. "I'm afraid that is precisely what I am, at least for the near future. And I am not willing to gamble on the lives of the hundreds of families tied to our lands."

"Nah. You've just always fancied war. I was hopin' you'd outgrow it."

"And you, my friend, delight in playing 'what if' games. I've enjoyed this foray into industry and agriculture and I will continue to be involved from afar—with your help. But I will be leaving for Paris, mark my words."

Little did the man know how close Nicholas had come to choosing just the path Owen suggested. But Nicholas was a man who rarely tempted fate. And while he was willing, due to necessity, to break his promise by marrying Charlotte, he would not change the original promise made so long ago to his father and brother. He would not change the course that would prove most beneficial to the dukedom.

Nicholas hated to use subterfuge on her, but he had decided that the ends justified the means. He found Charlotte just where her brother had said, at the graveyard, laying flowers on the bare earth of her father's grave. Kittridge had agreed to meet Nicholas at the village church in one hour's time, along with Rosamunde. As Nicholas approached the stone arches of the graveyard, he glanced down at the pocket watch he had removed from his waistcoat. He had but a quarter of an hour to convince her anew.

She looked so pale and reedlike in the black gown she wore. Her bonnet had fallen down her back, the ribbons tied at their ends around her slim neck. Brown wavy hair coursed down her back. The wind played havoc with her curls. She was so young and fragile.

She looked up when she heard his approach.

Nicholas faced her sorrowful expression. "Good day, Charlotte."

"Good day, my lord," she replied in her soft voice.

"Nicholas."

"Nicholas," she whispered. A lock of hair blew into her eyes.

He brushed the hair from her face and grasped one of her hands in his own. It was ice cold and very small in his calloused palm. "Is it so very hard to accept your future fate with me?"

She did not pretend to misunderstand him. "Perhaps a little."

"How much longer will it take for you to accept me, Charlotte? We have not the luxury of time, unfortunately."

"I do not know."

"You have already given your word."

"Yes," she said, looking at her father's grave.

He hated to force her. "Even my stepmother has accepted the inevitable. I believe she is secretly looking forward to the excuse to have a huge wedding breakfast. Her invitation list covers no less than eleven pages, although I am sure that few of the guests will descend from estates as far away as Scotland."

She continued to stare at her father's grave.

He sighed. "Your brother is anxious to be gone. And I am worried my father won't last another month," he said, lifting her chin to encounter her expression.

"I know," she said. "Do you think—?"

"Yes?" he encouraged her.

"I am not sure I have the courage to face the hordes of people Her Grace has condescended to suggest. And—"

"And—" he encouraged her.

"I had rather this not be a joyous occasion." She had a pleading expression. "I don't know if you can understand. I have little interest in pretending to be joyful when my father has just died."

He had to bend toward her to catch the last few words. "Charlotte, I would not tax you further. I have never expected you to feel delight on the occasion," he said.

"If you would prefer, we could go straight away to the church. I have the special license," he said, patting his breast. "And I have taken the liberty of asking your brother and Rosamunde to join us. I had hoped . . ." he said, feeling like a tongue-tied schoolboy.

She looked at him with huge gray eyes. For some unfathomable reason it gave him courage. "I had hoped you would do me the honor of marrying me this very morning."

"With only James and your sister present?"

"Yes. Well, and Charley too."

"Yes," she replied quickly.

"Yes?"

"Yes."

God help him, he felt like picking her up and swinging her around in circles, no matter this was hallowed ground. Instead, he raised her delicate hand to his lips and pressed a kiss to the back of her glove, squeezing his eyes shut as he did so. He wanted to turn her hand to brush a kiss on the sensitive underside of her wrist, but did not want to fluster her. She reminded him of a small wren, ready to fly away at the slightest provocation.

As they walked the short distance to face the vicar's domain, he kept a firm grip on her arm. A hard breeze forced a few of the less hardy horse chestnut leaves to the ground. They entered the sanctuary, and the sounds of their shoes against the slate echoed within the walls. Mr. Llewellyn entered from a hidden side door along with Charley, wearing his Sunday best. Rosamunde and Charlotte's brother had arrived well before the appointed time and sat close together in the front pew. They were conversing but broke apart with Nicholas and Charlotte's appearance in the nave.

Rosamunde handed Charlotte a small, beautiful bouquet. Nicholas guessed his sister had chosen the blooms from her private glass greenhouse for their significance: rosemary for remembrance, a single white rosebud for simplicity and girlhood, sweet william for gallantry, sweet violet for modesty, and a linden flower for . . . Nicholas looked at his sister and touched the heart-shaped leaves. With a knowing smile, he shook his head. Linden represented conjugal love. Rosamunde was a true optimist.

The short ceremony moved Nicholas in a way he had not anticipated. He promised before God and the people he cared for most in the world that he would honor and protect this woman with his life. And she promised to honor and obey him.

In the middle of the ceremony, she looked at him with the most trusting look he had ever encountered and he felt overwhelmed with an emotion he could not name. Lord, but she was beautiful. He was struck by her radiant air of goodness. She lowered her eyes to their hands when he slipped the slim gold band on her finger, his mother's wedding ring. Her lips trembled with unspoken feelings.

He lowered his mouth to hers to seal their vows, and then they were embraced by everyone, with only a few tears on feminine cheeks. After signing the church register, Nicholas invited the vicar and Rosamunde and Kittridge to join them in an impromptu late breakfast at the village inn. It was as unfitting a place for a future duke to celebrate his marriage as Nicholas could envision. It was perfect.

Charley was tapped to deliver an invitation to Owen and Sally Roberts from Nicholas, who painstakingly wrote the note in his primitive hand before leaving the church.

When the party entered The Quill & Dove, they created quite a commotion. Mindful of his wife's tender sensibilities concerning crowds, Nicholas ensured with a few gold sovereigns that the inn's doors would be locked. But word of the wedding spread as fast as the eager innkeeper's wife's lips could move. Nicholas arranged for the fast-growing number of curious villagers outside to partake in a bounteous feast under the shade trees while the wedding party enjoyed theirs in the privacy of the inn.

His little wife looked quite happy as she consumed a glass of rare champagne from the inn's deepest recesses. It was the first time he had seen a smile return to her unusual lips since that fateful morning three weeks before. Perhaps he would be able to coax her charming dimples to make an appearance as well, if he was lucky. He would endeavor to do so once they were in the bedchamber.

It was all so very strange to Charlotte. She knew she should be feeling shock and still sorrow, but looking at his classically chiseled features, Charlotte could not bring herself to feel anything but tentative excitement.

She had done it. *She had married him.*

Oh, it was wrong of her to allow him to break his vow to not marry, and of course he did not love her, but she could not help but feel wonder and a girlish thrill that they were tied together for life.

The innkeeper unlocked the door to allow Owen and his wife entrance. They bustled forth with great smiles on their faces.

"This calls for a toast," called out James, looking over-joyed. "To the blushing bride and chivalrous groom!"

"Hear, hear," seconded Owen.

Glasses clinked and the wine and champagne were consumed with gusto.

"And to those who could not be here to share in our happiness," whispered Charlotte almost to herself.

Nicholas turned to her and she realized he had overheard her. He clinked her glass. "I wish he were here too."

He had such kind eyes; the sort where a smile could be seen lurking in the crinkled corners without bothering to appear on his lips. Charlotte wished her marriage would be the happy ending found in all of those marvelous novels she had read by the mysterious "Lady." Would she find the happiness of Elizabeth Bennett and Elinor Dashwood? She feared she was more like the overly correct and timid Fanny Price of *Mansfield Park,* who would have never survived the rigors of life as a duchess.

She must venture to play the part of Elizabeth Bennett tonight in the bedchamber, as there was no one else she could so desire to emulate. Eliza would not be in fear. Charlotte rather thought the character would lead the way even if she had no idea what to expect.

Now she was becoming ridiculous, Charlotte thought as she listened to all the toasts made to their health and happiness and too many other topics. The champagne had gone to her head. Watching Nicholas's handsome form, just a footstep or two away from her, all thoughts of novels and heroines fled.

He moved with such controlled grace, without a single wasted motion. A bottle-green coat emphasized his immense shoulders and strong waist. She looked down the buff-colored breeches molded to the defined muscles of his legs. Charlotte's heart beat faster in her breast as she remembered what lay beneath all those elegant clothes. She had seen almost every inch of him when he was feverish so many weeks ago. And now, soon, very soon, he would know every inch of her. She felt as nervous as a cat caught under the bedcovers.

Nicholas closed the small gap between them and linked arms with her. It all felt so natural and right when she glanced down and noticed the gleam of burnished gold residing on his long tapered finger.

He was her husband. His gentle touch reassured her. Perhaps, just perhaps, everything would work out. She would try very hard to be the perfect wife. Then, with time, he might come to love her, to match the passion she felt at his touch and at his glance. As if he read her mind, he met her gaze and smiled.

Toasts were made to the dukedom, the brave heroes who fought under Wellington, the talented chef of the inn, the proprietors, and by the time a toast had been made to the vicar, Nicholas could see Charley getting wobbly in the legs.

Nicholas broke up the celebration before anyone became maudlin or singing broke out. As it was, Charley serenaded the foursome while they walked back to the abbey. The music brought back a familiar wave of battlefield emotions to Nicholas. He was surprised to feel somewhat nauseated by the chirping sounds. He said nothing to stop Charley because he did not want to hurt his young batman's feelings.

Nicholas was living too soft a life here. It was time to return to his old ways with the small addition of his wife. He looked down at Charlotte, who had to take two strides for every long one of his, and prayed that this evening's consummation would be completed without much suffering on her part.

The idea of breaching her maidenhead was daunting at best. Since Charlotte had been raised in a household of males, he wondered if anyone had ever discussed what was to be expected in performing her duty. One glance toward her brother's innocent expression made him doubt it.

And he would have to broach the delicate topic of avoiding the conception of a child. All of these worries meant very little to him, if he were to admit the truth. These thoughts were hard-pressed to overcome the great desire he felt looking into her clear gray eyes and at the gentle swell of her breast.

Chapter Fourteen

*"Poor fellow! He is quite distracted by jealousy,
which I am not very sorry for, as I know no better
support for love."*

—Lady Susan

She felt as good as naked standing in the transparent
nightgown, a gift from her irrepressible French cousin.
With a sly wink, he had insisted that it was just what was
called for on her wedding night. She felt herself blush anew
as she recalled all the wicked things he had suggested she do
to entice her husband. Charlotte had covered her ears in
shame and ordered Alexandre from the cottage under his
protestation.

"But Charlotte, *ma cherie*, do not let your French blood
be smothered by the frigid repression that seems to fill the
veins of most of these silly Englishwomen," he had called
out as a parting remark.

And so she had changed from her white cotton gown that
buttoned to the top of her throat into the revealing nightclothes made of silk and lace at least three times in the last
half hour. Nicholas had left her at the cottage after the up-
roarious breakfast, promising to return by sundown.

At the last moment, she lost her nerve again. As the silk
floated in a pool around her ankles, a soft knock sounded at
her small bedchamber in the cottage.

"Just a moment, *please*," she called out in a high-pitched
squeak.

The door opened at the precise moment when she was
tugging her old gown over her head. It billowed around her
on its descent. Had he seen her naked form? She was para-

lyzed with embarrassment. She quickly did up the front buttons.

"I am sorry, shall I give you a few more minutes, Charlotte?"

She pushed back her rumpled hair and tugged at her nightgown one last time. "No, no. I am ready."

Nicholas had changed from the sophisticated dress of this morning to dark evening clothes. He appeared as beautiful as a man could possibly be, all dark, mysterious elegance.

He came across the small chamber in three broad strides, picking up the discarded silk nightgown as he set the candlestick he had brought with him on her nightstand. "What is this?"

How mortifying. "Oh, it is nothing. Just a small gift my cousin delivered to me this afternoon."

"A nightgown?" he asked, standing a few inches from her.

"Yes."

He took one step closer to her. "I'm not sure I care for the idea of your former betrothed giving you such a . . . personal article, Charlotte." He paused and arched one eyebrow. "And yet you are not wearing it."

"Uh . . . no, I did not feel like myself in it, my lord," she said, looking at her toes peeking out of the bottom of her plain nightgown.

"My lord?"

"I am sorry, I mean Nicholas, of course." Oh, worse and worse. This was not going at all as Alexandre suggested. She was supposed to entrance him. Instead, she was awkward and *gauche*. It was just that it was so hard to focus on words when he was standing so close to her, looking at her through heavy-lidded mysterious eyes. A mere wisp of fabric separated her from his hands. Charlotte found it difficult to breathe normally as she watched him untie his neck cloth and drape it over her bed.

Nicholas indicated with his hand the small stool in front

of her simple dressing table. "Perhaps I could brush the tangles from your hair," he said.

She was sure he could tell her nervousness bordered on panic. Charlotte moved to the stool and dropped down onto it, grateful for the moment to collect herself.

He stroked her hair with the horsehair brush, from the crown of her head to the base of her back. Her scalp tingled from the pleasure of an action heretofore unknown to her. She could not remember anyone ever brushing her hair.

He dropped the brush on the stand after several long wordless minutes. She watched his large bronzed hands grasp her arms in the mirror.

"You are trembling. I hope you are not too afraid, are you?" His voice was steady and low. "I will be very gentle, but I daresay you already know there will be some pain involved."

"Yes," she whispered, unable to feign any of the nuances Alexandre had suggested.

"Charlotte, this is important. When were your last courses?"

If it was possible to be more embarrassed, she felt it at this moment. "A week ago," she whispered.

"You are certain?"

"Yes. Why do you ask?"

"I would not get you with child on our single *encounter*."

She had to harness every last drop of her reserves of dignity to not burst into tears. She would not let him see her sadness. So it was to be as he had proposed. One night—one night only to do the proper. She was as unattractive in his eyes as she had been the day he had first met her. He did not want children by her.

"Shall we proceed then, with the consummation of our vows?" she asked without a trace of emotion.

Nicholas looked beyond her shoulder into the mirror's image. Charlotte was very pale. He cupped her elbows and helped her to her feet, wrapping his arms around the front of her and burying his face in her flowing locks. She was like the same block of ice he had held in the graveyard this morning. He felt very unsure. He had never made love to an innocent, and hated the idea of hurting her.

He stroked her arms for a few moments, then turned her into his full embrace. He would bring her pleasure, slowly and lovingly. He wanted desperately to give her a small measure of happiness after her recent sadness. After everything she had done for him, he would give her passion. Tonight was all for her. He would loose his desire and hers as well, if it could be done.

He kissed the top of her head then pushed aside the thick curtain of hair to feather kisses on the soft, downy curls at the base of her neck. Nicholas felt her shiver. She weighed but a feather as he turned her and gathered her up in his arms to carry her to the bed.

"You are much more enchanting in this cotton gown than any amount of silk and lace. Your cousin has something to learn when it comes to the art of seduction, it seems." He felt her relax a bit in his arms.

"Thank you," she whispered, hiding her head in the crook of his arm.

With a quick movement, he thrust aside the bedcovers and placed her in the middle of the bed. Enormous gray eyes surveyed him as he went about the methodical task of removing his boots, coat and every article of clothing save his linen shirt. He was glad for her sake that his long shirt provided adequate cover for his obvious masculinity.

He joined her on the bed and pressed his lips onto her forehead, the tip of her nose, her cheeks, and finally settled on her gorgeous mouth. He kissed her for long minutes, patiently arousing her, enticing her body to respond to his experienced touch.

It took a long time.

Finally, she curled her tongue against his and moaned softly. Only then did he begin to undo the small buttons on the front of her gown.

"Should we not blow out the candle?" she asked.

He looked at her rosy complexion, bathed in the golden candlelight. "You would deny me the pretty vision I hold before me?"

"You do not need to say falsehoods to please me," she whispered.

"At some point in your life you made a very incorrect assumption about your appearance. I hope to persuade you to think otherwise. In fact, I shall put you on a strict regimen of no less than three compliments a day."

That brought a small smile to the corners of her lips.

"Ah, the dimples make an appearance. Just in time, I might add," he said with a chuckle.

An immense, deep desire dwelled in him. He reached beneath her neckline and felt her sharp intake of breath. His groin constricted when he touched the tip of her lovely breast and it hardened. Her skin was so soft, her breasts perfectly proportioned and firm. He looked at her face to see a fan of dark lashes splayed across her flushed cheeks. He wanted her to experience it all despite her shy nature.

As he lowered his head to taste the rosy pink confection of her breast, he massaged the other to tightened perfection. He laved and nipped the tender aureole, giving equal time to both breasts until she arched her back, involuntarily signaling her pleasure.

With deliberate movements, Nicholas slid his fingers up the side of her body, bringing the fabric of her nightclothes up along with his hands. Her eyes flew open but he was grateful that she resisted the urge to cover herself.

Dear God, she was perfectly formed.

All gentle, flowing curves and long slender limbs just waiting to be touched and awakened. He sucked in his breath, praying for control.

Without thinking, he drew his shirt over his head in one swift motion. Her gaze lowered and her eyes widened. He must patiently arouse her anew to dampen her fear and replace it with yearning. He stroked her arms and felt goose-flesh.

Nicholas knew without glancing that her legs were clamped together. He stroked her slender thighs over and over, trying to relax her.

"Dear heart, open yourself to me," he whispered into the delicate shell of her ear before gently biting her small earlobe. She trembled for a moment and released the tension in her legs, allowing him to spread her legs wide. His fingers sought her sensitive point of pleasure, stroking and massaging with the lightest of touches until he heard her breath quicken. Her flushed face began to twist from side to side, and he knew she was in a complete heightened state of arousal, lost to the world around her. His fingers continued their erotic dance, skin to skin, as he slowly circled the entrance to her and delved into the edge beyond.

"Nicholas, Nicholas. Oh, I need . . . I need . . . something," she whispered. "Please . . ."

The time was ripe, the air heavy with unrelieved tension. He moved his body to cover hers, forcing her legs even wider with his own. With tender longing, he entered her slowly, stretching the small, tight, very virginal passage until he met a barrier. God, but she was tiny, and she was like a delicacy before a starving man. She had become very still and tense all over again. He longed to gorge himself quickly, but did not.

He withdrew to massage the sensitive point of pleasure for long moments, and lowered his head to taste her breasts once again. The tension in his body was tight as a bow, and he could wait no longer. He must have her.

In one long, swift movement, he entered her as gently as he could muster and drove past her virginity until he could feel her inner muscles constricting all around his full length. He felt such exquisite pleasure it was almost painful. He paused and allowed her to get used to his invasion of her tiny body. He swallowed and prayed for regulation of his senses. Nicholas raised his head to look at her.

Her head was pressed back deep into the pillow, her puffy lips opened in unfeigned desire, her eyes closed.

"Are you all right, Charlotte?" he asked raggedly.

Her eyes opened ever so slightly. He was lost in their gray depths of emotion.

"Yes. Is it over?" she asked, it seemed to Nicholas somewhat sadly.

"No, my dear, it has just begun."

"Oh . . . Am I expected to do something?"

Nicholas smiled, glad the momentary distraction tempered the raw edges of his desire. "No, but I daresay if you move, this will be over before it has begun. Charlotte, you make me feel like an inexperienced boy, unable to muster any kind of control."

He watched a small smile tease the corners of her lips. "I am glad I please you."

He kissed her dimples and began the ebb and flow of a slow rhythm that made her eyes widen in surprise. He edged up her legs with his hands to wrap her limbs around his back, and then urged her to bind her arms around his neck.

She was all petite, charming femininity. As he drove into her, branding her as his own, he felt her body tighten about his own. Her small arms gripped his back in an effort to draw him deeper, deeper still. Then suddenly her body stilled, and at the peak of its straining she called out his name.

"Nicholas, Nicholas . . . Oh," she whispered, her breath caught.

He stroked deeply once, twice, then broke through the final fraction of an inch to fill her and release his seed into her very core. It felt like a release of years, powerful and overwhelming. He longed to crush her to him and burden her with the sudden realization of his great *love* for her.

He closed his eyes. That was the word. It had been so thoroughly wrapped up in a desire to protect her and nurture her that he had failed to see his feelings for what they truly were. He loved her. And he would love her always.

The question was whether he loved her enough to let her go, to let her live her life to its full potential without him to hold her back. He was not sure he could do it.

"I am afraid I am too heavy for you. You are so small."

"Don't go. Oh, please don't. It feels wonderful having you hold me," she said.

"Ah, my Charlotte," he said, and bit his tongue to hold back the words he longed to say.

He rolled off her and pulled her into his arms on her side. His shoulder provided a solid pillow. He longed to close his eyes and drift into what he was sure would be the most peaceful slumber, but he resisted.

"Would you like me to stay with you here tonight? Or shall I return to the abbey and leave you in peace?"

"Would you mind very much if I asked you to stay?"

His heart surged with joy. "Not at all. It would be my pleasure." He pressed her body closer to his own and felt himself falling, falling into a blissful state of peace.

She would never be able to fall asleep. Not on this, the most momentous day of her life. She would not be able to or want to miss a moment of feeling his arms around her. She felt something she had never experienced in all her years. She felt cherished. Oh, he did not love her as she loved him, but she did feel he treasured her, and she prayed she had performed her marital duties adequately, even though she knew he had done everything. It was a pity she would not have the chance to try some of the suggestions Alexandre had made.

She felt much more bold now that she understood the actual process, she thought in her traditional methodical manner. She had not realized conjugal relations could bring such unexplainable yearning and gratification. Now she understood why it was required to finalize a marriage. The act bonded two people together, body and soul, in a fashion impossible to reverse. Impossible to forget.

How could she live the rest of her life near him without wanting to experience this ultimate act again and again? It would become an obsession, which would lead her to madness.

She must accept his offer to live away from him or she would end up losing every ounce of pride and be reduced to begging for his attentions. But perhaps, just perhaps, he might not spurn her touches, this night only. She must make memories to last a lifetime.

And so it went.

He did not ignore her tentative touches. The rest of the night was filled with patches of sleep for him in between gentle lovemaking instigated by her. She forced herself to fling away the last vestiges of her bashfulness by touching and exploring every perfect feature of his body, first with her hands and finally, at moonset, with her lips, following his example. She was unsure who was more surprised by her boldness, he or she. But she hoped desperately that she had pleased him. He had groaned and whispered his delight over and over. Oh, please let him want to make love to her again after this one night.

She was very sore, but it was a pleasurable feeling nonetheless. She felt very womanly, very content. As the unwanted first tentacles of dawn groped through the curtains in her small bedchamber, she worried that by prolonging the sweet agony of the pleasures of the night she had not satisfied her thirst for memories, but whetted her appetite for more.

She turned her head to find his half-opened green eyes staring at her.

"I must look a fright." She touched her tangled locks.

"Quite the opposite. You look a veritable goddess of . . . of desire," he said, with a slow, devastating smile. "There, that is your first compliment today. And no, I see your look. You are not allowed to negate any compliments."

It would be very, very easy to allow herself to become reduced to the status of worshipful slave to him.

"All right. But I shall repay you with a fine breakfast, if

you will allow. I gave Doro the day off, as I could not bear to see her knowing looks this morning. So I hope you will be satisfied with day-old bread and coddled eggs."

"I can see you would be useful on the front lines by your willingness to cook the morning after your wedding night." His eyes twinkled.

Charlotte marveled at his rugged virility. His muscled, bronzed form lay against the white bed linen in all its tempting magnificence. Even the healed gash on his thigh and a various assortment of battle scars added to his powerful magnetism. His eyes darkened as he watched her looking at him.

He reached for her and dragged her against him once more. "But, I think I must have one last taste of you before anything else, and besides, it isn't anywhere near morning," he growled into her willing ear.

It had been easier to lose her inhibitions in the complete darkness when the candle had guttered. In the dim stillness of dawn, she observed his fully aroused male state and swallowed. She looked into his eyes and caressed his whiskered face with her small hand, so happy that he wanted her despite the reality of the receding shadows.

Suddenly, he stilled. "I think, perhaps, I have overstayed my welcome. Charlotte, you are too good. You must be very sore and uncomfortable. Come, my dear, if you will see to our breakfast, I will see toward a bath for you, my tender-hearted bride."

She looked down at the traces of blood on the sheets and felt shy again. She hastily rearranged the bedcovers. "As you wish. But I am very willing, more than willing to accommodate you first."

He stared hard at her, and finally pulled her once more into his arms, giving and taking in an age-old fashion that brought secret tears to her eyes in the final throes.

Chapter Fifteen

*"It was, perhaps, one of those cases in which
advice is good or bad only as the event decides."*

—Jane Austen

I told you, *ma cherie,* that you must leave all timidity out
of the bedroom," Alexandre said, while he slashed
through the face of the clay bust he had been working on.
"*Zut, alors.* This is the most frustrating craft. What if we relieve our tensions instead, by me showing you some of the
ways you could attract that cold-hearted Englishman back
into your bed?"

Charlotte sighed and continued to rework the noble forehead of her clay model. "Alexandre, I know you mean well,
and that you are flirting with me to tease me out of my
mopes, but really, I cannot find any humor in your comments today. I am sorry."

"Ah, but you do not know me very well, then. I do not
flatter where I do not see potential. And I find the idea of
teaching you a few methods of madness quite, quite intoxicating now that you are a more, shall we say, experienced
coquette? I promise you I could lead you to heights unknown," he said with a wicked grin. Alexandre wiped his
hands on the cloth, giving up his creative efforts. He came
around behind her and placed his arms around her waist.
"You are enchanting," he whispered into her ear.

She swatted him lightly. "And you are nothing but a
charming tease."

He nibbled at her neck and blew a kiss under her ear.
Funny, it did not feel as pleasant as when Nicholas had done
the exact same thing to her two weeks earlier.

Since then, after moving into the oppressive abbey and witnessing the departure of her brother, Charlotte had spent more and more time in her private clay room, away from her rooms in the abbey, which Nicholas never attempted to enter. For the first three nights after her wedding night, she had waited for him in her chambers, sure he would cross the threshold to take her in his arms again. They had shared so much that first night. She had been sure he would come to her. But, he had not.

On the fourth night, she had fortified herself with a large glass of secreted brandy and had gone, with shaky spirits, to his door and knocked loudly. Three times. He had refused to answer. So, she had her answer. He did indeed want the marriage of convenience he had originally proposed.

Alexandre fluttered light kisses on her neck, bringing her back to the present.

At that precise moment, Nicholas chose to cross the threshold of her sanctuary with nary a knock of warning. Her damnable cousin chuckled and released her after languidly running his hand down her arm, perilously close to her breast.

Nicholas stood stock still, taking it all in without a word.

"You have remarkably bad timing, my lord," said Alexandre.

"And you, sir, show a lamentable lack of good judgment."

Charlotte had never seen Nicholas appear so coldly contained. "You misunderstand, Nicholas. Alexandre was just keeping me company while I worked." She knew her voice was not well modulated. "He meant no harm."

"I see," he replied, looking back and forth between them. A long silence encroached. "And what have we here?" he continued, pointing to the bust in front of her. He began walking around the worktable. "You have decided to switch from birds to humans?" he asked, looking again to Alexandre.

Charlotte threw a damp cloth over the figure, hiding it from view, "Well, in fact, yes," she said.

"And I am not to have the pleasure of studying your work?"

"No," she said, looking down at her tools.

"I see. But your dear cousin does have that privilege," he said, with a hard edge.

"Yes."

"Well, I advise you to beware that he does not claim any other sort of privilege, my dear. For if I cannot demand fidelity, I can and will demand discretion."

"It will be with the utmost discretion that Charlotte and I continue to become reacquainted since our childhood, my lord," Alexandre said.

She longed to kick Alexandre and run from the room. The two of them were behaving abominably. If she possessed a witty bone in her body she was sure she would have been able to turn the moment and have them all laughing at the ridiculous set of circumstances.

She could feel Alexandre run his knuckles along her jaw.

Nicholas bowed and left the room. Only the sound of the outer door being slammed indicated the intensity of his anger.

"How could you? How am I ever to make it right? He has every right never to acknowledge me again."

"How could I not, *cherie*? You will thank me. You will see. If this does not get him into your, ahem, *culottes,* nothing will. Mark my words. And if it does fail, I assure you, I will be pawing at your door in three nights' time. Now that you have been awakened to the pleasures of the flesh, we cannot have you wilting again, can we?" He threw back his head and laughed.

Three miserable days followed, in which Nicholas remained as poker-faced as Stevens the butler, and the entire household at the abbey had become as depressed as the never-ending rain. Charlotte looked out the window of the library and could not decide if she felt more wretched because she missed her father or because her brother had left. Deep down she knew it was because of Nicholas. And try as she might to discourage Alexandre's continued witty remarks designed to further infuriate her husband, her cousin seemed to redouble his efforts. But he was the only one who paid any attention to her. Even Rosamunde was listless and inattentive. And the infuriating guests at the abbey continued to stay on.

Charlotte sighed. If the lot of them departed as well as her well-intentioned cousin, Charlotte believed that she had a small chance of forging a companionable if not loving marriage. As it stood, Lady Susan had augmented her efforts at securing Alexandre now that the heir was taken. And Alexandre continued to cause havoc with flirtations in every corner, upstairs and down.

The storms had effectively put a stop to the small but constant flow of ill or injured neighbors to the cottage. Charlotte had only been able to go see Mrs. Roberts, Owen's wife, who had been suffering from a mysterious illness for the last two weeks.

Charlotte was sad and bored, unused to idleness. She had sought the stillness and privacy of the library, knowing no one in the abbey shared her ardor for books.

But there were no novels to be found to tempt her. Only books of sermons, and history, and philosophy, all subjects that had fascinated her until she had delved into the forbidden pages of novels. Now she was insatiable. Nothing else would do. She longed to step into the shoes of a bold heroine like Elizabeth Bennett for several pleasurable hours.

Instead, she moved to the large desk and looked at the tall ledgers before her. She opened the one nearest to her and looked at the long rows of columns with dates, entries, and numbers. She understood little other than the nature of the simple entries. This one seemed to be filled with household expenses. She opened another and another, until six ledgers overspread the desk. She could not put her finger on it, but something was not right. It wasn't the numbers, or the dates. What was it?

Startled, she looked up to encounter the cold, hard gaze of Nicholas at the doorway.

"Good morning, my lord," she said, not knowing if she should rise to make a small curtsey or not.

"Good morning, Charlotte," he replied in his deep baritone voice, which had always made her insides constrict. "I did not know you had an interest in estate management," he said, arching an eyebrow as he walked toward the desk.

"I do not, but I couldn't find any book to interest me."

"So, naturally, you began reviewing Wyndhurst's ledgers?"

"I did not know they were forbidden to members of the family." She hated to sound defensive. "But then, I am not really a proper member of the family, am I?"

"I suppose you consider our vows before God quite meaningless, then? But then I forget, a learned member of the scientific world might hold different views. Especially one who has a handsome cousin to turn her pretty head." He looked angry now. "Ah, but you have deftly changed the subject. Why are you reviewing the ledgers? Do you not trust our family to ensure the proper care of this estate?"

"The real question is, do you? And if you do, then why?" she asked. "Something is obviously very wrong. Why do we eat like kings when there are entire families starving not a mile from the elegant gates of the abbey? These are people who have depended on the dukedom for generations. And why are all the habitations so poorly maintained?"

Once she began, she couldn't seem to stop the torrent of accusations pouring from her. She knew he was not to blame, but she had to hurt him. His continual refusal to touch her, even kiss her, something he had done before they had married, hurt her deeply. "I know you are trying to remedy some of the problems by starting the brewery, and the flock of sheep, as well as the other plans. But it is not enough, Nicholas. There are too many families, too many problems that need to be addressed and corrected. You are responsible for them, not your father, and certainly not your horrid brother or Her Grace. Tell me you are not using your family's ridiculous claims of your intellectual inferiority to stop you? You are one of the most brave and intelligent gentlemen of my acquaintance. Just because you can't read as well as other people doesn't mean you can relinquish your role as leader of your family." There, she had said it. The things that could not be said. That should not be said to the man she loved if she had any desire for him to return her love.

"And that is what you think of me? By your account my actions are reprehensible indeed."

Almost the same words Darcy had said in response to Eliza Bennett's spurning of his proposal. But she had not Eliza's backbone.

"Yes, and no," she replied, looking away from him. And then in a rush, "Oh, don't you see? You could do so much more—"

"More?" he interrupted her. "You think I should do more? I have served my king and my country, obeyed my father, tried to provide as well as I could for our neighbors with the means that I possess, and married you. What more do you want? I will never be able to live up to your standards, Charlotte."

She drew in her breath sharply, in pain. "I realize the honor you paid me by marrying me, and providing for me. But, you must remember that I tried to tell you it was not necessary, that I could provide well enough for myself. My defenses were weakened over the shock of my father's death when I acquiesced to your plan. I wish now that I had not. And by the by, I am sorry you feel the need to live up to my standards. I never intended my words to be taken that way."

"Well, I think enough has been said. I am sorry to have intruded. Perhaps it would be better if you did not take it upon yourself to review the ledgers again. And I will consider a plan that will alleviate the need for us to be under each other's inspection."

With that he was gone, and Charlotte threw herself into the leather high-backed chair. With an anger seldom expressed, she slammed the ledgers closed and rearranged them on the edge of the desk as tears ran unchecked down her cheeks. She must leave this horrible, depressing place. Nicholas not only pitied her now, he hated her.

She was so tired of it all. She missed her father and her brother. Worst of all, she couldn't bear the sadness within these walls, the loneliness, or rather, the aloneness she suffered despite Nicholas's presence and all the others. She must find Alexandre and beg him to take her away to London. Her cousin would find inexpensive lodgings for her until she could form a more suitable long-term proposition.

She could go back to her original idea of caring for an older lady. She did not think she could accept her husband's offer of the use of his elegant town house, not when she had criticized his actions so thoroughly. She could not feel beholden to him. She would not play the hypocrite.

There were very few items to pack in her old trunk. Aside from the beloved yellow gown, wrapped in tissue, and the two serviceable day gowns, Charlotte had nothing else save two mourning gowns, the bust of her mother and several drawings she had sketched of her father and brother. She would arrange for the medical books to be sent to her in London when she had permanent living quarters. She would leave all her other books behind. Even the novels. Especially the novels.

It had been two days since Charlotte had last seen Nicholas in the library. He had made himself as scarce as he had promised in anger. The words were imprinted in her memory: *"I will consider a plan that will alleviate the need for us to be under each other's inspection."*

She would not force him from his father's deathbed. *She* would leave. It had all been settled yesterday with Alexandre. He had left for London last night, and she would follow tomorrow. Surprisingly, he had been most willing to follow Charlotte's plans.

"La Susanne has become *insupportable*. Her diamonds are quite beautiful, yes, but she has become the most clinging little barnacle. All hope of frolic and amusement in Wiltshire evaporated when she banished her delightful maid. I suppose the description of a ménage à trois was too much for her." Alexandre had left with a kiss and a smile. "*Ma petite cousine*, you are not to worry another moment. I shall make you the gay duchess-to-be in town, whom everyone will be dying to meet. And we will live quite well with the funds your fusty, cold husband shall provide."

She had not had the heart or the nerve to tell him that she had no intention of entering the social whirl, much less accepting a tuppence from her husband.

A knock sounded at her bedchamber door.

The formidable form of Nicholas's grandmother brushed past and ensconced herself on a sturdy chair with what seemed to be a grim determination to remain fixed there for a long duration.

"It is as I thought, then," the older lady said, glancing at the trunk. "You are determined to leave him and ruin whatever chance of happiness this family had."

Charlotte took a deep breath, and continued to pack her nightclothes as well as her brush and pins. "I am sorry you have formed such an ill opinion of me, Your Grace."

"I have no ill opinion of you—only of your nitwit behavior. Don't tell me you subscribe to that silly notion that absence makes the heart grow fonder? Stuff of willy-nilly poets that is. If you leave, ten to one he will fall in with the duchess's fondest wish and never see you or anyone else in the abbey again. He will flee to battle if he can find a war to fight in."

"Even you do not have faith in his intelligence and ability." Charlotte closed the trunk and latched it.

"No, my dear. It is you who does not have faith. You are

a fool not to grab happiness when it is before you on a platter, yours for the taking."

"I do beg your pardon. You are one to talk. You are lecturing me on the importance of love when you—"

"Aha! I knew you loved him!"

"I did not say that."

"Well, do you?" the old woman asked.

"What does it signify? You love the vicar, do you not? And yet, you have not married him. And would I be right in guessing he has asked you on numerous occasions?"

The older lady's face turned a darker shade. "Why, that is none of your affair. We were talking about—"

Charlotte interrupted. "No. My ill-fated marriage is none of your affair."

"It most certainly is! Everything about this family is my affair," the dowager duchess harrumphed.

"Well, do not expect me to follow a course you are not willing to tread."

Her Grace sighed pitifully, and Charlotte hardened her heart. When had she discarded her timid personality for that of a bold and independent creature who cared little of what others thought of her and less of polite conversation?

"You're leaving with that trouble-making cousin of yours, aren't you? You will bring scandal on us all, as well as ruin my Nicky's life. But tell me this, once and for all, do you love the Frenchman?"

"No," Charlotte admitted. "Alexandre left last night. He has promised to secure lodgings for me in London. Really, this is for the best."

A loud rapping interrupted the conversation.

The butler entered with a flushed expression. "Your Grace, Lady Charlotte, the duchess asked me to request your immediate presence in the salon."

"Come, come Stevens, what is the matter? I have never seen you so ruffled. Is it my son?" asked the dowager duchess.

"No, no. I believe it has something to do with Lady

Susan. One of our chambermaids found a note on 'er bed. A bed that 'ad not been slept in, I might add," he said with a conspiratorial wink. "It seems the young chit, I mean lady, 'eighed off to London with that smooth-talking Frenchy," the butler said. In his excitement he was dropping his aitches and betraying his roots.

"What!" exclaimed Charlotte and Her Grace simultaneously.

Nicholas rubbed his eyes and tried to shake the gnawing headache that had invaded the edges of his mind. He had closeted himself in the library all day, refusing to allow anyone to enter, despite repeated knocks. Trying to decipher the ledgers was actually easier than he had thought; he could read the simple entries and the numbers. And he could add the figures in his mind. The problem was that the ciphers did not make sense.

It was the small numbers that caught his eye. Each time an entry was made for the farrier, it varied by ten to fifteen pounds. But in reviewing the stable charts, the number of horses shod never varied. And the variance did not occur in the off-season, when some of the horses' shoes were taken off for longer rests. Then the income from selling a small portion of the hay that had been recently harvested was off by five and twenty pounds. He was sure of this, because he had witnessed the sale.

Nicholas added Mr. Coburn's neat rows of figures three times. They did not add up. The expenses should have been two-thirds the stated amount. The profits should have been a quarter higher. When he glanced down at a notation involving the sum of five hundred pounds and its payment for rethatching tenant cottages, Nicholas squeezed his eyes shut and slammed his fist down on the ledger.

He had been a blind fool.

He had allowed his embarrassment and failures to evade the ultimate responsibility of his birth. Charlotte, of course, had been correct in all her accusations. He dragged himself to his feet and groped for the almost-spent candle, hating what he would have to do next, fearing how it might affect his father. But by the time he reached his sire's door, he had armed himself with ironclad resolve.

Charley, bless his soul, was asleep in the chair next to the duke's bed. He woke the boy and bade him go to his small chamber off Nicholas's own, then turned toward his father's bedside and saw that the older man's eyes were half open.

"What is it, my son? Is someone finally willing to tell me what all the running and thumping around is about? Everyone seems too afraid to tell me anything anymore, afraid I'll pop off at the smallest provocation."

"I don't know what you are referring to, Father. But I have come to discuss a very grave matter, something that will disturb you a great deal. But, I want to assure you that I will take full responsibility in seeing that everything is rectified in a satisfactory manner. I am only sorry I will have to break my promise to you to do so. But I must do this whatever your reaction will be. I owe it to my family, as well as to all the good people of the counties who depend on us."

"What is it, my son?" the father asked.

Nicholas sat on his father's bed and took one of his frail hands in his own. "Edwin and the steward have been draining funds from the estates. I have only reviewed the ledgers for the last two years, but in that time I estimate that over ten thousand pounds has been taken. For what uses, I have no idea."

The duke closed his eyes. A moment or two later his father waved his hand, urging him to continue.

When Nicholas was sure his father was alert enough for him to carry on, he did so. "At first, I thought it was just Coburn. I mean, why would Edwin take that which was already his?" Nicholas paused to search his father's face.

"Perhaps it is because I chastised him many times over the years for overspending. He has an addicted taste for high-flying."

"My best guess is that Coburn discovered Edwin's methods of taking funds, then blackmailed him into receiving money of his own," Nicholas said. "I confirmed Edwin's role when I found his signature approving five hundred pounds for rethatching all the cottages' roofs. There is not one rethatched dwelling in all of Wiltshire, I assure you. And Edwin toured the area with me."

"My son, you do not have to tell me any more. I believe and trust you. I have always trusted you."

"Father, I will remove Coburn and consult with the magistrate. I daresay this scandal will grow, as Coburn will surely try to blackmail us to keep Edwin's name out of the proceedings. I will not accept a scheme of this nature. But I fear this will cause you great embarrassment."

"It will not cause me pain, only joy in the knowledge that *you* will do what I always hoped," replied the duke in a ragged whisper.

"Father, do you understand me rightly? I will have to take control of the Cavendish estates."

His father closed his eyes again, yet patted his son's hand. "Nicholas, my son, I have waited so long to hear these words. I prayed for them. And now, as I lie here, my prayers have been answered."

"But I thought you wanted Edwin to oversee Wyndhurst and your other holdings. He was the more capable one. He was the one with the high marks from university. I was only capable of blasting our country's enemies to bits."

"No, Nicholas. You were always more capable than that. You are a leader of men. And you have integrity. And that is much more important than any intellectual pursuit."

"Well, then why didn't you tell me this and insist that I remain here?"

Nicholas had to lean close to his father's lips to hear him. "Because you needed to want to lead the people of our estate, and you did not. You needed to be willing to face the taunts and embarrassment of your one failing in life, and you weren't." His father squeezed his hand slightly. "And I would not force you to do it. You see, I am very similar to you. I faced difficulties learning too, although not as great as yours. If you did not think you were up to the challenge, I thought it better for you to choose a different course. But I never stopped believing in you."

"Oh, Father," he said. "I wish you had confided in me."

"No, Nicholas, you had to choose to become head of this family by yourself." His father's eyes opened and were watery. "And I was wrong about Miss Kittridge. I am glad you married her. She will make a fine wife and duchess, and will help you find your way if you allow her. I believe your pride is now up to the challenge. It shall be almost easy to let her be of assistance to you, for I have not seen a lady so in love with her husband." The duke seemed overcome with his long speech. He began to cough, but was too weak to produce more than a wisp of a sound.

Nicholas did not dare worry his father about the disastrous state of his marriage. He brushed a thin lock of white hair from his father's brow. "Father, you must rest now."

"No. I must know if you will now have the courage to have children," the duke whispered.

"I . . . I don't know, Father."

"Well, I made a mess of it. But, I do think you have the benefit of learning from my mistakes." The father's breath was becoming shallower.

"I never blamed you for any of it, Father. I blamed myself."

"It is time to stop blaming yourself. And I will do the same. You have much work to do." The older man raised his painfully thin fingers, and after fumbling for a moment, he placed something hard and cold in Nicholas's hand. "I have been wanting to give you this. It has been waiting for you. But I would not force it on you."

Nicholas looked down to find the long familiar signet ring in the palm of his hand. As it blurred before him, he squeezed his eyes shut, forcing himself to rein in his emotions.

"It has always been yours."

"Yes, sir."

The ring that had become too heavy and large for his father's thin fingers fit him perfectly.

"Now, my son, you have made me the happiest of men. Will you read to me the Twenty-third Psalm?" The duke indicated a bible on the nightstand. "I wish to rest a bit now. I am afraid I am worn out."

"Of course, sir." Nicholas rose to retrieve the bible, the ribbon indicating his father's favorite psalm. Nicholas knew the words by heart, but read the verse from the page to please his father, until he got through the first section and almost broke down. "Yea, though I walk through the valley of the shadow of death, I shall fear no evil; for thou art with me . . ."

Nicholas could go no further.

"Remember, my son, that I will be with you too, in your heart always," his father said on a slow exhalation.

"I will never forget. Father . . . I love you."

His father's breath rattled. "And I you . . ."

Exhaustion poured through every pore of Nicholas's body. He lay down next to his father and gently clasped his elder's cold hand in his own large warm one. Head pounding, he closed his eyes and remembered being a child and holding his father's hand then, Nicholas's small one engulfed by the powerful Duke of Cavendish's. A title he most likely would obtain all too soon.

The tears he had so successfully held in check silently coursed down the corners of his eyes, drenching his temples. He forced himself to relax his clenched chest.

Chapter Sixteen

"Think only of the past as its remembrance gives you pleasure."

—Pride and Prejudice

Goodness me." Charley jumped up from his bed when Nicholas entered the small chamber adjoining his own rooms. "Beggin' yer pardon, Lord Nick. Didn't hear you come in last night, or I would've performed my duties."

"I didn't retire here after all, Charley. I stayed with my father." At the inquisitive gaze of his faithful young batman, Nicholas forced himself to continue. "He is gone. He died just before dawn."

"Oh, Lord Nick."

"I know, Charley, I know." Nicholas accepted the embrace of his young charge, and they said nothing for long moments.

"I am glad then that I did not bother him with the ruckus going all around us yesterday," Charley said into Nicholas's shoulder.

"What ruckus?"

"Well, I don't know the whole of it, sir. Only that the overdressed frog left without a word the night before last, and a female went with him or after him."

"Which female, Charley?" asked Nicholas. He felt a certain stabbing sensation in his chest.

"I don't know. One of the ladies I think, sir."

"Mr. Roberts, the fever has broken, finally. Your wife, I hope, with good care will recover. You will have to be patient, as she will be quite weak after such a long illness,"

Charlotte said, and removed the compress from the woman's forehead.

It was very late, or rather, early, almost dawn. The distraught man had brought his wife to Charlotte's old cottage yesterday evening in the back of a crude wagon.

"I shouldn't have brought her in the wagon. It was too hard a ride for her. But I couldn't just stand by and watch her get worse," he said.

"No, Mr. Roberts. Don't blame yourself. I am sorry your note wasn't brought down from the abbey. You are lucky you found me here at all. I was packing a few last things before my journey." She looked down at the patient, who was sleeping peacefully for the first time in a fortnight. "I will send for Wyndhurst's finest carriage to transport her back to your home. And I will send Doro to nurse her. She will also be able to help you with your children and your meals. This will be a gift from me to you. Please don't say no."

"Thank you, my lady," Owen Roberts said, bowing awkwardly. "There's not many from the abbey who would lower themselves to care for my Sally. And I have naught to give you for me thanks," Mr. Robertses concluded.

"I am pleased to be at your service. Let's allow her to rest awhile. She is very comfortable here."

"If it be all right with you, Lady Charlotte, I would like to stay with my Sally until the carriage comes."

"Of course, Mr. Roberts," she said, rising to leave.

Doro was taking too long, Charlotte thought an hour later, while pacing the front room. It was almost full light and she had sent the maid to Wyndhurst's stables to make arrangements with the stable master. He was to bring to the cottage the carriage for the Robertses. In addition, the gig she had ordered for her own use was to be brought to the cottage as well, instead of to the abbey as she had arranged yesterday. Charlotte looked at the letter she had propped on the bookshelf for Nicholas.

When she had left for the cottage last night, the abbey

had been at sixes and sevens with the disappearance of Lady Susan and Alexandre. She had tried to calm them, explaining that her cousin had quit Wiltshire *alone* on an errand for her of the utmost importance. But that only served to make Susan's grandmother more hysterical. The old lady left in her carriage, wailing and bemoaning her worries and calling Alexandre every vile name she could concoct. Only the dowager duchess had remained calm, assuring the Dowager Countess of Elltrope that the family would employ every effort to find Lady Susan and help repair any damage to the young lady's reputation. Nicholas had been locked up in the library, blissfully unaware of the events.

The first letter Charlotte had written to Nicholas had been hurt and angry. The second, less so. The third was devoid of any emotion. It gave the address of her father's old solicitor in London and an assurance that she had made arrangements in town for a comfortable apartment and that he was not to worry about her furthermore. She expressed her sadness over his father's impending demise, and wished him a happy future in Paris. It was everything proper. There was only the smallest part of her that dared hope that he would fly to the solicitor in London and demand to see her. She squashed the thought each time it raised its relentless head.

Her thoughts fled at the appearance of the gig in the yard. With a sigh, she went to the front entrance, where her trunk lay waiting, and opened the door to her future.

"Mr. Coburn! What are you doing here? Where is the driver I requested?"

"Lady Charlotte, I am at your service." Mr. Coburn removed his hat and bowed down before her. "The duchess required Mr. Harper for some pressing errands this morning. I was planning a day trip to London this week or next, as the duke has asked me to attend to several things in town. I volunteered to drive you to kill two birds with one stone, so to speak."

She didn't trust the man, never had. But he returned her gaze with a pleasant, open expression. She could hardly refuse. It was a few short hours to London. She would take Doro, and arrange for another maid from the abbey to help Owen's wife. Mr. Coburn got down from the gig and began loading her trunk in the back.

"Well, then, Lady Charlotte, let me help you up."

There was something wrong. She could feel it in the pit of her stomach. She wouldn't go with this man.

"And where is the carriage for Mr. and Mrs. Roberts?"

"The other driver will be along any moment for them."

He urged her by the elbow before she halted. Why couldn't the other driver take her to London? "I am sorry to force a delay, sir. However, I must wait for Doro."

"There's no room for her, my dear Lady Charlotte. Her large bulk would never fit. Come, come let us be off now. If we wait much longer it will be full dark before we arrive."

In her distress, Charlotte did not notice a lone rider coming over the small hill in front of the cottage.

"You there, wait," Nicholas called out on his approach.

A moment later he verified it was indeed Charlotte near the gig with Mr. Coburn. What the devil? Something was very wrong.

Nicholas's horse slid to a halt in front of them. He remained on the animal, the pistol he always carried in the saddle near his hand.

"What the devil is going on here, Coburn?"

"Why, nothing out of the ordinary, my lord," replied Coburn, with an easy smile. "I am escorting your wife to London, per her request."

"Escorting my wife to London? Per her request? I think not. Charlotte?" Nicholas asked, looking at his wife.

"That is partially correct. I had made plans to depart. But not with Mr. Coburn. I've left you a letter in the cottage." She avoided his gaze. "I believe I will wait for the driver to arrive with the other carriage, Mr. Coburn, if you don't mind. I would prefer to go with him and I will wait for Doro too."

"But, my dear Lady Char—" began Mr. Coburn.

"Charlotte, get away," Nicholas shouted as he fired his pistol before the steward's weapon was cocked and visible.

The man yelped, and made an attempt to grab her, his hand bleeding. She evaded his grasp and fled to the safety of the cottage.

Nicholas leapt off his horse, grabbed the pistol that Coburn had dropped on the ground, and pointed it at the man.

"Mr. Coburn . . . How *kind* of you to offer to *help* my wife."

"If you're going to kill me, get it over with," said the man.

"If I had wanted to kill you, you would be dead, *my friend*. As it is, you are lucky I didn't maim you in a more satisfying part of your anatomy," Nicholas said, looking at the man's crotch.

"I guess I should be thankful, my lord."

"You will refer to me as 'Your Grace' henceforth, Coburn. As of a few hours ago, my title changed, as will yours. Now, I will give you precisely one minute to tell me what you were planning to do with my wife and about the embezzlement of funds from the Cavendish holdings," he said. "And remember, please, that the penalties for lying to a duke will not improve your lot."

The steward kept his gaze riveted to the ground.

"All right, Mr. Coburn. What have you to say?" Nicholas said, pulling his pocket watch from his pocket.

"Nothing, my . . . sir."

"I shall help you along then. According to Wyndhurst's ledgers, you have become rich, in my estimates, siphoning off thousands of pounds annually from the abbey alone. Actually I am amazed you still dare to be in Wiltshire. I was certain you had hightailed it out of here once you learned I was locked in the library. But then, perhaps I have caught you just as you were leaving? Planning to take my wife too for extra insurance, were you?"

"Your brother, he is the guilty party, not me."

This was going to be easier than he thought. Self-incrimination was a beautiful thing.

"Perhaps you are correct, Mr. Coburn. However, he is not here. And he was not the one who was about to put a pistol to my wife."

Nicholas heard a sound from the doorway and did a double take upon sighting the form of Owen Roberts. "I won't even ask what you are doing here, Owen. Your timing is impeccable."

"Glad to be of service. I heard your question to Coburn, here, and thought you might want to know that there's been some gossip in the village, there has. Seems someone heard that Coburn bought a prettyish sort of estate for his, er, his mammy in the next county. Mr. Coburn is a kindhearted soul to be providin' for his mammy, don't you think?"

Charlotte was peeking from behind the large man.

"That's an out and out lie—" said Coburn.

"Not another word," said Nicholas. "Owen, find some rope to bind Coburn's hands, will you?"

"I tell you, it is your brother who is guilty. This was his idea," Coburn whined. "But perhaps we can work something out, Your Grace. Surely you would not want to implicate your own brother. I would be willing—"

"I am sure you would be, Coburn," interrupted Nicholas. "However, I shall leave it to the magistrate to decide. Until then, you shall spend a night in The Quill & Dove's strong room."

Owen was tasked with securing Coburn's hands with a bit of rope. Charlotte disappeared for a moment and returned to wrap a small piece of cloth with ointment on Coburn's hand.

"It is just a flesh wound, Mr. Coburn. You are lucky. It should heal in a fortnight," she said.

"All right, enough lollygagging, Coburn. Into the gig, now. That's a good man," Nicholas said, then turned to Owen. "Will you take him, then?"

Charlotte spoke up. "I see Doro coming, Mr. Roberts. I will have her stay with Mrs. Roberts until your return."

"All right," Owen replied.

"After he's secured, may I count on you to find the magistrate and tell him what happened? I will call on him tomorrow morning after I arrange for my father's burial."

Owen clapped him on the shoulder. "I'm sorry, that I am. There's been no' a moment to say it."

Nicholas accepted Owen's firm handshake and avoided the man's gaze. "Thank you."

Owen urged the horse forward, and Nicholas turned in time to overhear his wife's explanations to her maid. Doro shook her head and clucked as she entered the cottage, murmuring her horror at the morning's events and promising to watch over Sally Roberts.

Nicholas strode over to Charlotte, who stood with her back to him. He resisted the urge to place his hands on her shoulders.

"Did I understand correctly, Nicholas? When did your father die?"

"Very early this morning."

Her shoulders began to shake, and he turned her and pulled her into his arms. She cried and then shook her head, pulling away from his embrace. "I should be comforting you." She wiped her hands across her tear-stained face.

"You've earned the right to a good cry, after what Coburn did." Nicholas fingered his breast pocket. "I'm sorry Charlotte, I dressed in haste, and have no handkerchief to give you. Damn Coburn's hide. I lost ten years of my life when I saw him reach for his pistol."

"I guess that will be the last time he draws on a Rifleman," she said, smiling through her tears.

He made a motion for the cottage door. "Let me retrieve a handkerchief from your maid."

"I have one in my pocket." She drew forth a large handkerchief.

The white-on-white embroidered initials on it surprised

him. "Why, this is one of my own," he said. "How fortunate."

"I could not bear to return it to you. You lent it to me long ago."

He took it from her and dried her tears, then forced her to blow her nose. She did so in a loud, childlike fashion.

"Will you accompany me back to the abbey, Charlotte?" He hesitated. "You weren't really leaving for London, were you?"

"I thought it was for the best," she said, not looking at him. "But I will not leave right away. I will stay for your father's funeral, of course. I would not be so disrespectful to his memory. He was the kindest of men. But after, when you plan your own departure—"

"There you are!" shouted Charley, coming down the rise overmounted on a huge chestnut gelding.

Nicholas had to grab the reins when Charley could not bring the animal to a stop.

"You are needed at once, Lord Nick, I mean 'Your Grace.' " The boy was completely out of breath. "Her Grace is in such a state. Stevens sent me to find you, and to ask Lady Charlotte, I mean Her Gr—, oh, you know who I mean, to bring some smelling salts. Oh, do hurry, please, afore she tears the abbey down with her screamin'."

Nicholas turned to Charlotte, shaking his head. "Will this day never end? It is only eight o'clock in the morning, and yet it seems like it should be nightfall. We will continue our conversation a bit later," he said, taking her arm to urge her toward the abbey. "But Charlotte, promise me you will not make any plans to leave before we do so. Come, it's time to face the worst of it."

"You!" his stepmother shrieked as Nicholas entered the elegant sitting room off the duchess's bedchamber. Both Edwin and her lady's maid had to physically restrain her from attacking him. She pointed an accusing finger at Nicholas. "You dare to show your face in my rooms? You,

the murderer of your own father. And you," she said, looking beyond his shoulder to Charlotte. "You vulgar little
French mushroom. I knew you would be the death of him.
My dear, beloved Richard," she continued, and then crumpled onto the chaise longue. The maid handed her mistress a
new handkerchief.

Nicholas looked down at her. She made for such a pathetic creature. The duchess had seemed to be made of steel
will and unquestionable authority when she had moved into
the abbey so many years ago. He had tried so hard, for a
decade, to gain her approval, a feat that a young boy of eight
had not known was unattainable. And now, lying before
him, she was just an old woman, filled with nothing but ha-
tred and venom. He felt only pity.

"Madam, I shall choose to ignore your unfortunate comments as you are consumed with grief. However, I must ask
you to exert some effort to regain a measure of sanity in the
presence of others. If that cannot be accomplished, then I
must ask your maid and Stevens to leave us."

Stevens bowed, and the maid curtsied her acquiescence.

"Already giving orders are you, *Your Grace*?" Edwin
said.

"Yes, as a matter of fact, I am," Nicholas replied. "Do
you have difficulty comprehending why, Edwin?"

His half brother looked at him through half-closed eyes.
"Why, I have never had trouble *following* orders. Quite to
the contrary. I have been obeying our father's orders since
birth; a trait I thought we shared. But clearly, I am very
much mistaken. Now that our father is gone, you will break
all your vows to him and ruin us all because of your ignorance."

Nicholas looked at Edwin's cynical, pompous mask and
turned to Stevens and the maid. With a nod, he dismissed
them and returned his attention to his half brother.

"Edwin," he said, and paused to collect his thoughts. "I
have found, in my many years serving the Crown, that there
are three kinds of evil in the world. The first type is plagued

with insecurities and jealousies that lead individuals to behave badly. The second kind seems to be relentless in an attempt to acquire power and control. And finally, the third type is demonstrated in the sad cases of people who were born with criminal tendencies," Nicholas continued. He glanced down the length of his nose to see the furious expression on Edwin's face.

Nicholas raised his hand to stop him from speaking. "Have no fear. I will not ask you to tell me into which category you fall. The only reason I do not is because of the memory of our father."

Nicholas caught a swift, dark movement from the corner of his eye. His stepmother had hurled herself headfirst from the chaise longue and was now barreling into his stomach. He tried to catch her thin arms as she struck his chest with her fists.

"You stupid ox," she screamed at him. "You dare to call Edwin evil? You are the devil incarnate. My dear Richard is not even cold on his deathbed and already you dare to try to take control of the family and insult my son, who is your superior in every conceivable way. I knew you would break all the promises you made as soon as you came back. You are nothing but a bad seed that should never have been born. You killed your father with your scandalous marriage to this—this penniless foreign nobody with pretensions of grandeur. Let me go! Or am I next on your list?"

Nicholas released her and took a step back. "Madam, it was not my intention to hurt you. As long as you can restrain yourself there will be no further need for me to do it for you."

"Your Grace, may I offer you some laudanum for relief?" Charlotte asked quietly. She had been one step behind him all this time.

"You! Why I wouldn't accept one drop of anything from you. You have been in league with this demon all along. All those potions and concoctions you gave dear Richard. If there was any justice I would have both of you before the magistrate on charges of conspiracy to murder my husband."

Charlotte stepped back and looked at the carpet. There was something about her graceful posture and the lovely tilt of her head, that made Nicholas want to take her in his arms and spirit her away from the evil that permeated the walls of this cold abbey.

Suddenly, she tilted her head back and looked at him. She had the most trusting, loving look on her face. She radiated goodness. It hardened his resolve.

"Madam, my grandmother and Mr. Llewellyn were with me very early this morning, just prior to the time of my father's death," he paused to take a deep breath. "They were called in to witness an addendum to his last will and testament. I have asked the vicar to come later this afternoon to discuss the changes with you so you will not be surprised during the formal reading of the document following the funeral three days hence." He stopped when he felt a small, warm hand curl into his own. He realized his fingers were clenched and cold. "But I do not want you to live in suspense and worry. You and Edwin are to remove to Carston Hall in Yorkshire—"

"Why am I not surprised that you would exile us to the cold, boggy north?" Edwin interrupted.

"I chose Carston because it is the estate's second-largest property. If you would prefer, I will allow you to choose the smaller manor house in Shropshire."

"Well, Mother dear, I suppose we must be grateful for the unexampled kindness *His Grace* is seeing fit to bestow on us. I for one will enjoy watching from afar the total ruin of the Knight family fortune. Although, I expect with Mr. Coburn remaining as the competent steward, it will take longer than expected. May I be permitted to ask *Your Grace*, if we will be allotted our own portion of funds to control? At least we will be able to invest wisely to ensure our own future comfort and well-being," he said with an air of supreme confidence.

"I am again sorry to burst the bubble of your illusions, Edwin, but your Mr. Coburn is, at this very moment, cooling his heels in the strong room of The Quill & Dove. There is the matter of many thousands of pounds missing from our estates, which *you* and Mr. Coburn will be required to explain," Nicholas said, before staring hard at Edwin. "Now, Edwin. I would not have you misunderstand me on this last point. You and your mother will be given a generous stipend each month that you shall not exceed. Have no doubts that no debts of yours shall be paid that exceed the stipend. I will attempt to exonerate your name from any scandal Mr. Coburn's actions produce. But, I will not agree to any blackmail.

"I shall forgive your gross mistakes this one time. But understand me well, if you and Her Grace," Nicholas said, nodding toward the duchess, "behave properly, I shall reward you both with a season in town every few years or so. Make the mistake of continuing your malicious behavior, and you will reap your reward, which will include a substantial change in your standard of living. Do I make myself clear?"

The young man's face had exhibited every color of the rainbow during Nicholas's lecture. He was surprised Edwin had not exploded in anger. But Nicholas had underestimated his half brother's reserves of control when self-preservation was at stake.

"And lest there be any doubt about the future, I will sign a document this morning transferring all unentailed wealth and properties to my wife upon my demise. And I daresay it goes without saying that any sudden change in my health would be investigated, starting with you both. Now, may I count on you to not make complete spectacles of yourselves by disgracing me and my wife while you stay here for the funeral?" He continued without waiting for an answer. "For the next time either of you utters an ungracious word to me or my wife, I shall be forced to change my mind about allowing you a generous portion and not including you in the investigation concerning Mr. Coburn."

Edwin had turned white in his shock. He looked like a child who had received a well-justified whipping. "Yes . . . sir."

The proverbial bully had turned coward.

"Very good, then. I shall leave you to recover and send a maid to attend to Her Grace."

Nicholas stood stock still as the pause lengthened into an uncomfortably long silence. He stared at his half brother until Edwin was forced to show his respect by a slight bow. With that, Nicholas quit the room alongside Charlotte.

His arm had never felt so rock-hard as it did just now while they walked past the tiered formal gardens of Wyndhurst Abbey toward the cottage. The loud crunching sound of the pea gravel beneath their steps filled Charlotte's ears. The air was cool, signaling autumn's commencement as the dark red roses made a final fragrant showing before the killing frosts.

Charlotte felt very shy in his commanding presence, unsure of what to say. She dared a sidelong glance at his rugged, handsome profile and saw the grim set of his mouth while they headed into the teeth of a strong wind that promised to pierce the heavy gray clouds all around. They entered the taller grasses, swirling madly in the breeze, and startled a pocket of field grouse, who flew away, their long tails fanned in flight.

They walked in silence; he seemingly lost in thought, she wondering what he was thinking, not confident enough to utter a word. Within sight of the cottage, Nicholas halted.

"Charlotte," he said, turning to face her. "I am sorry for everything you have had to endure since coming to this godforsaken place. From the hostile reception, the death of your father, your forced betrothal, through it all you have been a model of grace and all that is charitable and good. And I, well, I was all that is the opposite."

"I am not sorry I came," she interrupted in whispered tones, while looking at the ground. "And it is not true what you said. You are all that is courageous and kind. I know that because of your excellent character. You took pity of me, but there was no need. I did not want your pity. I only ever wanted your . . ." Out of the corner of her eye, Charlotte could see that he had bent down to try and catch her words.

"My what?" he asked.

"Oh, never mind. It doesn't signify. Shall we go into the cottage? I have something for you. I wanted to give it to you before I left."

He took her hands in his own and bent to kiss them. She felt like an awkward girl staring into his impossibly handsome face.

"What did you only ever want from me, Charlotte?"

She released his hands and began marching, in the longest strides her legs would allow, to the whitewashed cottage beyond. She could hear him walking beside her.

"Tell me you only ever wanted *my love*, dearest," he said, his deep baritone voice floating in the wind.

"I cannot," she said, horrified that he had guessed her greatest desire. "I only ever wanted your respect, sir."

"Well then, that is too bad."

She swung around to face him, anger flooding her body, forcing the tears that had threatened to spill back into their small recesses. "Yes, it is too bad. I was never able to gain anything but your pity. Now, please, I beg of you to leave me alone. I think it best that I leave you here, actually. I will send the item I have for you with Doro. Will you please, I beg of you, arrange for a carriage to take me to London the morning after your father's burial? I think it best that I leave then," she said.

He threw back his head and laughed.

It was outrageous. He was outrageous. She had never seen him act with so little concern for her sensibilities. She ran to the door. At the last moment, she was snatched back into his arms.

"Darling, you do not think I would let you go now, just when you have almost admitted that my fondest wishes have been granted?" There was a shining light in his laughter-filled green eyes.

"Put me down!"

"Not until I hear from your beautiful lips precisely how long you have loved me."

"I did not admit that."

"Then it is a shame. You shall have to live with a man who loves you to distraction while you only tolerate him. I shall not let you go away, my love."

"Oh, Nicholas," she said. "Please don't make fun of me or of our situation. You have never loved me. You have only ever pitied me."

"Yes, you are right, of course. I was feeling only pity the day I first met you and railed against your nursing, and again only pity as you helped me begin to learn how to read, and pity alone on our wedding night, as we made love in every way imaginable. It was all done in pity."

"I beg of you not to lie to me. It would only lead to great unhappiness," she said, looking away from the intensity of his gaze. She pushed at his strong shoulders in an attempt to release herself from his embrace.

"Oh, no. I shall not let you go. I have not given you the requisite number of compliments today. First, you are the most delicately beautiful lady of my acquaintance."

She sighed in sadness, refusing to believe.

"Second, you are the most hardheaded—no, rather, impossibly hardheaded wife, even if it is a beautiful hard head. And by the way, I take great offence that you would even think for a moment that I would lie to you. It is a very lowering thought just after you complimented my great character. And finally, I do hope Doro and the Robertses are not still in this cottage, as they and you would be most embarrassed by what I plan to do to you very, very soon," he said, then laughed heartily. "That is, of course, a roundabout way of telling you how attractive I find you," he said.

"Well, hmmm, still no dimples. What more can I say? That I have loved you since the moment I met you? No, I can see you will not believe that. Well, then, I can assure you that I have loved you ever since you responded quite eagerly, I might add, to my first kiss. And if not then, then the time you looked quite lovely covered in blood and straw when you saved both mare and foal. But I was sure I loved you after you forced me to take responsibility for my family, thereby allowing my father to die in peace." The last was said in quiet, all laughter drifting away.

"Please stop . . ." she said, resting her head on his cravat.

"Charlotte, I love you. And I will not let you go away from me. So, I am afraid you are stuck with an ignorant ox of a husband who was too stupid and blind to tell you all this before, and who now requires you to tell me you will stay and help me make the Knight properties once again the finest in Christendom, whether you are able to tell me you love me or not," he said quietly in her ear.

At that moment, the haunting call of a mature cuckoo could be heard. She refused to encounter his expression, so she hid her face in the folds of his linen. "I do love you, Nicholas. You know I do, and always have. I will never stop loving you. And I am so proud you have faced down the familial cuckoos who usurped your rightful place. I feared it would never happen, and that you would return to the military life while I lived apart from you."

Nicholas nudged open the door and released her over the threshold. He cupped her face within his hands and kissed her until she entwined her arms about his neck. She broke away and continued, "I have a small wedding gift I have been wanting to give you."

"And I you," he said, looking at her with a heartwarming expression. "You first."

She took his hand and led him into the clay room. The large bust she had created with painstaking care was in the corner, a damp cloth hiding the sculpture. Charlotte uncovered it to reveal a perfectly formed bust of Nicholas's head and chest.

She glanced toward him and saw the surprise and delight in his expression. "I hope you are pleased with it. It is not quite right, I know. I did not capture—"

"You captured it all," he said in awe and wonder. "I only hope I can live up to the heroic and intelligent gleam in these noble eyes," he said, then chuckled.

"I am so glad you like it."

"I had thought it was a bust of your irascible cousin."

"I know. I am sorry he acted toward you as he did," she said.

"Actually, I am pitying him, now. Of course, I was feeling differently when I assumed it was you who had gone off with him. But once I knew it was the lovely Lady Susan, well—" Nicholas said, scratching his head, "—I daresay he will be hard pressed, as a gentleman, to disentangle himself from parson's mousetrap. That would put a quick end to his humorous nature."

Charlotte shook her head. "Knowing Alex as I do, he will not only convince Lady Susan of the foolishness of her bold flight but find a solution to avoid her complete ruination— that is—if she ever finds him."

"I know I should feel more compassion for your cousin but at this moment I can think only of you, here with me," Nicholas said, cupping her face with his hands. "Although I daresay my conscience shall get the better of me soon enough and I shall go riding helter-skelter toward London in search of the pair of them. Perhaps I can persuade dear Edwin to help me. But enough of that. We have waited long enough for our own happiness."

Charlotte felt awash in feminine excitement mixed with newfound boldness and confidence. The first raindrops sounded like pebbles hitting the rushes of the cottage. A moment later, the skies let loose the full fury of the heavy clouds and lightning flashed.

"But first you must have your present. I am afraid it is not jewels or pearls, as would be much more fitting. It is a kiln, my dearest, newly constructed for your use. Not very romantic, I know."

"A kiln," she said in wonder. "You had a kiln made for me? Why it is exactly what I most wanted! Thank you, oh, thank you, Nicholas."

In her exuberance, she flew into his arms and kissed him using every wicked technique her cousin had suggested.

"Well, if I had known you would react like this, I would have given you the silly brick oven ages ago," he said, after pulling reluctantly away from her. "Now what say we ascend to your chamber above and pray that this storm does not let up for a fortnight?"

"Or two," Charlotte responded, looking up into his loving eyes.

"Or three," he said, as he laughed and swung her up into his arms, where he swore she would always remain.

Epilogue

"You have delighted us long enough."

—Pride and Prejudice

$\mathcal{A}$s the last few notes of a concerto died away in the air of the room, the gleeful laughter and clapping of two young children could be heard.

"All right, my loves, your father has favored you with not one but three pieces of music, and it is long past your bedtime," Charlotte said, looking up from a letter in her hands.

"But Mama, Father promised us a story too," said a little girl of six, with the same dark looks and emerald eyes of her father.

"And I'm starving. Nanny promised to bring me an apple and cheese," wailed the younger brother, whose countenance matched his mother's.

Nicholas looked at the happy scene before him. "Now Solange and Richard, your delaying tactics are well known to us. But I suppose," he paused when he saw the delighted smiles overspread their innocent faces, "we can have a brief, very brief reading lesson and story as we wait for Nanny."

Nicholas walked the two children to the long table and began asking them the names of the old fired-clay letters he and Charlotte had formed so long ago in the cottage. He patiently corrected them when the sounds of the letters did not correspond with their shapes.

He glanced up to catch the loving, proud gaze of his wife. Their eyes met, and Nicholas was filled with the joy he had never dreamed would be his.

Nanny appeared at the doorway of the west salon, bearing

the promised apples and cheese. The children rushed to her with the endless hunger of the very young.

"Dearest?" inquired Charlotte.

"Yes, my love?" He walked over to sit on the arm of her overstuffed armchair.

"Shall we invite Mr. and Mrs. Llewellyn for supper tomorrow night?"

"I think a visit with grandmamma and the vicar is very much in order, now that they have returned from Italy. It is a wonder she did not burst in on us this afternoon when they returned."

Charlotte laughed. "I assume she has someone, a very special someone, who occupies her uppermost thoughts."

"Ah, yes. The vicar. He is an old rogue, is he not? I suspect St. Peter will have many questions for him when he meets him at heaven's gates. Knowing Mr. Llewellyn, he will charm him into acceptance," Nicholas said, shaking his head.

Nicholas could see the happy glow of laughter in Charlotte's large gray eyes. She still appeared to him as a girl of seventeen instead of five and thirty. "And we should have Mr. and Mrs. Roberts to celebrate the transfer of the brewery to him as he has worked devilishly hard."

"Oh, I love impromptu parties! You must give Charley the pleasure of laying out your finery tomorrow. It is only proper, on his final night," Charlotte said. "I am so glad you acceded to his request to apprentice with Mr. Babcock, here. I think he will make an admirable steward for one of the other properties in a very short time."

Charlotte paused to brush a lock of his hair from his brow. Her touch brought the familiar wave of pleasure to him.

"I fear your stepmother, Edwin, and Susan would expire from shock at the idea of common folk invading the hallowed grounds of Wyndhurst Abbey."

"Yes, well, I for one take comfort in knowing that we have provided the three of them enough fodder over the years to warm their conversations at every meal in the wilds of Yorkshire. But, I have been pleasantly surprised by their behavior since Edwin and Susan wed, although I suppose I should not be. Living so far removed, with her ten thousand a year, it would be next to impossible for them to overspend. In fact, I had thought to send them word that I would make good on my promise. Do you think the shock of an offer to use the house in Bath would be too much?"

A gurgle of laughter escaped her. "I don't see why not."

Nicholas reached down for the letter on his wife's lap. "What does your cousin have to say for himself? Still showing Lady Sheffield the delights of Paris in the springtime?"

"No. I'm afraid he has wearied of that lady and of Paris. He talks of coming to visit us. Let's see," she said, looking at the letter. "He writes, 'I shall bestow on you and your husband my presence if you can assure me that Edwin and Lady Susan will not make an untimely appearance. I should not want to have to disappear again for a year, although I cannot say my year in Biarritz and St. Jean de Luz was not well-spent.' "

"I do believe, dearest, that you are not translating the last part very well. There seems to be a somewhat delicate reference to a certain lady and what he did to her anatomy. He may come as long as he does not contemplate any part of your anatomy."

Charlotte smiled and folded the letter.

The two children piled into their mother and father's laps. "Now, Father, you promised us the story," said Solange, with the same commanding tone Nicholas used.

"Why, you know I cannot read, my sweet," Nicholas said, looking into the serious expression of his daughter and mussing the top of her dark hair.

"That's a great bouncer, Father. Now read our favorite story again, please," begged his son with large gray eyes.

"Yes, the one about the girl who saves the knight who is then saved in return," Solange said, handing her father a storybook.

"Ah, yes, *A Passionate Endeavor*, my favorite, too!" he said, smiling at Charlotte as he opened the book.

The soft touch of Charlotte's hand glided through his hair. He closed his eyes and felt her gentle kiss on his forehead.

"Once upon a time . . ."

Author's Note

In November 1896, an English doctor published *Congenital Word Blindness*, the first description of a learning disorder that would come to be known as dyslexia. Until that time and beyond, many children and adults were cruelly labeled "slow to learn" and much worse.

In today's more enlightened world, many theories abound as to the cause and treatment of dyslexia. While researching the many different techniques employed to teach individuals with dyslexia, I read about an unusual method that used clay and large solid forms of letters to help certain dyslexics learn to read. This technique was the inspiration for several scenes in *A Passionate Endeavor*. However, I must add that I have no firsthand knowledge of the program's actual success. If you would like to read *The Sunday Times* (London) article that provided the inspiration, please go to: http://www.times-archive.co.uk/news/pages/tim/2000/03/21/timfeabam03003.html. There are also many more library books and sites on the internet with helpful information.

One final note: There is a scene in this book during which the hero suggests a knowledge of the female reproductive cycle. In fact, during the Regency period, it was mistakenly believed that conception could only occur at the beginning of the cycle, very much like other mammals. It is no wonder some women, in the past, had ten or more children! It was not until the early twentieth century that this concept was proven incorrect, thereby introducing a more successful rhythm method.